Shave Ice Paradise

a novel

Shave Ice Paradise

a novel

Mark Daniel Seiler

OWL HOUSE BOOKS
AN IMPRINT OF HOMEBOUND PUBLICATIONS

OWL HOUSE BOOKS
AN IMPRINT OF HOMEBOUND PUBLICATIONS

Quantity sales. Special discounts are available on quantity purchases by corporations, associations, bookstores, and others. For details, contact the publisher or visit wholesalers such as Ingram or Baker & Taylor.

Published in 2020 by Owl House Books
Cover Design and Interior Design by Leslie M. Browning
Cover Image by Tithi Luadthong
ISBN 9781947003682
First Edition Trade Paperback

Owl House Books is *an Imprint of Homebound Publications*
WWW.HOMEBOUNDPUBLICATIONS.COM

10 9 8 7 6 5 4 3 2 1

Owl House Books, like all imprints of Homebound Publications, is committed to ecological stewardship. We greatly value the natural environment and invest in environmental conservation.

ALSO BY THE AUTHOR

Sighing Woman Tea
River's Child

Prolepsis

Officer Moreno peered over the rocky ledge. A woman in a black and gold *kimono* lay motionless on the floor of the cave sixty feet below.

"Hello! Are you all right?" Moreno climbed down to the motionless figure and felt the cold neck for a pulse. It wasn't her first dead body.

An owl swooped over the body without a sound. "A *pueo*," Moreno whispered.

Officer Gutierrez crawled through the cave opening and brushed the sand off his knees. "Don't touch the body, Moreno! Wait for the detective."

Gina

Life and death are one thread,
the same line viewed from different sides.
–Lao Tzu

"It's too late to cancel." Mrs. Tanaka stared out the window at the heavy rain.

"Yes," Reverend Mori agreed. "We must do our best under the circumstances." As a Buddhist, he accepted that death was part of life, though, in that moment, it did little to negate the feeling in his chest. "Life is not the same without Auntie Nalani."

There was no respectful way to cancel the event. A temple member was already on his way to the airport to meet grand-master Genshitsu Sen. The grandmaster and his entourage had endured the nine-hour red-eye from Kyoto to perform the tea ceremony commemorating the 35th anniversary of the Tea Society of *Wai Nau*.

Gina finished sweeping the temple steps and began dusting the teak pews with a damp cloth, while her father made last-minute adjustments to the flower arrangements in front of the altar. When Gina's mother died, Auntie Nalani had always been there. Gina wished she could cry, but the weight pressing down on her heart wouldn't lift. "I'm finished, Chichi," she told her father.

A temple member donated two large white orchids, which Reverend Mori carefully placed to either side of the golden Buddha. After trimming the end of a long anthurium stem, he took a step back to study the arrangement. "Did you vacuum the threshold, daughter?" He knew by her silence that she had forgotten. Was she unable to appreciate that Grandmaster Sen had spent the last fifty years of his life offering peace to the world through a bowl of tea?

Unrolling the stiff cord from around the old silver vacuum, she sucked up the piles of termite droppings that accumulated daily in the grooves of the sliding shoji doors. The century-old temple was slowly returning to the earth. "A lesson in impermanence," her father had observed. Earlier that very morning he had scraped off a large mushroom growing on the side of a rotten foundation post. Gina wrapped the unwieldy cord around the vacuum once again and tucked it in the closet. "I wonder how many more times I'll pull you out before the Grandmaster arrives?" she asked the silver Hoover.

Gina bowed before the altar and lit three sticks of incense to Amida Buddha. She slid open the shoji doors on the east side to let in the light breeze. "Hmm! More termite droppings." She quickly brushed the termite frass away with her dust cloth just as Chichi appeared from his office in his black ceremonial robe. It was just like him to wear his old drab robe during the most important event held in the temple in her lifetime. She wanted to chide him but understood it was his way of showing respect to the Grandmaster. She smiled and fixed his tie. He had shaved his head earlier that morning. "To have hair is to worry about hair," she joked. Last Sunday, Chichi gave a dharma talk about the freedom of not having hair. It saved time, "Plus, I save money on shampoo," he pointed out merrily.

The ceremony was to start in less than half an hour, and the temple was empty. As she feared, all their days of preparation would go unnoticed. Her generation had lost interest in coming to the temple. The few remaining elderly members came on Saturday for *Fujinkai,* the Woman's Club. The older women were the *enno shitano chikaramochi,* the power behind the scenes. The *Nisei,* the second generation of Japanese immigrants to arrive on the island, held fast to tradition. Though Buddha accepted that change was the only changeless thing in the universe, the older generation was comfortable with things remaining the same. When Gina was born, there were nearly three hundred Buddhist temples in Hawaii, now fewer than eighty remained.

Mrs. Sato and Mrs. Tanaka arrived just before eleven, sitting in their usual places in the back. They looked out of place without Nalani sitting between them.

Chichi held two chunks of sandalwood incense above the altar candle and then blew on them to make sure they were lit before carefully placing them in the incense burner.

Grandmaster Sen strolled the temple grounds, pausing to admire the lotus blossoms in the pond.

Korematsu, the Grandmaster's assistant, entered through the side entrance and quietly prepared the tea utensils, pouring rainwater from a wooden pail into the iron *furo,* the portable brazier.

Gina sat behind Mrs. Sato and looked at the empty pews. On her twelfth birthday, Auntie Nalani began teaching her *wabi-sabi.* As part of her training, she practiced the tea ceremony. Gina remembered carefully scooping tea from the *natsume* container. Try as she may, before the powdered green tea reached the bowl, it would spill. The more Gina struggled to be careful and precise, the more she knocked things over. The terrible morning she dropped the cast iron lid on the black lacquered tea table signaled an early end to her tea training.

Korematsu hung a scroll behind Chichi's flower arrangement. The beautiful kanji characters read, *ichi go, ichi e*. "One time, one meeting." It was a poet's declaration, "This rare moment we now share, will never be again." Behind the simple movements of preparing tea was a deep mysticism. Traditionally, the guest sat in the place of honor where they could view and appreciate the scroll and flower arrangement. It could be a single blossom of a common weed, elevated by being placed in a vase in the *tokonoma*.

The host sat with their back to the beauty and served the guest.

At two minutes to eleven, a green Robert's tour bus pulled up. The air brakes hissed, and the doors flapped open sending a rush of humanity flooding through the east entrance. Two middle-aged Japanese women squeezed in on either side of Gina. She greeted them, "*Ohayo gozaimasu*. Good morning." They didn't acknowledge her.

When Grandmaster Sen appeared from the side entrance, a hush fell on the guests as he knelt on the tatami mat.

The women to Gina's right whispered in Japanese, "Sen is the fifteenth Grandmaster going back to the 16th century."

Like her father, the Grandmaster wore a simple black *kimono*. The graceful movements of the gray-haired man, the tenderness with which he set the bamboo ladle atop the *kama*, mesmerized her. He slowly folded the tea towel and ritually cleansed the lip of the tea bowl. She felt the world begin to slow.

Gina knew how happy it would make Auntie Nalani to see the temple full. She was eight years old when her mother died. The morning after the funeral, Auntie Nalani was waiting on the front step to walk her to school. When the school bell rang, Nalani was waiting by the crosswalk to walk her home. If someone drove too fast on *Mana'olana* Road, Auntie's gentle smile magically slowed the vehicle to a crawl.

Gina sat entranced as Grandmaster Sen gently whisked the tea into froth. His movements, neither fast nor slow, seemed to Gina to take place in-between time. He carefully set the steaming cup of tea on the tatami in front of him, a symbolic offering to Auntie Nalani. As he placed his palms together making a formal *gassho rei*, the temple guests mirrored him, all silently bowing their heads in deep respect.

After the ceremony, Gina served refreshments. She overheard the bus driver telling Mrs. Sato that the visitors had only just arrived from Japan. They had made the long journey to witness Grandmaster Sen perform the tea ceremony. A woman explained half in English, half in Japanese, that the nine-hour flight was well worth it. Seeing the grandmaster in Japan was next to impossible, as rare as a private audience with the Pope, or the Dalai Lama. Gina cleared the tables when the crowd thinned. She washed out the serving bowls while Mrs. Sato dried.

"I need to talk with you, Gina," Mrs. Sato said.

"Okay."

"Later, in private."

When they had finished cleaning up, they sat under the big monkeypod tree nestled beside the temple. "It's Auntie Nalani's funeral the day after tomorrow," Mrs. Sato said quietly.

The younger woman understood the look on Mrs. Sato's face. Nalani had been Mrs. Sato's dearest friend. "I'm so sorry for your loss, Mrs. Sato," Gina said.

"I need your help."

"Of course. I'm helping Chichi with the preparations for the service. Let me know whatever you need me to do."

"Something isn't right," Mrs. Sato blurted out.

"Ask Chichi." She reached for a more respectful way of addressing the older woman's concerns. "Reverend Mori will be happy to make any changes—"

"No, it's not the funeral. Something isn't right about Auntie Nalani's . . ." Mrs. Sato couldn't bring herself to say, *death*. "The police said Nalani-san fell into the *Mana'olana* sinkhole. It makes no sense. Nalani-san has never been to the sinkhole in her life. Why would she go there? And her bag? Where is her bag? She never left her house without that ugly bag of hers."

"That's true," Gina remembered the faded gray bag with the plastic hoop handles. When she was little, she thought the shiny green handles were made of real jade.

"They said Auntie fell and hit her head."

"I'm very sorry, Mrs. Sato. I wish there were something I could do."

"You could find Nalani's bag."

"I'm not sure that—"

"Remember when you found my Pickles? He was lost for two days," Mrs. Sato reminded Gina.

"Your dog crawled under your couch. All I did was sit down, and Pickles whimpered. Scared me half to death."

"Remember when you found Miyahara-san's pruning shears on the roof?" Mrs. Sato countered. "Or Ray-Ray's cooler when the tide carried it out into the bay?"

It was well known that Gina had a gift for finding things. If someone lost a pair of glasses or their phone, she found the missing item without fail.

"And Ben Fuji's tackle box down by—"

"This is very different. Ben's tackle box didn't die. If the cause of Auntie's death is in any way suspicious, then you must appreciate the seriousness of the situation. We must let the police do their job."

"But they're not doing anything." Mrs. Sato broke down into tears. "Will you speak with your friend Carla? She works for the police department. Please, Gina-san."

Gina caved. "All right, I'll speak with Carla."

10-84

. . . to prove, and to help one bear,
the fact that all safety is an illusion.
–James Baldwin

When the call came over the radio the previous morning, Officer Carla Moreno was in Kimo's store pouring a fresh cup of coffee. Abandoning her cup on the counter, she rushed out to her cruiser. Before hitting the siren, she realized she didn't know where she was going. She thought about the cruiser's GPS and then ran back into the store. "Hey, Kimo, where's the cave?"

"Go the cane road down to *Mana'olana* Beach, past the horse stables," Kimo gestured giving her the lay of the land. "Turn through the gate, take one left to Perry's beach house. Cross the footbridge. The sinkhole is beside *Mana'olana* stream."

"Thanks, Kimo. I've lived here all my life and have never been to the cave."

"More like one big hole." Kimo didn't want Moreno to get her hopes up.

Officer Moreno took the old cane road, and parked near the beach house and walked along the *Mana'olana* stream. Large and agile, she easily crossed the rope bridge. The sandy trail led to the upper rim of the cave. She could hear the pounding surf on the other side of the dunes.

Well before the first Hawaiians settled the island, a millennium of rains had turned the high sand dunes into soft limestone. Over time, underground springs carved a massive cave. Eventually, the ceiling of the cave collapsed, leaving a deep crater.

Officer Moreno peered over the rocky ledge. A woman in a black and gold *kimono* lay motionless on the floor of the cave sixty feet below.

"Hello! Are you all right?" Moreno ran down the trail. The metal entry gate was unlocked. She crawled on her hands and knees through the narrow cave entrance until there was room to stand. The ceiling of the cave led to a natural amphitheater opening to the sky.

"Hello." Approaching the motionless figure, she felt the cold neck for a pulse. It wasn't her first dead body. The older woman's *kimono* was damp to the touch. She pressed the call button on her radio. "This is Puna 6. I have a 10-84, repeat, 10-84, a deceased female in her mid to late seventies. Over."

"10-4 Moreno. Gutierrez is two minutes from your 6. Paramedics are en route. Over."

An owl swooped over the body without a sound. "A *pueo*," Moreno whispered. Though Hawaiian owls preferred daylight, the sight of the rare bird shocked her.

Officer Gutierrez crawled through the cave opening and brushed the sand off his knees. "Moreno! Don't touch the body. Wait for the detective," he barked. "Proper procedure is to secure the perimeter of the scene."

Moreno ignored him.

"Hey, rookie! Secure the perimeter. That's an order."

"Okay. Stay with her."

"Rookies follow orders; they don't give them."

Moreno headed back to the top of the sinkhole just as a long-haired tourist came charging up the path. Upon seeing the big woman in uniform, he jumped straight in the air, turned in his tracks, and ran back toward the beach.

"Stoner," Moreno said, under her breath. When the paramedics arrived, she met them at the footbridge. "Hey, Walters, good to see you."

"Hi, Moreno. We heard over the radio, suspicious death." Walters had worked with the rookie on dozens of calls.

"Yeah, we're waiting for the detective," she explained. "I'll show you the entrance to the cave. It's a tight squeeze."

* * *

An hour later, Detective Sergeant Alvaro finally arrived. He walked by Moreno as if she were invisible and joined Gutierrez. Four years in Afghanistan bought her some respect, but it didn't change the fact that she was a rookie and a woman. Alvaro looked over the edge at the body below. "This is the same spot where Johnny Depp jumped off the cliff in *Pirates of the Caribbean IV*." Alvaro never tired of telling the story of meeting Capt. Jack Sparrow when he was on "milk duty" guarding the set against crazed fans.

It irked Moreno to see Alvaro taking his sweet time. She wanted to yell, "Time is of the essence!" Preserving physical evidence was vital in any investigation. The sun had reached the body making it more difficult to determine time of death.

"We should put up a tent over the body," Moreno suggested.

Ignoring her, Detective Alvaro leaned over and whispered something to Gutierrez. They both laughed.

Before the medical examiner arrived, Moreno was ordered to return to the station and write her report. Not wanting to give Alvaro and Gutierrez the satisfaction of seeing her upset, she walked calmly to her cruiser and drove away.

The Wai Nau Times

Advertisements contain the only truths
to be relied on in a newspaper.
–Thomas Jefferson

A grubby *haole* in a dirty black coat parked his shopping cart full of plastic-wrapped bundles against the curb. Renee Algar, the receptionist, set down her nail file and slipped the latest People magazine in the pencil drawer just as the front door opened. She did her best to smile, "May I help you?" *What's he doing wearing that long coat in the middle of summer?* The homeless man smelled like a dumpster.

"I'd like to put an ad in Lost and Found," he said.

"Let me get you a form. It's twenty-five dollars for the first twenty letters," Renee explained.

"Oh." The homeless man shuffled his feet and stuck his hands in his coat pocket. "How much for a letter to the editor?"

"Those are free. I'll get someone to help you with that." Renee held the phone against her ear with her shoulder and punched three. "Judy, to reception." Renee was anxious to be rid of the odoriferous man. Every day another hippy *haole* stepped off the plane and started living on the beach.

The editor emerged from his office. "Judy's running an errand. I'm Sam Hara. How may I help you?"

"T. McKenna. Pleased to meet you." The two men awkwardly shook hands. "I'd like to submit a letter to the editor."

"Well, you've come to the right place. I'm the editor."

McKenna pulled a wadded up piece of paper from his coat pocket and attempted to smooth it out on the countertop.

"Let's take a look." The editor-in-chief read the note aloud: "Lost, female calico cat, six claws on her right front paw. Call 632-0610." He adjusted his glasses. "I'm sorry, Mr. McKenna, but this belongs in the lost and found. It's twenty-five dollars for the first twenty words."

"May I borrow a pen?" McKenna asked.

"Sure thing. Here you are." The editor grabbed a pen from his breast pocket and studied the face behind the long stringy hair and matted beard. "It's the policy of the *Times* to ask for photo ID before publishing letters."

"Oh." McKenna finished scratching something out on the scrap of paper before reaching into his other jacket pocket. He rolled a rubber band off a thick wad onto his wrist and shuffled through his collection of tattered business cards. He held up his Hawaii driver's license.

"Thank you." Sam glanced at the ID. "Okay, Mr. Terence McKenna. Let's see what you've got here." He read the revised version: "Lost, female calico cat, six claws on her right front paw. Please help me find my cat. Stray cat feces carry *Toxoplasma gondii*, a parasite deadly to marine mammals. Save a monk seal and whale today! Call: 632-0610." Sam made a couple of notes on the bottom of the paper. "Is this your phone number?"

"No," the homeless man said, already halfway out the door. "But I can be reached there."

Renee wanted to scream, "Close the door! You're letting the cool air out." Instead, she continued to pretend she was typing something of great import.

"Thanks, Mr. McKenna, for coming in. I can't guarantee your letter will make tomorrow's paper, but we'll do our best," Sam promised.

"Thank you, sir."

Renee came around her desk and ushered the smelly *haole* out the door and pulled it closed.

Sam ignored the look on Renee's face, stating for the record: *I'll never recover*. "I hope that derelict never comes back," she said, under her breath.

As far as Sam knew, Renee got her wish: the homeless man never again set foot in the *Times*. What neither of them knew was that they had just witnessed the beginning of T. McKenna's prolific and historical writing career. Nothing would ever be the same.

The Sinkhole

I want to be with those who know
secret things or else alone.
–Rainer Maria Rilke

"Where's the fire?" Gina yelled out the driver's side window. The red Mustang blew by disappearing in a cloud of dust. She swerved dodging the deep craters littering the old cane road. Something happened to the mind of the tourist when they left the pavement. A primal switch flipped. Trashing their rental car was a small price to pay if it meant getting to the beach a few seconds earlier. Another red car zoomed by. Gina coughed on the cloud of dust that hung in the still air. The obnoxious '90's tourist bureau jingle popped in her head, *Wai Nau? Because tomorrow may never come.*

Chichi's old Subaru, "Sooby," theoretically had air conditioning, but Gina refused to roll up the windows to use it. When she swerved to avoid a deep pothole, she almost sideswiped a convertible that decided to pass on the right. "That does it!" she yelled at the sunburned tourists. She made a sharp left, abandoning the old cane road, and headed for the rodeo grounds. "Safer to walk the rest of the way."

She parked Sooby in the shade of an ironwood tree and headed across a recently plowed field toward the sound of the crashing waves. A giant gear with rusty teeth, its circumference nearly as great as Gina's height, had been left propped against a lava rock wall, an artifact of another age when sugar was king. Clouds in the shape of a summer hat sat above Moana Ki, the sculpted black basalt ridge to the East. She walked through the miniature desert left in Moana Ki's wake. Just as she met the trail, a string of horses and riders came through the brush. She stepped aside to let the riding tour pass.

"Howdy!" The guide tipped his hat. "Watch yer step, missy," Cowboy Billy offered his no-nonsense advice in a heavy country drawl.

Gina soon discovered what the man in the ten-gallon hat was talking about. The trail had recently been blessed with steaming fragrant offerings.

The cowboy's tall tale to the tourists traveled on the light breeze, "The lil' lady from Arkansas gave me a hickey bigger than a rodeo buckle . . ."

Gina wandered down a side path that overlooked one of her favorite places on the island, *Mana'olana* Beach. She paused and took in the shifting colors of the magical landscape unlike any place on earth. *Mana'olana* meant "hope" in Hawaiian: a fitting name. The light and shadows played over the turquoise water framed by a long white beach. Gina picked her way through large boulders to the mouth of the stream.

A young man was crouching on the opposite bank filling a glass vial with muddy water. She wondered if he was a plain-clothes officer taking forensic samples of the scene. Everything seemed oddly normal. There was no yellow crime tape.

Curly looked up and saw the young woman staring at him from the opposite bank. She wasn't smiling. He hoped she wasn't pro-dairy. The fecal bacteria in *Mana'olana* stream was a thousand times the legal limit. Any more cows in the valley and the runoff would be a disaster for the coral reef. In the silence, he readied himself for an earful, or worse, an ear tag. He suddenly realized he was staring. "Hi," was all he could think to say.

"What are you doing?" she asked.

Here it comes, he braced himself. *At least there's a moat between us.* "I work for the Department of Land and Natural Resources. I'm taking water samples that will be sent to a private lab to determine water quality."

"You're not with the police?"

"D.L.N.R. does have enforcement officers. I'm a riparian biologist. For some unknown reason, they don't allow biologists to carry firearms."

Gina stifled a laugh.

Through the canopy of trees, a ray of sunlight found her eyes. Her features were simple, nothing to add or take away, a face that naturally smiled at rest. He realized he was staring again.

She gave the *haole* boy the once over. He had the look of a freshman trying to remember his locker combination. "You know this is a crime scene? I'm not sure you should be stomping around without permission."

"Are you pulling my leg?" He couldn't tell. She looked Japanese, but he knew better than to assume. Discounting the serious look on her face, she was seriously attractive. Without further explanation, she headed upstream along the opposite bank. He screwed the cap on tight, sealed the small bottle in a padded envelope and ran to catch up. "What do you mean by crime scene?" he called over the water.

"A woman was found dead." Gina clenched her jaw, turning her face into a mask.

"Seriously?" He hurried across the footbridge and followed her up the sandy path.

Gina stopped at the rim of the sinkhole and looked over the edge. "How far down would you say?" she asked.

"Sixty, maybe seventy feet. Is this where it happened?"

"I think so," she said.

Her stern look was gone. Tears brimmed on her lower lashes and fell on the tiny black freckles on her cheeks.

"Look, I don't want to be rude, but I'd love it if you took a step back from the ledge. You're making me a little nervous." He saw the muscles in her jaw bulge. "Please," he added. She looked ready to lose it. He guessed that she knew the woman who died. "I am sorry for your loss. I'll be down by the river if you need anything."

She watched him turn to go. "What did you say your name was?"

"Julius, but everyone calls me Curly."

She smiled. "I'm Gina."

"Look, I didn't mean to intrude, I'll—"

"You're not. It's . . . My Auntie Nalani was found—" she couldn't say the word.

"I'm really sorry." Curly knew locals called anyone older "auntie" or "uncle" as a sign of respect but, gauging by her reaction, he thought the woman who died must have been family.

She wondered if he was from O'ahu. "Where'd you go to school?" she asked.

"White Bird." Curly was well acquainted with the question. It was a semi-polite way to ask: where are you from?

"The Mainland?"

"Yes. Idaho."

She suspected as much. "How long have you been working for the Department of Land and Natural Resources?"

"Three months. I just moved here."

A real haole boy, all right, she thought.

Curly noticed the awkward silence. The harder he tried to think of the right thing to say, the harder it was to think of anything at all.

"The police say Auntie fell by accident."

"And . . . you don't think so?"

"As far as anyone knew, she'd never been to this place in her life. Auntie didn't drive, so she must have taken the shuttle bus and walked all the way here from the Four Seasons." Gina pointed west. "The police searched for Nalani's handbag but didn't find it. Auntie didn't have any money, so it couldn't have been a robbery. Her handbag might help me figure out what happened."

Curly wasn't a complete stranger to trouble, and this had trouble written all over it. "Sounds like a job for the police."

"Obviously." She looked around and held out her arms. "I don't see them. Do you?" She looked up the trail toward the stables. "If you were in a hurry where would you hide something around here?"

"So, now I'm a suspect?"

"The sooner you confess, the better." She allowed herself a small smile.

"If I were in a hurry, I'd chuck the bag in the stream."

"Great minds think alike. We need a way to drag the stream bottom."

"Volunteers clean the trail on weekends." Curly headed down a side path, Gina in tow. He flipped over a moldy tarp that covered a wheelbarrow filled with rusty garden tools. "This rake might do the trick. I need to grab something in my rig."

Curly found a hank of rope tucked under the driver's seat and ran back to the stream. He tied one end around the rake head and tossed it into the stagnant water. It immediately snagged a tree root, and he had to wade into the muddy brown water to free it. On the very next toss, the rake caught something. "Not again." He slowly reeled in a heavy, waterlogged branch. He sat on the bank, out of breath, ready to give up.

Gina wrapped the end of the rope around her wrist and threw the rake into the middle of the stream.

"Five hundred years ago, the ancient Hawaiians had their own sustainable system of agriculture using the fresh-water streams to grow food," he explained.

"The *ahupua`a,*" she replied, surprised. There was more to this *haole* boy than she first thought. "Do you know much about traditional Hawaiian culture?"

"No, not really," he admitted. "But I know that we're practicing, *laulima,* many hands working together."

"You're just sitting there, I'm doing all the—" She tugged on the rope and fell face-first into the stream.

Curly laughed and then dove in, helping her up the steep bank. He couldn't help but notice how the wet fabric of her dress became translucent and clung to her skin. The rope and rake were gone. Wading around, he felt something on the muddy bottom. "Hey, are these handles jade?"

"You found it!"

He climbed up the bank and handed Gina the waterlogged bag. She carefully tipped it, draining out the brown water.

Curly's eyes clung to the wet cotton dress around the gentle curve of her hips.

Gina rummaged around in the soggy handbag.

"Shouldn't we call the police?" He realized they had just found evidence relating to a suspicious death.

"Don't worry. I'll hand the bag over." She reached in and pulled out a bra.

"Okay, I'm done."

"Take it easy, big guy. It's a bra. You probably didn't know Japanese women don't wear underwear when they're wearing a *kimono*."

"Look, it's not—"

Gina pulled out a small bound book. "It looks like a recipe book." A loose page fell out as she opened it.

Out of reflex, Curly reached for the soaked paper and caught it before it hit the sand.

"Hey, I thought you were done?" she asked, watching him carefully unfold the wet paper. She glanced at it. "It's a recipe for oxtail soup."

Prima Facie

Facts are stubborn things; and whatever may
be our wishes, our inclinations,
or the dictates of our passions, they cannot alter
the state of facts and evidence.
–John Adams

Officer Moreno didn't recognize the number on her phone. "Hello: Officer Moreno."

"Hi, Carla, it's Gina Mori. How are you?"

"Hey, Gina. *Howzit?*"

"We need to talk."

"I'm working. I'll call you at the end of my shift. We can grab a bite."

"What can you tell me about Auntie Nalani's death?" Gina asked.

"Nothing."

"Oh. Well, I'm down here at the entrance to the cave and the gate is locked. Do you have a key?"

"Gina. It's a crime scene."

"Oh, wait, the lock isn't fastened. Never mind. See ya, Carla."

"Gina! Don't go in the cave! I'll be there in twenty minutes."

Gina hung up.

"Damn it!" Moreno made a U-turn in Benny Rita's driveway and gunned it toward the South Shore. As badly as she wanted to use the siren, she knew it would only make matters worse.

When Moreno saw the gate was locked, she knew she had been played. She found Gina holding onto a tree branch, leaning over the edge of the cliff above where the body had been found.

"Mrs. Sato told me you guys didn't find Nalani's handbag." Gina leaned further over, hoping to spot a clue.

"No comment." Moreno wondered how Mrs. Sato knew about the bag and then remembered Officer Gutierrez had a big mouth. "Hey, *Lolo*! Stop hanging over the edge. You crazy or something?"

"Do you have photos of the body?" Gina asked.

"You want to get me fired? I can't share evidence of an ongoing investigation. Look, I know you loved Auntie Nalani, but you need to go home, Gina."

"I'll hand over the bag if you let me see the crime scene photos."

"You found the bag? Seriously?"

"Can I see the photos?"

"That's blackmail."

"Sharing is caring." Gina smiled.

"Girl! You are definitely going to get me fired."

"Or promoted. Just think how impressed your boss will be when you show him the handbag full of evidence."

"What kind of evidence?"

"You first."

"I should arrest your ass."

Gina held her wrists together. "Book 'em, Danno."

"It's not funny, Gina. You shouldn't even be here."

"I heard you were first on the scene, *prima facie*. Did you notice anything?"

"Girl, don't even start with the Latin." Moreno shook her head. "Now that you mention it, the ground was damp where you're standing, right by that cut branch. But it hasn't rained in weeks. The victim's . . . I mean, your aunt's *kimono* was damp."

"How damp?"

"Soaked through. Well, at least her back. I was securing the perimeter when they turned the body over."

"Why would Nalani and the ground be damp? Was it tea?" Gina wondered.

"No. I heard Detective Alvaro mention later that the tests indicated fresh water."

Gina picked up the green branch. "The leaves have been stripped and both ends of this branch have been recently cut." She looked behind her. A six-inch stub was left on the trunk just above her head. She held up the cut branch to the stub. It matched.

"It's just a branch, Gina." Moreno was out of patience. "Where's the bag?"

"You're sure this is the exact spot where Nalani fell? You say the ground was damp, but nowhere else?"

"Yeah. Why? What are you thinking?"

"I don't know. I need to see the photos of Nalani."

"Give me the bag, and I'll see what I can do," Moreno held out her hand.

"I don't have it with me."

Moreno shook her head. Gina was an old friend, but she was pushing it. "My shift ends at five-thirty. Meet me by the baseball diamond in *Koa* Park. Bring the handbag."

"Thanks, Carla."

Koa Park

All I need to make a comedy is a park,
a policeman and a pretty girl.
–Charlie Chaplin

Curly found Gina in the park an hour before sunset, sitting behind the dugout on a rickety picnic table. A crowd of wild chickens gathered, hoping for food scraps. He was there to witness Gina handing over the bag to the police as she promised.

"So, your boyfriend's a cop?" Curly asked.

"Something like that."

"Did you bring the bag?" Curly didn't see it anywhere.

"Relax. I have it."

Moreno drove up in a '69 Honolulu blue Camaro.

Curly was impressed. He figured a hot girl like Gina would have a real dude as a boyfriend. Even from across the ballpark, as soon as Moreno stepped out of the car, there was no mistaking her for a man. By the time she made it to the infield grass, it was clear Gina's friend spent all her free time in the gym.

"Who's he?" Moreno asked, without looking at the scrawny *haole*.

"That's Curly. Did you bring 'em?" Gina asked.

Moreno spread the copies of the crime scene photos out on the grungy picnic table. "I hope you realize that any mention of this will cost me my job."

When Gina saw Nalani lying dead on the ground, she closed her eyes and held her breath.

Curly kept his distance, reminding himself that he was only there to make sure the bag was handed over. He was pretty sure removing evidence from a crime scene was illegal.

Gina opened her eyes and took a close look at the photographs. "Who found her?"

"A Canadian tourist from Saskatchewan. The detective in charge of the case interviewed him. That's all I know." Moreno was well aware that showing Gina the photos could get her fired. "Why do you think Nalani was wearing a *kimono*?"

"As far as I know, the only time she wore her crane *kimono* was when she performed tea ceremony at the little *Murakami* Teahouse."

"Where's that?" Moreno had never heard of it.

"It's a tiny traditional teahouse at the end of River Road. The aunties call it Love Bites Teahouse." Gina noticed the difference in the color of the silk. She compared the various photos of Nalani on her back and her stomach. "I think you can tell where the golden silk is wet and where her *kimono* is dry. Look, around her shoulders, above her *obi* is dry. Why is her *obi* tied like that?" Gina wondered.

"What do you mean?" Carla picked up the photo and took a closer look.

"Auntie is wearing the crane *kimono* she brought with her from Japan as a young woman. Her *kimono* is a one-of-a-kind treasure, but it pales in comparison to her *obi*. It's priceless. She would never have tied it like that. It should be high and tight, like a corset."

"I thought an *obi* tied in the front meant you were a prostitute," Carla remarked.

"That's a myth. If auntie had someone to help her, she would have preferred the knot in the back. It means she was alone when she dressed. Nalani would have tied her *obi* neat and tight; she took great pride in such things. There's no way she tied it like that. It would be deeply disrespectful, not just to herself, but to the artist who made the *obi*."

Curly took a step closer. *What's an obi?* he wondered.

In the beginning, Gina believed it had been a terrible accident. She knew Mrs. Sato was having a difficult time with the death of her oldest and dearest friend. For that reason, Gina agreed to find out more about Auntie Nalani's death. It was possible Nalani threw her handbag into the river. It was possible that she hurled herself over the edge of the cave, or stumbled and fell in the dark. But it was not possible that she tied her *obi* in such a careless way. "Someone else must have been there before or after Nalani's death. It's the only explanation."

The moment Moreno saw the body, she knew in her bones that it was not an accident. After she got back from Afghanistan, she didn't think anything on sleepy *Wai Nau* would bother her. In her gut, she knew Gina was right. Auntie Nalani had been murdered. "I just remembered something." Moreno looked at Gina.

"What is it?"

"When I was with . . ." Moreno paused to find the right words. "When I was waiting for the detective, sitting beside Nalani. A *pueo* swooped right over us. It was eerie, the soft feathers were completely silent."

Gina drew in a breath. "The *pueo* must have been auntie's *aumākua*." She could tell Curly wasn't following. "The owl was auntie's spiritual guardian."

Curly nodded but kept his doubts to himself.

Moreno used her cop voice, "Hopefully, I can figure out a way of introducing your theory to Detective Alvaro without getting my ass fired. Maybe Mrs. Sato can take a look at these photos and notice that someone else may have tied the *obi* for Nalani. Now, where's the handbag?"

"It's right here." Gina pulled it out of her grocery bag.

"You realize that you interfered in a police investigation. The chain of evidence has been broken. That's a crime. I should arrest both of you. Where did you find the bag?"

"I was helping Curly pull a dead branch that fell into the *Mana'olana* stream. By some miracle, the plastic jade loop caught on the limb and—"

"Bullshit, Gina." Moreno shook her head in disgust. "Just give me the bag." She went for the weak link. Moreno's eyes bored into Curly. "Did you remove anything from the bag?"

Curly fidgeted. "I don't know what's in the bag." It was the truth.

"I'm letting you both off with a warning. This time." Moreno walked back to her car without a goodbye.

"She seems pissed," Curly said, sheepishly. "And . . . what's this about you helping me pull out a dead branch?"

"Should I tell her you found the bag?"

"Nope."

Letters to the Editor

I don't care to belong to any club
That would have me as a member.
–Groucho Marx

Editor: "Mr. McKenna, why did you decide to become your own private club?"

Member: "It was a deeply personal decision. One morning I woke up and realized just how special I am. After that, it was impossible to live with direct contact with the general public."

Editor: "Did you have to file any paperwork to become a one-person private club?"

Member: "One of the many privileges with membership is the ability to cut through red tape."

Editor: "So, there are no legal documents that prove your club exists?"

Member: "On the contrary, there are mountains of paperwork. I can tell you the annual dues are quite steep. Fortunately, the tax advantages alone make it worthwhile."

Editor: "May I see some documentation?"

Member: "Unfortunately, only members are allowed to access the club's records. I'm sure you understand."

Editor: "Do you live here full-time, Mr. McKenna?"

Member: "I have residences all over the globe, but I call *Wai Nau* my home."

Editor: "Why set yourself apart from the community you call home?"

Member: "I am a part of the community—a very special part."
Editor: "Do you ever get tired of being special?"

Member: "No, not really."

Editor: "Will you be seeking other members to your private club?"

Member: "I belong to the most exclusive club in the world. Why would I ruin it by accepting another member?"

Editor: "Good point."

* * *

Curly met Gina at Kalo's Cafe. They stood at the counter to order. To be polite, Curly waited, but Gina couldn't decide what she wanted. His patience used up; he ordered a cup of coffee and a piece of macadamia nut pie. He paid Kalo and took a seat by the window.

"*Pili nakekeke*," Kalo said, as he poured the hot water for Gina's tea.

"Uncle, you know I don't speak Hawaiian."

"*Pili nakekeke*." Kalo translated, "Loosely tied."

"Meaning?"

"Your man over there, he's not on the island for long. Here today, gone tamari." Kalo winked.

"Easy, Uncle, we're not getting married. And cool it with the wise sayings. I get enough of that at home."

"Haha! Good one, Gina." Kalo shooed her away when she tried to pay.

She chose the better of the two wicker chairs. "That's half a bottle of Karo syrup you're woofing down."

"I was going to share." Curly took another bite of mac nut pie washing it down with black coffee.

"Did you see the paper this morning?" Gina asked. "That Tafari McKenna is so conceited."

"The letter to the editor guy?"

"Mr. *I'm-My-Own-Private-Club*. What an idiot." Gina made a face. "They're not even real interviews."

"I think it's meant as political satire. He's parodying the proposed private Avalon Club the Chinese billionaire wants to build on the North Shore."

"Yeah, I get that." She grabbed her fork and hacked off a big piece of pie. "But does he have to be so arrogant?"

"It's social commentary," Curly explained. "People move here and act like it's the Mainland."

She gave him a look.

He realized it was ridiculous to argue what it means to be "local" with someone born and raised on the island. "Yeah," he decided. "That Tafari is a total jerk." He watched helplessly as Gina took another big swath of pie.

"Wow, this pie is way too sweet and the mac nuts are stale," she complained.

He looked with conspicuous disappointment at the remaining crumbs.

"So, here's what we have so far," Gina began in earnest. "We know Auntie Nalani was murdered, and whoever did it tried to make it look like an accident. Why was she dressed in her finest *obi* and *kimono?* I called Nalani's best friend, Mrs. Sato and asked if Nalani was performing the tea ceremony the weekend she was killed. Mrs. Sato said she didn't know of any bookings that week. Another explanation is Nalani was meeting someone special.

Auntie lived alone. Mrs. Sato told me that Nalani never talked about having a lover."

"The police are investigating. There's nothing to be done." Curly was more than ready to give up.

"We need to find out what Nalani was doing in the days just prior to her death. It would help if we could see the coroner's report."

"Aside from getting arrested by your amiable and scary girlfriend Officer Moreno, if you haven't noticed—I have a full-time job."

"Take some vacation time," she suggested.

"I just started three months ago! I don't have any vacation time. I'm sorry, I can't risk losing my job."

"Fine. No problem." She set her fork down and sipped her tea. "*Pili nakekeke.*"

"What?"

"I said, my shoelace is *loosely tied.*"

Auntie Ōta

Dead my old fine hopes
And dry my dreaming but still . . .
Iris, blue each spring.
–Shushiki

Gina needed to search Auntie Nalani's house before it was disturbed. There might be a clue explaining why Nalani went to the cave. Searching her home meant asking permission from Nalani's older sister, Auntie Ōta.

*   *   *

A temple member owned Eddie's BBQ. Gina arrived five minutes after ten. She found the stern old woman sitting alone. "*Ohayou gozaimasu*. Good morning, Ōta-san." Gina's smile was met with a look that said, "You are late."

Gina sat down and concentrated on keeping any emotion from showing.

Auntie Ōta was a living museum. "More Japanese than Japanese," her contemporaries whispered. Auntie Ōta's anachronistic attitude prevented her from noticing when her peers were giving her the business.

Gina remembered Mrs. Sato comparing the two sisters. "Nalani is gentle as pineapple rain. Her older sister's practiced softness is hard as stone."

Teri, the head waitress, had married into the restaurant right out of high school. She showed up early and stayed late. Teri outworked everyone. After ten years, Teri was still treated as an outsider and a gold digger. The other aunties would say loud enough for any to hear, "What does she know about hard work? Nothing."

Teri accepted her fate and never complained or even indicated that she noticed her mistreatment. Out of habit, she brought a pitcher of water to the back table. Teri took one look at Auntie Ōta, set the pitcher down on an empty table, and bowed. After quietly removing the water glasses and silverware, she retreated into the kitchen, found the finest teapot and shined it up with a clean dish towel.

Gina knew there was no neutral place to meet Auntie Ōta. The fierce old woman was staring at her with a look that said, "Mind the upholstery." There was no choice. Gina needed to look around Nalani's home. If Ōta-san had cleaned the house, it might already be too late.

Teri brought a pot of tea and hesitated, unsure if she should pour.

Auntie Ōta motioned for her to set the pot on the trivet, and with a glance asked, *Why would you pour the tea before it has the proper time to steep?* "Bring Gina-san some milk for her tea." It was well known how Reverend Mori spoiled his daughter. The girl lacked even basic manners, which would be forgivable if she wasn't such a lazy girl. Everyone knew she was fired or quit every job she had ever had. Auntie Ōta pursed her lips together and refolded the cloth napkin on the table properly.

"Thank you so much, Auntie Ōta, for meeting me. I am very sorry for your loss." At the mention of Nalani, Gina noticed a warmth emanating from the older woman.

Auntie Ōta regained a firm grip; she would not allow herself to be sentimental in front of Reverend Mori's child.

Teri set a small pitcher of milk on the table without a sound and kept on the move.

Ōta-san poured the tea.

Gina looked up. Auntie's face had softened. She waited for the older woman to drink first.

They sipped their tea in silence.

"You forgot your milk," the older woman chided.

"You have an excellent memory, Auntie. Yes, when I was young, I used to put milk in my tea." Gina smiled and waited for the silence to wash away the shame. She reminded herself why she had set up the meeting. "Nalani-san was teaching me wabi-sabi."

"I was not aware you were studying anything," Auntie Ōta said, without inflection.

"I apologize." Gina bowed. "I left my copy of Okakura-san's *Book of Tea* in Auntie's house."

"I will bring it to you." At least the girl was trying to do something with herself. Auntie Ōta recalled the dent in the black lacquer tea table. Wasn't it this same girl?

"Thank you, Ōta-san. But, I wouldn't want you to mistake my copy for Nalani-san's. They are very much alike."

"The spare key is under the mat. Do not forget to lock the door when you leave."

* * *

By the looks of it, the driveway to Auntie Nalani's little house had not seen a vehicle or a pair of shears for years. The narrow ravine was filled with a dense cloud that sifted a gentle mist onto the windshield. Gina did her best to keep the wheels out of the ruts. Monstera vines wrapped acacia trunks, climbing to find the sun. Gina rolled her window up and drove slowly; hoping the scraping sounds on both sides of Sooby weren't doing any lasting damage to the paint.

She parked beside a persimmon tree and walked the path to the little house. The rotted front porch steps were more of a means to display Auntie's potted orchids than a way to reach the front door. Gina stepped carefully around the pots, moving a dry pink dendrobium under the drip-line of the roof. The key was under the mat as promised, but the door was unlocked.

Gina didn't remember the furniture, yet immediately recognized the smell of Auntie's house. She hadn't been there since she was in middle school. The living room was neat, completely free of knick-knacks. The kitchen was spotless, everything in its place. She tried to focus on why she had come. Maybe there was a note or piece of mail that would help her to piece together the days before Nalani's death.

A green lamp and black rotary telephone were the only two items on the desk. No message machine. Gina sat in the desk chair and opened the top drawer. White envelopes were glued shut from the humidity. In the second drawer was a choice of fine stationery and handmade rice paper. Auntie's generation wrote letters, ink on paper. The second drawer contained an impressive collection of stamps. The beauty of the bonsai and lotus stamps tempted her. "Would you mind terribly, Auntie, if I took a sheet of them to remember you by?"

Outside the window, a white-rumped shama's melodious song blended with the light rain on the roof metal. Gina walked around the sparse room and tried to clear her mind. She wondered if subconsciously she knew what she was looking for. "It must be right here in front of me."

Near the east window, a pair of worn tatami mats; one for the guest and the other for the host, were neatly built into the floor. She wandered around the empty house until finally settling on the tatami. The faded silk brocade border was soft and smooth as the day it was made. She opened the slender wooden box that contained Auntie's tea utensils: a plain clay teapot on the bottom shelf, four mismatched tea bowls on the shelf above.

"A different shape of tea bowl for every season," she remembered Nalani explaining. In spring and summer, a wide-open bowl is appropriate. In the cooler months, a thicker bowl with a narrower opening keeps the tea hot. All the items looked to be castaways from different sets. She opened the *natsume* tea caddy and smelled the pungent tea powder, imagining it to be the finest tea in the world. Without thinking, she walked to the kitchen, filled the kettle and lit the gas flame with a rusty flint striker. As a little girl, she dreamed of serving tea in Love Bites Teahouse. That was before she had dropped the heavy cast iron lid on the polished lacquer table—the first of many dreams to die young.

She went outside and picked a sprig of wild honeysuckle and placed it in a small vase in the *tokonoma*. The hanging *Tatejiku*, scroll, had Gasan style characters that read, "*wa kei sei jaku.*" Harmony, respect, purity, and tranquility.

She sat with her back against the scroll and flower arrangement. When the water reached a boil, Gina put her hands together and made a formal *gassho rei,* the traditional bow of respect. As a young girl, Gina asked her father, "Why do we always bow?"

"Don't expect. Just bow," Chichi replied.

As if guided by the spirit of Auntie Nalani, she opened the tea caddy and used the bamboo tea scoop to gently sculpt the powdered tea into a miniature Mt. Fujisan. She ladled hot water in the tea bowl, ritually cleansing it, and discarded it into another bowl. Gently scooping a healthy amount of tea into the plain bowl, she poured hot water over the tea and listened for a moment before whisking the powder into a green froth. She set the bowl of tea in front of where the guest would sit, in the place of honor where they could admire the flower arrangement and scroll.

The rain dripped off the rusty tin roof. When she opened her eyes, it was dark.

Wai 'apo Stream

If you go anywhere, even paradise,
You will miss your home.
–Malala Yousafzai

Gina took the 7:30 A.M. bus to Kalo's. She entered with a pirouette and smiled at Kalo waiting for his Hawaiian greeting.

"Gina girl. Did you hear about Ray-Ray's new girlfriend from the Mainland?" Kalo asked, nearly jumping out of his seat.

"No. Why? Is she—"

"No one has seen her," Kalo informed her, as if it were a matter of national security.

"Okay," Gina didn't get why it mattered. "Hot tea please, Uncle." She dropped a fiver in the tip jar and returned Kalo's mock expression of outrage. "When I see Ray-Ray, I'll pump him for information on his mystery woman."

That seemed to satisfy the big man.

Curly waited until he saw Gina and then pretended to eat his pie as fast as possible.

"Hilarious." She gave him a peck on the cheek, sat down and nonchalantly picked up her fork and took a big bite. "Can I come to work with you today?" she asked with her mouth full.

"You bet." He tamped down his excitement. "I'm planning to take water samples of *Wai'apo* stream. I need to swing by my place and get my water test kit."

"Sounds fun."

After pie, Curly hurried out to his rig to rake the mess on the floorboard under the seat.

"Good enough." She hopped in, clearing away enough room for her feet. "I'd be more worried if you were a neat freak."

They drove west as the mist from the hard night's rain rose in the clear morning sky.

"So, you're interested in stream biology?" he asked.

"No, not especially."

Does that mean she likes me? He glanced over, trying to get a read on her. It was no use— she was a complete mystery. He tried not to get his hopes up but it was impossible.

She could tell he was staring. "Watch the road, big guy."

When he pulled into his driveway, the front door was wide open and the lights were on. "Typical," he muttered.

Gina jumped out, curious to check out Curly's *hale*. She kicked off her slippers in one fluid motion and followed him inside. "Whoa!"

"If I knew I was having company, I would have cleaned up," he said, embarrassed.

"Your place could use some sprucing up as well," she teased, combing her fingers through his tangled hair.

"Very funny," he said, indignantly, pretending he didn't enjoy the attention.

"Is that your surfboard?"

"No, it's my roommate's." He wanted to add, *my same buddy who left the door wide open and the lights on. And yes, those are mostly his empty beer cans.*

She smiled, picturing Curly teetering on top of a surfboard. "It's really stuffy in here. Why don't you open a window?"

"They're stuck."

She tried cranking open a jalousie. "Where's your WD40?"

"My what?"

"Did you have servants in Idaho? How do you not know about WD40?"

"Because I'm a Russian spy. My handlers sent me here to find out why you're so rude," he replied.

There was a pool of water in front of the incontinent refrigerator. "You got anything to eat around here?" She opened the refer door and quickly closed it. "Comrade, I think something perished in there."

"I can't believe you're hungry again. We just had breakfast."

"Pie is not breakfast."

"Maybe food will help with the rudeness."

"Take me to Harada's Market. I need musubi."

He grabbed his water testing kit on the way out the door.

When they got to Mau Loa, he waited in the truck while she ran in and grabbed a can of WD40 and some snacks.

Chickens scurried out of her way in the parking lot. She jumped in the cab and tossed him a warm musubi. "Okay, back to your place."

"Why? You're gonna woof that musubi down in three bites."

"Now who's being rude?"

Curly made a U-turn and headed back to Lani Kai. He laughed when he noticed the old bumper on the rusted-out Chevy pickup in front of them was tied on with orange bailing twine. *All it would take was hitting a deep pothole for it to break free of its lashings,* Curly thought.

When they pulled back into the driveway, Gina opened the squeaky front door and sprayed the rusty hinges before setting to work on the window cranks. "When you spray this stuff, don't get any on the glass or you'll never get the oil off," she advised. As she cranked open the louvered panes, the flat skeleton of a squashed gecko fell on the sill.

Curly gathered his roommate's laundry off the bathroom floor and threw it in the linen closet just as she came through the door.

Within half an hour, Gina had cranked all of the windows open, letting in the cool breeze. "Your screens are rusted through. You know how to replace screens?"

"Yeah," he lied.

"Have you ever replaced a screen?"

"I'll figure it out," he declared with bravado. "You must be starved. I'll buy you a gelato."

"Deal. You can keep the rest of the can." She set the WD40 on the coffee table. An opened notebook drew her eye.

Curly raced over and snatched it up. "My roommate's diary."

There was something about his expression that made her wonder.

"I'm leaning toward pistachio," Curly said, as normal as possible. His heart skipped a beat as he realized how close he had come to disaster. "What about you? Coconut gelato?"

Gina wondered about the odd look on his face. *It must be your diary,* she thought. "I'm leaning toward lilikoi shave ice. You buying?"

"You did most of the work," he admitted.

"I think you mean, all the work."

They hit Sherry's Shave Ice Shack on the far side of Mau Loa. *Sherry's* was a little hole-in-the-wall on a back street. Ever since the *Ultimate Wai Nau Guide Book* gave *Sherry*'s five stars, there was an ever-present long line out the screen door.

After a twenty-minute wait, Curly watched in amazement as Gina polished off a double lilikoi with a scoop of vanilla ice cream. "When you're finished, we can grab some emergency rations before we leave town."

"Hilarious," she said, sarcastically.

"If possible, I'd like to stop between meals and take water samples at the mouth of the *Wai 'apo* stream. My boss, Tanner Horn, has been trying to get permission to access the upper drainage but so far I've only been able to survey the mouth of the stream. The valley is private property up to the locked gate, a mile beyond the *Pali* golf course."

"I went fishing in *Wai 'apo* reservoir once when I was a kid," Gina remembered getting jabbed by a dorsal fin when she tried to remove the hook out of a peacock bass's mouth.

"Duane Lin, the Chinese billionaire financing the Avalon Club, has purchased nearly all of the valley, including the reservoir. I'd love to get a look at the earthen dam. The health of the stream depends on how much water they let through."

"Uncle Kahawai lives in the lower valley. Can we stop by and see him on the way?" Gina asked.

"That would be great." Curly was excited to be able to gain access to *Wai 'apo* stream.

"Take Old Quarry Road toward *Wai 'apo* Beach Park."

Though the deep potholes rattled the fillings in his back teeth, Curly loved the old road that wound tightly along the coast. Spotting the towering basalt *pali* through a break-in the mist, he knew they were getting close to Wai'apo stream. The signature silhouette of the high cliff had been used in dozens of movies since the war.

"Take this driveway," Gina pointed.

"The one with all the *No Trespassing* signs?" Curly reluctantly turned up the narrow drive. "Are you sure?" More than once he had driven down a driveway, only to find himself face to face with an irate local. Stink eye was one thing, but he had been physically assaulted on a couple of occasions. The Hawaiian state emblem on his rig was not always welcomed by those who believed they were living in the Kingdom of Hawaii. Some Hawaiians viewed the US government as illegal. It didn't help matters that he was a *haole* with a Mainland accent.

Gina could tell Curly was getting nervous. "Relax. Uncle's place is just ahead, right after this banyan tree."

The fence line opened to a wide green meadow. An old plantation cottage built on tofu blocks sat near the far tree line, the rusty red roof blended with a huge African Tulip in bloom.

Gina hopped out of the cab and waved. Curly saw a large figure sitting in the shade of the lanai. As they crossed the meadow, Curly let out a relieved breath when he saw the old man's gentle smile.

"Gina girl! It's been too long. How you been keeping?" the big man asked.

"Fair to middling."

"And who is this rascal?" he asked.

"Uncle Kahawai, this is my friend Curly. He works for the state. I'm helping him to survey your stream today."

"Survey? Hmm?" The old man sat down, as if suddenly tired. "Yes, they will be building soon enough."

"Not that kind of surveying," Curly explained. "Gina has volunteered to wear a snorkel and mask to survey the health of the stream bottom."

"I did?" she asked, surprised.

"The water's plenty chilly this time of year," Kahawai laughed.

"There is a nice swimming hole a short walk from here."

Kahawai got to his feet with help from his carved guava walking stick.

Gina noticed the older man was having trouble walking. "What's wrong, Uncle?"

"My left knee is *buss up*," Kahawai explained in pidgin that his knee was hurt.

"Sit back down for a moment," she insisted. "Let me see."

Curly watched as Gina examined the big man's knee, going through a sequence of strength tests.

"Does this hurt?" she asked.

"Plenty," Kahawai smiled and grimaced.

"Uncle, you need to go see your doctor. It looks like you have a torn meniscus." She saw the incredulous look on Curly's face. "I majored in physiology in college," she explained, not wanting to get into why she quit.

"I can walk." Kahawai grabbed his walking stick and headed for the stream. Curly and Gina flanked him, ready to offer an arm in support.

"Do you know the meaning of *Wai 'apo?*" Kahawai asked Gina.

"Wai is water," Gina remembered that much.

"*Wai 'apo* is water caught on top of a taro leaf," Kahawai explained. "We Hawaiians gather this sacred water to use in our ceremonies."

Curly was delighted to meet an old Hawaiian who knew about the traditional ways. He liked how Kahawai viewed *Wai 'apo* stream as millions of drops of sacred water. A thousand questions swirled in his head, but he decided it was better to listen.

"*Wai 'au 'au,*" Kahawai pointed to a deep pool that sat behind a giant boulder. "This is where I bathed since small kid time." A light rain fell, swirling in the breeze like tiny snowflakes.

"What did you mean, Uncle, when you said, 'they will be building soon?'" Gina asked.

"When my parents died, the land passed to me. My father worked in the pineapple fields. Small kid time, none of these trees were here, this was all pineapple down to the coast road."

Gina remembered when the cannery closed without warning. "Did you lose your job when the cannery closed?"

"No. Luckily, I got a job on the docks when I was a teenager. I was a stevedore for forty-five years. I'm retired now with a decent pension, but with land prices climbing to the sky, I can't afford my taxes."

"Uncle, you're not thinking of selling?" Gina asked.

"No choice." He looked across the green meadow. "You're looking at the new *Wai Nau* Polo Grounds."

When Curly read the Times article about the proposed Avalon Club, he thought the polo grounds must be a marketing scam. Looking across the deep grass and wildflowers of the meadow, the idea seemed surreal. *Who the hell plays polo?* he wondered. "This looks like prime bottomland," Curly asked, wondering why it was fallow. "You could grow anything."

"Yes, if I had water," Kahawai agreed.

"I don't understand?" Gina pointed to the stream running right through the meadow.

"The water rights are tied up with the developers," Kahawai explained. "I'm not allowed to divert water from the stream."

Gina fumed. "I never knew any of this, Uncle. You need an attorney."

"I asked my friend Jaco, who is a retired judge. He told me the attorneys for the developers can keep a lawsuit from going to trial for five years or more. With the taxes doubling and tripling, I don't have that kind of time. If I sell now, I'll have money but no place to live."

When the rain began falling in earnest, Curly decided it was best to cut the workday short. They bid their farewells to Uncle Kahawai and ran for the truck.

Gina didn't say a word on the ride home.

"Are you okay?"

"Just thinking, that's all."

Tom Scrum

It is not economical to go to bed early to save candles
if the result is twins.
–Chinese proverb

Gina borrowed Chichi's car and braved the old cane road, dodging red rental cars the full seven miles out to *Mana'olana* Beach. She parked Sooby under a poinciana tree and walked through the cool shade of the *haole koa* bushes that covered the high dunes. There was a chance that the tenant staying at Perry's beach house had seen something around the time of Auntie Nalani's death. The only problem being the disgusting tenant Tom Scrum. A legendary letch, locals affectionately called him Scro-Tom. Gina reminded herself that Tom was sleazy, but not dangerous.

The winding path spilled on to a white sand beach arcing in both directions for miles. She could see the roof of Perry's beach house. She waded in the shallows and decided to take a swim to cool off from the hot, dusty ride. Swimming against the current to the reef, she spotted a school of triggerfish. She floated on her back and saw the sun glint off of a pair of lenses on the lanai of the beach house. Wrapping her aqua blue sarong around her wet two-piece suit, she donned an oversized pair of pink sunglasses and strolled down the beach, looking lost.

The older man hid his binoculars and waved.

She waved back. "Hello! Could I please use your bathroom?"

"Sure thing, come on up." *She looks like a local girl,* Tom thought. He gave her his best bleach-white smile. She wasn't wearing a wedding ring. "Are you visiting from the Mainland?" he asked.

"Yeah, the Bay Area," Gina said, topping the stairs. She had rehearsed her character and cover story the night before. "I'm Minnie."

"Welcome to my *hale,* I'm Tom. A pleasure to meet you." He slid open the screen and pointed, "The bathroom's the second door on the right." He watched her backside for a moment before grabbing a bottle of Barefoot Bubbly champagne and orange juice from the fridge, pouring two mimosas with time to spare.

As badly as Gina had to pee, she couldn't bear the thought of her bare bum on Tom Scrum's toilet seat. She waited a minute and flushed while pulling open the squeaky medicine cabinet containing: one large bottle of Viagra, two boxes of Clairol Natural *Instincts* for men, a stick of Old Spice High Endurance deodorant, a small black bottle of Dior *Sauvage* Eau de Toilette, Tom Ford "Raven" eyeliner and mascara, and a wide assortment of condoms and other unmentionables. "High end," she said to her reflection as she silently pushed the mirror closed. "High-end creepy," she added, as if her comments might be used out of context. "A real catch," she whispered, as she sauntered her way back to the living room, reminding herself to get back into character.

"I thought you might like a cool refreshing drink after being out in the sun." Tom handed her the crystal flute.

"Oh, how thoughtful." She took a small sip and followed him out to the lanai. She sat with her back to the water. "I read in the local paper that a woman was found dead near here. Did you know her?"

"No."

"So, you didn't find the body?" Gina teased, hoping to keep the conversation going.

"Evidently an old woman was wandering around in the middle of the night and fell into a sinkhole."

"So, it happened right near here?"

"So, Minnie, you're from the Bay Area?" he asked, changing the subject.

"Just outside Berkeley."

"Is this your first time visiting *Wai Nau*?"

"Yep."

"Are you a student?" he asked.

"I write mystery novels. I'm working on a murder mystery set on a tropical island. I was really hoping to meet someone who knew the woman who died, or saw the body," she said, disappointed. "You've been really kind. I should get going. Thank you so much." She got up to leave.

"A novelist! How interesting. Now that you mention it, I did see a woman the evening before they found the body."

Gina sat back down, "Really!" she said, enthusiastically.

"She came out of the trees just over there." Tom pointed back toward the sinkhole. At least now he had an angle. She was a mystery buff. He could work with that.

"An older woman?"

"Actually she was . . ." he almost said, "Built," before pausing to think of a more mysterious way of phrasing it. "I saw her from a distance. She looked in very good shape. Around five-nine, blonde, late twenties/early thirties."

"Wow, you have a really good memory," she gushed. Gina was getting a kick out of watching Tom work his debonair magic. She was grateful it was a woman that came out of the trees. Had it been a man, Tom would more than likely have zero recollection. "Sounds like a tourist."

"I don't think so. She climbed into a souped-up beige Accord." Tom didn't want to get into how he was watching the woman through his binoculars. "I remember her because she flipped her cigarette in her mouth and lit it." Tom mimicked the flip.

"Wait? She tossed her cigarette in the air and caught it with her lips?"

"Yes. It was very sexy." Tom's eyes lit up.

Gina sipped her mimosa. "Have you told the police?"

"Of course," Tom lied. "Are you vacationing alone?"

She could tell he was getting suspicious of all her questions. "I don't know if you read mysteries, but—"

"I love Agatha Christie," Tom said.

"Agatha Christie! She's brilliant. I love how there's always so many suspects in her stories. Are you sure there wasn't anyone else around the evening before the body was found?" Gina smiled and thought about touching his knee and quickly changed her mind. "It's for my novel," she pleaded.

Tom wanted to land this fish. "Well, now that you mention it, I remember seeing Al Johnson's boat in *Hokua* Cove right over there." Tom pointed north. "It was odd, cause Al usually heads out into deep water to fish for tuna."

Gina took off her oversized pink sunglasses and smiled.

There's something about this girl, Tom thought.

"You're trying to work out if I'm local. Am I right?" she asked, looking him in the eye. "Local girls come with so much baggage."

"I thought you looked familiar."

Gina shook her head in mock sympathy. "Local girls look for

two things in a man: Does he have a house? And, does he have a job?"

Tom's mouth dropped open.

"Trouble is—you don't have a house or a job."

"Excuse me?" He gestured at the house and then to the ocean behind her.

"Sorry, Tommy, I happen to know that you're house sitting for your cousin, Trevor Perry, whose family owns this place. Every local girl on the South Shore knows your cousins are rich, but you're a shirt-tail relative, a senior citizen with no job, pension, or prospects." As she got up to leave, Gina hoped a fly would land in his open mouth.

Tom stared at her ass as she walked away. "Plenty more fish in the sea!" he called after her. He poured the rest of her drink into his glass and looked up the beach.

A Shift in the Wind

The sea finds out everything you did wrong.
–Francis Stokes

Gina swung by Kalo's to pick up Curly. She was anxious to ask Captain Al Johnson why he had come ashore on the evening of Nalani's death. After just experiencing cocktail hour with Tom Scrum, Gina wasn't keen on booking a deepwater cruise without backup. Curly wasn't exactly imposing, but two was safer than one.

Curly had never seen Gina drive. He would never say it to her face, but Gina had two left feet. There was no hiding the fact that she was clumsy. He had been in a serious accident when he was ten, and as a result, was a nervous passenger. He found himself getting anxious as he waited at Kalo's.

Gina pulled into the parking lot and waved to him.

"I can drive," he suggested.

"Hop in. I want to get to the Port *Panoa* marina before the fishing boats leave."

Curly climbed into the passenger seat of the old Subaru wagon and buckled up. "Is this your car?"

"It's my dad's. He doesn't drive much. Old Sooby is going to be thirty next year, and she only has thirty-five thousand miles."

Curly checked his seat belt and realized his hands were sweating. He was impressed when Gina signaled before pulling out onto the highway.

Before they made it out of town, a tourist rolled through the stop sign without looking left.

Curly instinctively put both hands on the dashboard and braced for impact.

Gina braked immediately as if she foresaw that the Mustang wasn't going to stop.

He caught himself watching her every move. Her hands were on the wheel at ten and two o'clock. When she came to a stop at the light, it was like silk, the same when she accelerated, easing out the clutch, flawlessly breezing through the gears.

"What's going on?" she asked.

"Nothing."

"What's with the look?"

"It's your driving," he admitted.

"What about my driving?"

He could hardly say that he thought she had two left feet. "It's just that . . . I'm a terrible backseat driver. I get nervous if I'm not driving."

"I didn't know you were such a control freak," she teased. "You want me to turn around? We can take your truck."

"No. You're a great driver."

"Thanks," she said, noticeably relieved. "I used to drive cab. I still fill in once in a while for friends."

"Why am I not surprised?" *What job haven't you done?* he thought. "Gotta say, cab drivers are famously crappy drivers. Seriously, where did you learn to drive?"

"Long story short, when I got my learner's permit, Chichi, my dad, let me practice driving Sooby." She laughed. "Well . . . let's just say, he arranged for me to help him deliver eggs to the temple members."

"I don't follow."

"My first time driving a stick shift, Chichi sat right there, with five flats of eggs on his lap. I'd step on the accelerator and popped the clutch and kill it. "Be careful, daughter," he said, clutching the eggs. We drove all around the island for weeks delivering eggs. When I knocked on the door of the first house, you should have seen the surprised look on the Auntie's face. It took me a couple more stops to work out Chichi's Driving School method. I still drive like there are five flats of eggs sitting on the passenger seat."

Gina took the windy bypass road in hopes of avoiding the morning traffic through Waikoko. She tapped the brakes going into a tight ninety-degree corner, accelerating out of the turn. A blond shirtless man was in the middle of the road. She pumped the brakes, just as the man pumped his right foot. She realized he was on a skateboard. "You've got to be kidding me?" She had come dangerously close to running the *haole* over. She waited until she could safely cross the double yellow and sped past.

"Hey wait, Gina! That's my roommate."

"That's your roommate?" She reluctantly pulled over.

When Hutch recognized Curly, he kicked his board up on the dismount, tucked it under his arm and climbed into the backseat. "Wow! Who's the babe?"

Curly cringed.

"The Babe can hear you." Gina turned around and gave Curly's roommate the stink eye.

"Dude, she hot!" Hutch reached around the bucket seat and punched Curly in the arm.

"And, she is sorry she is such a careful driver," Gina said, stomping on the accelerator, half-wishing she'd run him over.

"She can drop me at Mona's Burgers and Brew," Hutch said to Curly.

"Or not," Gina muttered under her breath.

Curly looked over at Gina and mouthed, "I'm sorry."

"What's her name?" Hutch asked.

Before Curly could jump in, Gina spun around, "Why don't you ask her?"

"Dude she is smokin' hot, but kind of high maintenance."

Gina slammed on the brakes and pulled over. "Okay. Out!"

Hutch looked perplexed.

"Curly, tell your friend to get out," Gina said, in no uncertain terms.

"Hutch, get out. I'll explain what a dumbass you are later."

"Totally high maintenance." Hutch grabbed his board on the way out and slammed the car door.

Gina stomped on the gas and looked in the rearview mirror. The infuriating *haole* was already scooting down the middle of the road.

"He's an old friend from high school," Curly said, apologetically. "He's sleeping on my couch till he finds his own place."

Gina didn't say a word.

"I'm sorry. Hutch is a jerk. He gets nervous around women. I said I'm sorry."

They rode the rest of the way to the harbor in uncomfortable silence.

Gina parked in the shade near the paddling club. They walked around the marina looking at the boats. Sailboats always sent Gina's imagination out into the beyond, the gentle swaying of high masts lulled her into calm. She recognized the old man fishing off the end of the pier, "Uncle Pantaloon! How you been?" Gina hugged him.

"Little Gina! It's good to see you."

Pantaloon lifted the lid on his five-gallon bucket, proudly showing off his catch for the day.

"Uncle, do you know Captain Al?" Gina asked.

"The *Sugar II*," the old fisherman pointed to a thirty-foot Twin Vee Powercat and frowned. "Mind how you go, there's a dark cloud over that boat."

"Thanks, Uncle. Not to worry, we'll be careful," Gina promised and gave Pantaloon a kiss on the cheek.

The captain of *Sugar II* smiled and welcomed them aboard. "Watch your step, young lady. How can I help you?"

"Are you Captain Al?" Gina asked.

"Yes, that's right."

"I'm Tiffany, and this is Pete," Gina smiled and shook the captain's hand.

"Just so you know, Tiffany, I'm not booking any fishing trips this month. I'm doing a little maintenance on my sweetheart." Captain Al brushed his hand over the teak hatch he had just finished sanding. "Come below out of the wind."

Curly followed Gina into the small cabin.

Capt. Al pulled open a floor hatch and grabbed the boat key that was sitting on top of the bilge pump.

"Good hiding place," Curly remarked.

"That's not the reason I keep the key here. If you forget to turn the bilge pump off you can burn up the pump, drain your batteries, or worse, set your boat on fire. I always turn the key on when I come aboard to pump the bilge. When I leave, I switch the power off and put the key back on the pump. Force of habit."

Gina thought Capt. Al sounded like a pretty savvy boat captain until the wind shifted and she smelled the alcohol on his breath. Maybe it was from the night before, either that or Captain

Al liked a splash of coffee with his bourbon first thing in the morning.

"So, what can I do you for?" the captain asked.

Gina couldn't think of an indirect way to ask. "*Sugar II* was seen in *Hokua* Cove on the night before Nalani Ōta was found murdered. We were wondering—"

Captain Al's eyes widened, and his face turned red. "You need to beat it. Get off my boat. Now!"

Curly stood between the irate captain and Gina. "Take it easy. We're leaving."

"Did you see anyone that night?" Gina asked, over Curly's shoulder.

Captain Al shoved Curly in the chest.

"I said we were leaving. Don't touch me again," Curly warned and backed out of the cabin.

Gina hopped onto the floating pier. "You can talk to us, or you can talk to the police."

"I've already told the police everything. Now, piss off!"

Gina caught up to Curly who was hoofing it back toward the car. She smiled and said wryly, "Salty old dog."

Curly laughed, even though he was upset.

"I liked him more than your roommate," she quipped.

"So did I."

Speed Thrills Auto Parts

I'm always getting this junk mail plopping through my door inviting me to a 'car boot sale,' but I never wear boots in the car.
–Michael Shepherd

After getting nicked in the left ear at Freddie's barbershop the last time he got a trim, Curly asked Gina if she knew another barber.

"There's Bev's. I can drop you off."

"Great."

Gina drove across town on the back streets and pulled up to the curb. "That's the place."

A pink neon sign in the window flashed, *Bev's 'bove da Neck.*

"Don't you want to come in?" he asked.

"Not a chance." She had always had a fear of hair salons.

Curly reluctantly walked up to the glass door and pulled it open. He was greeted by a wave of ammonia hydroxide vapors and a chorus of "Oh là làs."

"Aloha." A short, blonde Bev personally welcomed Curly into her lair. She led the way to her Belvedere styling chair with a kind of criminal intent, a furtive gate as if she'd just robbed a liquor store in broad daylight. In his mind, he turned and ran for the door, as his body walked calmly across the room and sat in the black vinyl recliner.

The other hairdressers immediately ceased whatever they were doing and came over to introduce themselves and admire his cowlick. He was used to it. No one actually knew his given name. Julius who?

"I'm Bev. What's your name?"

"Curly."

This brought forth a warm hum. The absence of a wedding band on Curly's ring finger momentarily set the furniture on fire. "How do you like it?" Bev giggled curling her shoulders in like Marilyn Monroe.

"Umm? Just a trim would be good."

"Relax, honey." Bev leaned his head back against the marble shampoo bowl and rinsed his hair with warm water. It felt good. Curly could see Bev glancing up at the TV. The unmistakable organ music of a daytime drama held the room as Bev gently massaged his scalp.

The customer in the next chair getting a perm asked if Jenny knew about Robert's affair. The narrative turned to the important question: who was the father of Jenny's baby. Half the room was certain that it was Robert's baby. Bev was convinced that Anthony, the Latin pharmacist, was the real father.

Curly realized he was in mortal danger. If he let slip that he didn't know who Jenny was, a nicked ear would be the least of his problems. The close-up shots lasted an eternity.

"So, Cutie, how did you hear about my salon?" Bev asked.

"My girlfriend." Curly could have sworn the water instantly turned ice cold.

"Oh? Where does she get her hair done?" Bev asked as she dried his hair.

"I'm embarrassed to say that I don't know." Curly raised his voice above the hair dryer.

"Is she local?" Bev flipped off the dryer.

Though there were faint sounds of scissors snipping, it was clear to Curly that the stylists and the customers wanted a name and they wanted it now! In a panic, he blurted out, "Is Jenny going to marry Robert?"

"Are you kidding?" Bev shook her head in disgust, pointing an accusing finger at the TV. "Robert's such a coward. Jenny doesn't even know he loves her."

With a narrow black comb in her left hand and a short pair of ivory-handled scissors in her right, Bev worked her magic. When she was finished, she handed Curly a mirror. "What do you think?"

Curly ran his fingers through his hair. "You're an artist. What do I owe you?"

"Shampoo and a trim is fifty even, honey."

Curly had never paid fifty bucks for a haircut in his life. He had to admit, it did look and feel great. He dug two twenties and ten out of his wallet. "Thanks, Bev. It was nice to meet all of you."

"Anytime, sweetheart." Bev squeezed his hand and held it for an awkward few seconds.

Gina sat in Sooby in front of the salon and fumed. "What's he doing in there? It's been forty-five minutes." Waiting was by far safer than going in to get him. Either because she was cheap, or because of her deep-seated fear of hair salons, she had always cut her own hair. She looked at her plain black hair in the mirror. "Not too bad, she said, turning her head around, never sure if it was even in the back.

When Curly finally emerged, the storefront window quickly filled with the silhouettes of five different hairstyles. Gina looked at their astonished faces as Curly hopped in the beat-up old wagon. She kissed him on the lips to claim him as her own before speeding away.

"Wow. I guess it's worth it to pay a little extra."

"Was there a line or something?" she asked. "It was nearly an hour."

"Did you know Robert is the real father, and Jenny doesn't even know it?"

"You're a brave man," she said and meant it. "Before we stop by the auto parts store, I need to swing by my place and feed Ananda, my cat."

Curly tried to hide his excitement. He was dying to see her place. "Sure, that's fine." He played it cool.

Gina's little house was on Honi Street, one block south of Perry Plaza shopping village. It sat between *Roy's Rods and Tackle* on the corner and a brightly colored fuchsia house that looked like an unlicensed daycare. The yard was filled with an odd assortment of bikes, a faded plastic pool, and piles of toys.

Gina pulled into the gravel drive. "You want to come in?" she asked.

Curly popped his seat belt. "Love to."

Clumps of wild amaryllis ringed the small yard. The trunk on her jade plant was the diameter of an elephant's foot. A low shed roof over the front lanai sheltered three black leather office chairs. Curly didn't think anything about it until he went inside. Surrounding the makeshift coffee table of stacked pallets was a beat-up sofa and three more black office chairs. He stifled a laugh.

He followed her into the kitchen where two more identical black office chairs were tucked under a small glass table. He let out an involuntary giggle.

"What?" She gave him a sharp look.

"Nothing."

"You can't smirk like that and then say, "Nothing."

"It's just . . . I didn't know about your fondness for office furniture."

"Oh." Her face softened. "I used to work at the transfer station. People throw lots of good stuff away."

Curly remembered when he dropped off his trash how all the county workers sat in black office chairs in the shade. "Okay, makes sense."

A wide assortment of gourmet olive oils and balsamic vinegars lined the long kitchen counter. Trying to solve the puzzle, he pointed to all the bottles.

"I clean condos on Wednesdays. Tourists fly here for three days and buy tons of groceries."

"More perks of the job."

"Exactly."

Grabbing the box of dry cat food off the counter, she headed out the back door. She was tempted to show Curly her rain barrel. Outdoor showers were common, but there was nothing to compare with washing and rinsing your hair in rainwater. She filled Ananda's bowl and ladled a little rainwater from the barrel into his water bowl.

Curly wanted to snoop around, but couldn't even manage to get up the nerve to peek into the refrigerator. He sat in the closest black office chair and scooted around the kitchen tile.

Gina came in from the backyard. "Tuck in your feet." She gave him a spin. "Close your eyes."

He closed his eyes and gave into the sensation of the room spinning. He wondered if Gina really liked him, or if she just needed his help. They were having fun and he didn't want to risk messing it up, whatever it was. He imagined the spinning chair to be a roulette wheel. He decided when he came to a stop and was facing her, he would tell her how he felt. As he slowly came to rest, he opened his eyes, looking directly at the refrigerator. "Perfect." He chuckled.

Gina reached into a bottom drawer for a green glitter gift bag, and selected a cold-pressed Greek olive oil, pairing it with an award-winning Italian balsamic. She handed it to him. "Congratulations on your chair spinning expertise. You're our grand prize winner!" she announced.

"Thanks."

"Ready to check out the car place?" she asked.

"Oil and vinegar, *and* I won a new car?"

"Something like that. Tom Scrum said the woman he saw the evening before Nalani's death drove away in a souped-up Honda Accord. There's only one high-end parts store on the island."

He stood up, still a little dizzy, and carried his prize out to the car, hoping her present was a secret message.

Gina drove across Perry Plaza shopping village to *Speed Thrills*.

From the outside, the parts store looked like any other franchise in a strip mall. Curly pulled open the glass door for Gina.

"Chivalry's not dead," she pronounced.

Despite the door chime, the two salesmen remained oblivious to the new customers. The two men looked so much alike in their matching aloha shirts, Curly took a second take, wondering if they were brothers. Their identical haircuts glistened with product, adding to the illusion. He thought he recognized Bev's handiwork.

"I think we should have brought Moreno," Curly whispered. He was used to buying the odd quart of oil or a new set of wiper blades, but this parts place was a whole different level. Everything on display was eye candy for your car.

"Look, your favorite." She pointed to the black car bra prominently displayed on the grill of a BMW.

"Very funny."

Gina vogued beside a life-size cardboard cutout of a woman in a bikini grasping a wrench.

Curly ignored her, wishing she would quit acting up in the store.

"You're cute when you're embarrassed," she teased.

They strolled along a long row of shiny magnesium rims.

"These black rims are called 'murdered,'" she explained.

"How would you know something like that? It's disturbing."

"*Howzit?*" the closest twin behind the counter asked. "Can I help you find something?"

"You carry an HKS twin sport dual axle exhaust for a 2019 Honda Accord?" Gina asked.

Curly pretended he understood what she had just said.

"The dual exhaust for the V-6?" the salesman asked while tapping the keyboard.

"Yeah." Gina pushed her breath out as if she wouldn't be caught dead driving a four-cylinder.

"That works best with the ceramic headers." The other twin chimed in, holding the phone against his shoulder.

"So I've heard." Gina smiled, giving it a little extra. She took each of their business cards, reading their names in a sultry voice, "Steve Jade and Kai Shin."

Curly did his best to hide how uncomfortable he felt watching Gina flirt with the two men.

Gina leaned over the counter. "This skinny blonde, who drives a beige LX-S Coupe, told me her turbo spools quicker. And, even the lower range is smoother with this setup."

"Your friend is correct. The reduction in backpressure makes a huge difference in acceleration," Steve, the nearest twin pointed out. "The stock exhaust on the LX-S is junk."

"You know the blonde I mean; she drives a beige LX-S Coupe?" Gina pounced.

"Maybe. What's her name?" Steve asked.

"All I know is, she blew by me on the straightaway at Halfway Bridge," Gina sounded upset.

"That sucks," Kai, the other salesman said. "I can get you ten percent off if you order the set today."

"This blonde really thinks she's hot," Gina had an ax to grind. "She flips her cigarette into her mouth." Gina mimicked the flip.

"You say she drives a beige LX-S with an HKS twin sport dual axle exhaust?" Steve asked, and then looked at his twin for confirmation. "There are lots of Accord coupes on the island." He shrugged his shoulders. "Sorry, can't say I remember a blonde wahini with a beige Honda. Maybe it's her boyfriend's car," he offered. "So, with ten percent off the whole package, it will run you twelve hundred and seventy-five dollars, plus shipping."

Gina slid down her shades. "That's a bit dear."

"Cheaper than a DSM. If you really want to get into the game," Kai threw down the gauntlet.

"I wouldn't be caught dead driving a Mitsubishi," Gina shot back.

"Whew! Burn!" Steve howled. He wasn't very impressed when the two drove up in the junker Subaru, but this girl was fiery. "I can get the set here in a week?"

"Thanks. I'll think about it." Gina made for the door with Curly in her draft.

He jumped into the passenger seat. "Holy shit! I didn't know you knew anything about cars."

"I used to be a parts runner for NAPA."

"I should have guessed. What in the hell is a DSM?"

"Diamond-Star Motors. You're the guy; you're supposed to know this kind of stuff." She was disappointed, hoping to get a real lead. "I bet this place sells a lot of high-performance mufflers. Still, you'd think those two guys would remember a tall blonde who works out and drives an LX-S coupe."

"What are you saying?" Curly asked.

"I'm saying—it's time to visit the drag strip."

Slow Your Roll

If everything seems under control,
you're not going fast enough.
–Mario Andretti

"I'll meet you there." Moreno hung up. She didn't want to show up at the track with a *haole* in the backseat. She had a reputation to maintain.

Gina called right back, "I think it would be best if we ride together; we'll blend in better."

"If you bring Curlers—we're not blending."

"We're at Kalo's. See you in a few." Gina hung up before Moreno could get in the last word.

Ten minutes later, Moreno reluctantly pulled into Kalo's.

Gina pulled the passenger seat forward, and Curly climbed into the back.

"Mind the leather," Moreno barked.

"Have you seen the coroner's report?" Gina asked.

Moreno pulled onto *Hoku* Highway and punched it. Both back wheels squealed, the sudden acceleration pressing Curly into the leather upholstery.

"Well?" Gina insisted.

"Don't even." Moreno rolled her eyes. "You know I can't discuss an ongoing police investigation."

When they arrived at the drag strip, Curly started to get excited. He had never been a gear head, but he was looking forward to seeing what the classic Camaro could do on a straightaway. Not wanting his life to end in a giant fireball, he was relieved when Moreno stopped at the front gate.

"Out!" Moreno used her thumb for emphasis. "Don't give me that look, Gina. You two gonna mess with my time." Moreno didn't want to get into the whole weight-to-load-ratio thing, knowing she was built for comfort, not speed. Her Camaro SS, on the other hand, was built for comfort and speed.

"I'm good with watching from the stands," Curly weighed in.

"It costs money," Gina pointed out.

"I'll buy." Curly offered as if there was ever a question. He stood in line and bought the cheapest tickets available, while Gina bought a lilikoi shave ice with a scoop of vanilla ice cream. They found their seats in the high aluminum bleachers.

Gina took a taste. "Whoa! Way too sweet and sour! My lilikoi syrup is the real thing." She took a bite of vanilla ice cream to round off the tang.

Moreno was three cars back in line. When a souped-up Nissan pulled in the other lane, her heart began to pound. The coupe's tinted glass was too dark to be street legal. She couldn't see the driver, but she recognized the aftermarket chrome airfoil. She was pretty sure she had written the pimply-faced owner a speeding ticket in the recent past. She felt herself becoming aroused as they pulled up to the starting line. A spotter helped snug her front wheels up to the line.

Moreno eased the stick into first gear and relaxed her clutch foot. The yellow light flashed three times, and the light turned green. She stood on the accelerator pedal and listened to the sound of her paycheck burning up as her rear tires bit into the pavement. Two blinks later, she dropped into second gear and fished-tailed. Out of the corner of her eye, she could see the Nissan pull ahead. She double-clutched and hit third, spooling well into the red before slamming her into fourth with a chirp.

Gina jumped to her feet, her remaining shave ice landing on Curly's lap. They both cheered as Moreno blew past the Nissan.

Moreno looked over her right shoulder as she crossed the finish line. Her challenger was a full car length behind. She let out a deep breath and tapped her dash with affection, "Never doubted you, Baby."

Curly was surprised by Gina's reaction. "I thought we were being low-profile."

"We're blending." She pursed her lips into a small mea culpa.

Curly surveyed the scene below. "No shortage of beige Accords, just like your boyfriends at the auto parts said." He wasn't sure the point of coming to the track, but he had to admit, he was thrilled when Moreno crossed the finish line.

"Speaking of the twin assassins, there's Steve Jade and Kai Shin." Gina pointed to the crowd mingling around the black Nissan that Moreno had just bested. She watched closely as the street racers talked story. They all looked pretty amped up. "Definitely a tweaker crowd. They're not hopped up on double lattes."

Curly knew meth was a huge problem on the island.

Gina noticed a folded bill in a tall teenager's palm as he shook hands with Kai. Then the teen shook hands with Steve, the other clerk. "Did you see that?" she whispered to Curly. Kai had passed a small paper packet to the teen.

"What?"

"I'll tell you later." She was pretty sure the packet being palmed was meth. Now that she knew what to watch for, Gina's eyes followed Steve and Kai as they did business in plain sight. She realized, even if they were arrested, they couldn't be charged because the money and the meth were separated. It suddenly became clear that Speed Thrills was a front for distributing methamphetamine. "You gotta hand it to them—truth in advertising."

Gina scanned the crowd for tall blondes. She noticed a couple of girls smoking. Tom Scrum said the woman he saw near the cave flipped her cigarette in her mouth.

Moreno hit the scales, pulling up to the timeslip shack. It took her a minute to recognize her old classmate in the drive-up window. "Hey, Tanner."

"Nice run, Moreno." Tanner stared at Moreno's breasts.

"Thanks. What's my time?"

"Sorry, the clock's got a glitch today. You want to go again? On the house. They're gonna glue the track at 11:00."

Spraying VHT on the track for better traction would improve her time. "No chance 'em. My tires still plenty hot," she explained.

"Hot and spicy." Tanner raised his eyebrows. "With some wrinkle-walls, no one could touch you. You're a touch light on your backside. That's why you were so soft out of the gate."

Moreno blushed. "You think my backside light? For reals?" Moreno couldn't hide her delight at being called skinny.

"Just enough junk in the trunk." Tanner winked and handed over her timeslip. "You had a perfect RT time, 0.500."

"Why you never give me my time already?"

"Cause you know, Baby. You always like to go again," Tanner whispered.

"Nevah kiss and tell." Moreno locked on to his eyes, pursed her thick lips and parted them slowly before stomping on the accelerator. Driving around in circles looking for Gina, she spotted Gutierrez, one hand holding a beer, the other wrapped around Kammie Sato. He ignored his arm candy and shot his signature smile at Moreno.

Moreno pretended not to notice. Gutierrez was the trifecta: handsome, great body, and he was an earner. When she was in Afghanistan, she'd seen plenty of pretty boys wet their pants during a firefight. She looked past the prince and spotted Gina in the nosebleed bleachers. She honked and waved. "I won the race!" she yelled. "You're supposed to come and congratulate the winner!" She could forgive Beaver Cleaver; it was obviously his first time at a drag strip.

Running on Empty

You might be a redneck if . . .
The blue book value of your truck goes up and down
Depending on how much gas it has in it.
–Jeff Foxworthy

Gina went to the *Wai Nau Times* and scoured the back issues for clues. She skimmed a front-page article the day after Nalani's death, about two divers Sammy Morita and Jay Long that had gone missing, their bodies never recovered. Next, she carefully read through the Arrest Log section in the weeks before Nalani's death, concentrating on drug busts. A meth lab was found in an abandoned house in *Kai Pali,* but there were no arrests. She was going to have to figure out a way to keep an eye on the auto parts store. She had been a parts runner before; maybe she could get her old job back? She decided it was probably too dangerous since she had already asked about the cigarette-flipping blonde.

The only other significant event in the arrest logs was an assault charge filed on a *Malama Mana'olana* protester by the Sun Dairy Group the week prior to Nalani's death. The proposed dairy site was on the other side of the stream from the sinkhole. Maybe there was a connection. Lacking any other leads, she decided it was worth following up.

After making some calls, Gina found out that the site manager of the proposed dairy, Kyle Scott, lived north in *Wai'oli,* just north of the construction office. She called Carla and pitched her plan.

Moreno listened and silently shook her head. She was in no hurry to get mixed up in another one of Gina's hair-brained schemes. Not that there was much choice, someone needed to keep a close eye on Gina. It didn't help that Detective Alvaro was an arrogant prick who had frozen her out of the investigation. According to Alvaro, she was only qualified to fetch coffee and malasadas. Gutierrez and Alvaro were too proud to admit that without Gina there wouldn't be a murder investigation.

Moreno reluctantly agreed to help Gina do a little recon. They found a turnout on the old cane road and waited. Five minutes after five, Kyle Scott drove by on his way home from work.

"Is that your guy, the construction manager?" Moreno asked.

"Yep. I think it's time for Minnie to ride again," Gina said.

"Minnie who?" Moreno asked.

"She's a student from Berkeley, vacationing alone," Gina used her innocent lost voice.

Moreno rolled her eyes. "I almost feel sorry for this Kyle guy."

That night, Gina cut off an old pair of shorts up to the crotch and likewise sacrificed the collar of a perfectly good T-shirt, cutting the neckline as low as she could handle. She stood in front of the mirror and did her best not to pass judgment on the woman looking back at her. "A girl's gotta do what a girl's gotta do." She splashed some water on her face as if she could wash away the indignity.

The next evening at a quarter to five, dressed as Minnie, Gina parked Chichi's Subaru on a straight stretch of the old cane road north of the Sun Dairy construction trailer. She propped open the hood and waited.

Moreno parked nearby in the brush with a clear line of sight. Earlier that morning she gave Gina a small can of pepper spray. "Keep your right hand in your bag holding on to the spray. If the guy touches you, shoot the buggah in the face." She knew Gina would go through with the ridiculous plan whether she helped or not. At least this way, she was only a minute away if anything happened.

Gina called Moreno on her cell. "Hey, Carla, can you hear me?"

"You on speaker?"

"Yeah. My phone's already in my handbag. All set."

"Don't take any chances. If you get a bad feeling, say the code word: Chicken Wings." Moreno instructed.

"Chicken Wings?"

"Yeah like, 'I could really eat some chicken wings right now,' and I'll be there in forty-five seconds. Got it?"

"Yeah, except . . ."

"Except what?" Moreno was ready to call it off.

"Now I'm hungry."

Kyle slowed down to pass the stalled car. When he saw the girl, he hit the brakes and rolled down the passenger side window. "Looks like you could use a hand."

"I think I'm out of gas," Gina said.

"Jump in. I'll take you down to Kimo's."

"Thank you so much." Gina climbed in. "I'm Minnie."

"Hey, Minnie. I'm Kyle. Happy to help. What are you doing way out here?"

"I work for SDH, the company that's working to get a local dairy on the island. I'm sorry I can't tell you any more." Gina took out a tube of pink lip-gloss from her handbag. She slowly rolled the shiny gloss over her full lips, pressed them together and parted them as if blowing a kiss.

"It's okay," Kyle reassured her, struggling to keep his eyes on the road. "I work for Sun Dairies. I'm the security supervisor for the project."

"Wow! So, you're management! I just started last week with the PR department. It's my job to take on the idiots who oppose the dairy. Who doesn't want fresh local *Wai Nau* milk to drink?" She smiled, concentrating on batting her lashes, a skill she had never quite mastered. Her face itched from the makeup and her eyes stung but she resisted scratching them.

Kyle's eyes wandered. When his side mirror started slapping branches, he swerved back into the middle of the dirt road.

"It's so frustrating." Gina crossed her long legs and inched closer.

Kyle started to sweat.

"I wish someone would find those troublemakers and crack 'em. Maybe some Tongans," Gina suggested.

"I've had a couple of run-ins with the nature worshipers," Kyle said, proudly.

"No kidding? Did you kick their ass?"

"I've towed their cars a couple of times." Kyle smiled, remembering the looks on their faces when they discovered their cars were gone.

"Oh, is that all?" Gina said, disappointed. She rolled down her window and looked out.

Kyle could see Minnie was losing interest. "Don't tell anyone. A couple weeks back, I caught this guy coming out of the construction trailer."

"Did you beat him up?"

"I chased him down to the beach and had it out."

"What happened?"

"I made it pretty clear that if he ever showed up again—" Kyle was tempted to show her the scar above his eye, but realized it was better not to go into the seven stitches or the fact that the guy was only five-two. He must have been a surfer. "I think it's safe to say; he's not coming back anytime soon."

"Did he steal anything?" Gina asked.

"I'm not sure," Kyle lied. An important soil perc test had failed, so Sun Dairy paid a local firm to make sure the second test came in with the right figures. The manilla file with both tests was the only thing missing. It was as if they knew what they were looking for.

"So, they broke in but didn't steal anything?" she asked.

"Let's just say, Butch Connors was raging the next day." Kyle began wondering about all the questions.

"Yeah, Butch. He can be a real jerk."

"Butch is her nickname, cause she's butch. Who did you say your boss was?"

"Yeah, that bitch Butch. She wishes she was a guy." Gina laughed. A wave of adrenaline shot through her. Her right hand was gripping the little can of pepper spray so tight, she couldn't reach for the door handle.

Kyle stomped on the brakes. "I think you better get out, Minnie, or whatever the fuck your name is."

"Yeah, I could really use some chicken wings!" She jumped out and slammed the truck door.

Kyle punched the accelerator forcing Gina to dodge flying gravel.

Moreno immediately pulled up. "You okay, Minnie?"

"I need food. Let's hit Rey's taco truck." Gina jumped in. "We need to track down somebody from *Malama Mana'olana* who broke into the project trailer last week. It could be important."

When they got to Rey's, Gina ordered three ono fish tacos and a large diet coke. Gina sat down and handed Moreno her drink. "What's going on with the investigation?"

"You definitely do not understand my job. I'm a rookie, not a homicide detective. If I so much as glance at the Nalani case file, I could get suspended," Moreno explained, again.

"So, have you heard anything?" Gina asked.

Moreno was frustrated. Gina didn't seem to understand the risk she was taking. "It's easy for you. You've already lost your dream." Moreno regretted the words the minute they escaped her lips.

Rey called her name and Gina picked up her basket of tacos at the window. She sat across from Moreno and ate in silence, thinking about what her life would have been like if she had finished college. She told herself at the time that she was forced out. For the last five years she had replayed it all a thousand times. She was the one who quit.

Moreno sipped her diet soda, feeling bad about jumping on Gina. If her job wasn't on the line, she would have apologized.

"Oh crap!" Gina jumped to her feet.

"What is it?"

By the time they got back to Chichi's car, it had been towed.

* * *

After paying the ninety-five dollar impound fee to get Chichi's car back, Gina spent the evening piecing together the information she had gleaned from Kyle Scott. He had mentioned that Butch Connors was upset about the trailer break-in. Something important must have gone missing. She remembered her old classmate, Victoria Summers, worked for *Malama Mana'olana*, the citizen's group fighting the industrial dairy. Victoria wasn't exactly a shrinking violet. Gina steeled herself and made the call.

"Hi, Victoria. This is Gina Mori. I was wondering if you could help me. I heard a rumor about a break-in at the construction site of the proposed Sun Dairy site. I would very much appreciate speaking—"

"*Malama Mana'olana* is not involved in any criminal activity," Victoria set the record straight. "We are a legitimate legal organization." She didn't question where the two perc test documents had come from that proved the dairy was fudging the numbers. "*Malama Mana'olana* supports local agriculture. We support a local dairy with 200 cows but oppose an industrial dairy of 2000 cows in *Mana'olana*. It will be an environmental disaster for our drinking water, for our beaches, and for tourism—the island's main source of revenue."

"I understand and share your concerns," Gina assured her.

"Donations for legal fees are always welcome," Victoria suggested.

"Yes, of course," Gina was back on her heels, suddenly feeling like a cheapskate. "If you were to hear anything about a theoretical break-in at the construction site, I'd theoretically be interested."

"Have a nice day, Miss Mori." Victoria hung up.

Gina couldn't tell if Victoria was cranky because she knew something, or because she didn't. Or, because she was just naturally irritable. It was another dead end. Kyle had said that Butch was upset about the break-in. "She must know something. We need to draw her out. I better ask Curly," she said to herself. "Moreno is not going to like this."

The Turk

Happiness is a simple everyday miracle,
like water, and we are not aware of it.
–Nikos Kazantzakis

Gina called Curly and invited him to lunch. "I'll buy," she promised on the phone. Those two little words made Curly nervous. If she was buying, something was up. He swung by her house, she was waiting under the lanai.

"Where are we going?" he asked, as she jumped in the cab.

"Kepa Beach."

"Where's that?"

"Just on the other side of Perry's Ford."

"Great," he said, trying not to sound ungrateful. He knew the free lunch was going to cost him. Technically he had an hour lunch break, now he was driving thirty minutes one way to Kepa Beach.

Gina gave an edited version of her encounter with Kyle Scott, the onsite dairy manager, leaving out how she got the information from Kyle, instead, focusing on her plan of action.

Curly listened, squeezing the wheel harder and harder as they drove through the thousand tall coconut palms of the old Perry Estate. When he couldn't take Gina's hairball scheme any longer he interrupted. "So, let me get this straight: you want to pretend to blackmail a woman named Butch, using information you don't have?"

"I know it sounds a little far-fetched, but remember, Butch Connors has no way of knowing that we're not the ones who broke into the construction trailer. It's simple; we pretend to have damaging information and ask for money in exchange for our silence."

"Aside from going to jail, what do you hope to gain by blackmailing Sun Dairy?" Curly asked.

"We're pretending to blackmail them, not actually blackmailing them."

"A distinction without a difference." He was tempted to point out that so far, none of her schemes had uncovered anything useful. "It's a miracle I still have a job. I can't keep doing this crazy stuff."

"You're right. Sorry, I shouldn't have asked." *My Auntie Nalani was murdered. I don't expect you to understand.* After the fiasco with Kyle Scott, Moreno would definitely shoot down the plan. She needed help, but it was clear she had pushed her friends to the limit.

"Take one left." Gina pointed. "Right here!" she said a moment too late.

Curly stood on the brakes and turned the wheel, overshooting the gravel drive. "Thanks for the warning, co-pilot," he said sarcastically, as he drove over the curb.

The gravel parking area was a stone's throw from Kepa Beach. Mismatched tables with ratty umbrellas pitched at various angles surrounded a bright purple food van parked under a massive monkeypod tree.

They parked and walked past a green Toyota pickup that was left running with the air-conditioning on. Gina glanced at the local couple eating at a nearby table. "It's nice to see young people so concerned about the environment." It bothered her how often people left their cars running to keep them cool.

Curly read the menu on the side of the van. "Gyro?"

"It's pronounced, *hero*," Gina corrected.

He didn't recognize anything on the menu. "Risking my job to make sure you're well-fed," he complained. "Must be a weekday."

"It's lunchtime. Don't you get a lunch break?" she said, defensively.

"Yeah, but I'm pretty sure I'm not supposed to drive clear to the other side of the island to eat."

A woman in a turquoise muumuu in front of them was picking up a large takeaway order.

"Falafel is good for the soul," the chef declared through the window.

The auntie stuffed a fiver in the tip jar and grabbed the two big to-go bags. "Thanks, Hot Feet."

Gina stepped up on the wooden platform to order. "Falafel is good for the soul? Really, Hafeed?" Gina teased.

"Hey, it's true," the chef shot back. "Nice to see you, Gina. What would you like today?"

"Two specials, please. When the rush is over, we need to talk," Gina said.

"Have a seat. I'll bring your food," the chef said, enthusiastically.

Gina found a table away from the others. "Hafeed is from Turkey. He used to have a restaurant in Jeddah, Saudi Arabia."

"How does a Turk end up with a Greek food van in *Wai Nau*?" Curly asked.

"Hafeed is an international chef. He studied in Europe and is certified to cook Italian, French and Asian Pacific. He used to work at the Four Seasons on O'ahu. That's about as high-end as it gets unless you have your own gourmet restaurant."

"What happened?"

"Like any chef worth his salt, Hafeed can show a clove of garlic who is boss. But when it comes to women, let's just say . . . he's a romantic. Hafeed fell in love with the hotel manager's daughter, a huge error in judgment. He had to go into hiding."

"I can relate," Curly mumbled under his breath.

"What?"

Hafeed emerged from the van carrying four plates. As he set them down, he explained each dish to Curly, "This is Baba Ganoush, and this one is tabouli."

"The tabouli is very green." Curly noticed.

"Yes, my tabouli is fresh parsley and mint, with a little bulgur wheat, olive oil, and lemon. This one is falafel of course, and this is tahini with pita." Hafeed disappeared back into the van.

"He's not making more food is he?" Curly was concerned.

"These are the pupus." Gina dipped her finger in the baba ghanoush and tasted it. "Oh my!"

"Why are we here, besides to stuff ourselves?" Curly wondered.

"The Turk has special gifts," she explained between mouthfuls.

"Such as?"

"He's a night owl."

"That's a special gift?" Curly took a bite of tabouli. "Wow! Tasty."

"In order for my plan to work, someone has to stay awake and watch."

Hafeed arrived carrying two large plates. "Sumac crusted *Opakapaka* on saffron rice with grilled *opi'i*."

"You have outdone yourself, Hafeed." Gina took a bite of fish. "Oh, lovely."

Hafeez looked at Curly. "What's the matter? Why are you not eating?"

Curly was completely stuffed, but he picked up his fork and got busy. The fish was like nothing he had ever tasted.

When Hafeed saw Curly's face light up, he relaxed. He lived to watch people enjoy his food. "I'll be right back."

Curly took out his wallet and checked to see how much cash he had. "I'll buy." He knew she invited him, but he didn't want her paying for a four-course meal.

"Put that away, unless you want to set him off," Gina shouted in a whisper.

"At least let me leave the tip," he argued.

"I may have done Hafeez a small favor in the recent past. Trust me; don't even think about paying."

"Why is he working in a van? This is the best food I've ever eaten."

"Here he comes with dessert."

"Oh no!" Curly said under his breath.

After finishing the last bite of Turkish delight, Curly leaned back in his plastic chair. Never had he experienced more pleasure and pain from a meal. He watched Hafeed bring a rather plain looking plate of food to a nearby table before closing up shop for the day. When he was finished, he joined them in the shade.

Curly rubbed his aching belly and thanked Hafeed for the amazing meal. "I saw you serving what looked like a sandwich and fries to that table over there."

Hafeed shrugged. "Like any artist, you play to the audience. If they want grilled cheese, you make them grilled cheese."

Gina brought Hafeed up to speed on their suspicions concerning Auntie Nalani's death. "We know that someone broke into the job site trailer less than a mile from where Nalani was killed."

"We don't know for sure that she was killed," Curly interjected.

"Was the break-in the same night as Nalani's death?"

"We're pretty sure." Gina brushed off Hafeed's question. "We know the dairy people are very upset about the break-in, but we don't know who it was, or if anything was stolen."

"What? That's it?" Hafeed asked, gripping his face with both hands.

Gina suppressed a smile. Whenever Hafeed was upset, he would become overly dramatic.

"This is like preparing a banquet from an old shoe. You have no ingredients," Hafeed stated the obvious.

"The difference is, Hafeed, your imaginary banquet guests don't know that we have no ingredients."

"This is beside the point," Hafeed argued. "When the food fails to arrive, the customers will burn down your restaurant."

"It's simple. We call our dairy friends and tell them we broke into their trailer. We tell them we need a thousand dollars to keep quiet about what we found," Gina explained.

"I'm not seeing how this helps," Hafeed had heard the story of making stone soup, but this was going nowhere.

"Trust me, Hafeed, if they have something to hide, they'll respond."

"Yes, by burning down your restaurant," Hafeed said, under his breath.

"Can you round up a voice-activated recorder and a camera with a telescopic lens by tomorrow?" Gina asked Hafeed.

"No problem."

* * *

The next day when Hafeed closed up his van, Gina was waiting.

"Where's your boyfriend?" Hafeed asked, climbing into the Subaru wagon.

"Curly's not my boyfriend and he's busy tonight."

Hafeed gave her a knowing look. "Lucky guy."

Gina wondered if he meant Curly was lucky not to be involved with her, or lucky not risking jail time? She drove to the Port *Panoa* marina and parked near the public bathrooms.

"We need to hide the recorder near that payphone." Gina pointed.

Standing on his tiptoes, Hafeed placed the digital recorder on a brick ledge above the payphone. He did a couple of tests until he was satisfied it was working.

Gina scouted the treeline a hundred yards up the grassy embankment. "If we park in the Methodist church parking lot up the hill, we should be able to follow the irrigation ditch, hide in those trees and then exit discreetly without being seen."

"There's a streetlight," Hafeed pointed. "So taking photos shouldn't be a problem. What's the plan again?"

"It's simple. I'm going to call Butch Connors from this payphone and tell her to bring the cash here at midnight or else. When she shows up, I call the payphone. You snap pictures, and the voice-activated recorder will pick up anything that happens after she hangs up. Got it?"

"Yeah, I got it," Hafeed admitted. "We'll get five years in jail for blackmail if we get caught."

"Relax, we're not going to touch the money. And we're not going to get caught."

Gina picked up the receiver with a handkerchief, punched the number in the phonebook for Sun Dairy and asked for Butch Connors. A few minutes later Butch was on the line.

"Hello, this is Beverly Connors. How can I help you?"

"Bring a thousand dollars in cash to the public bathrooms at the Port *Panoa* Marina midnight tonight, or Sun Dairies will be on the front page of tomorrow's paper."

"Who is this? What's this about?"

"The *Times* would love to get a hold of what I found in the construction trailer." Gina hung up and wiped her prints off the receiver.

* * *

Just before midnight, Kyle Scott parked in front of the payphone. He got out and looked around. Both bathrooms were locked.

"Crap," Gina said under her breath. "It's Kyle." She was hoping to speak directly with Butch Conners.

When Hafeed saw Gina's reaction to the man getting out of his pickup, he began to panic.

"Relax, Hafeed, stop holding your face." She dialed the number.

When the payphone rang, Kyle picked up the receiver. "Hello."

"Do you have the cash?" Gina said, an octave lower than her normal voice.

"Yes." Kyle looked over his shoulder, wondering if they were watching him.

"Listen carefully. Stick the money beneath the brick under the bench behind you. Then, drive to Joe's Drive-in. Unless you want me to go to the *Wai Nau Times*, do exactly as I say." Gina hung up.

"Who is this?" Kyle asked, before hearing the dial tone. "Shit!" He took out his cell phone and called Butch. "There's no one here. They called the payphone by the bathrooms and told me to leave the money under a brick and drive to Joe's Drive-in."

"Leave the money and drive to Joe's. I have a good view of the bathrooms from where I'm parked. When they show up, they'll get more than their money's worth," Butch promised as she scanned the lit area of the parking lot below with her binoculars. She was more interested in catching the blackmailers than whether the two soil perc tests were sent to the *Times*.

Hafeed snapped a few pictures of Kyle from their hiding place up the hill in the tree-line.

"Let's get out of here," Gina looked around, wondering if Butch was watching.

"That's the first sensible thing I've heard you say all day." Hafeed followed Gina around the paddle club's equipment shed and along the irrigation ditch to Chichi's Subaru parked in the church parking lot. As they sped away, Gina kept a watchful eye in the rearview mirror.

"That was hectic," Hafeed let out a relieved laugh.

* * *

Two days later, Gina returned to the harbor just as the tourists were coming off the sunset cruise boat, steering clear of the bench where the money was hidden. She picked up the phone receiver and pretended to dial. Then she casually reached up on the ledge and recovered the voice recorder. She sat in the Subaru and listened to Kyle's phone call to Butch. Gina wondered what Butch meant by "getting more than their money's worth."

Gina drove to Hafeed's for lunch and played him the recording.

"I thought it was going to be a complete waste of time," Hafeed admitted. "It's not exactly a smoking gun, but you were right. The dairy people have something to hide. Whether it has anything to do with your Auntie's death, we still don't know. What do we do now?"

"We figure out a way to sweat Butch Connors. We need to find out more about her."

"This *wahine* is already plenty pissed off."

"Pissed off people make mistakes," Gina said confidently.

"Like killing the world's greatest chef?"

"Yes, that would be tragic," Gina agreed.

"So, what's the next move?"

"We need to break-into Butch's house."

Hafeed held his face with both hands. "You need to take a step back, Gina. You're out of control."

The Blue Van

Then I remembered what my Mom said about eating Bitter melon. If I keep eating this will I get used to it? Will I learn to like it? Somehow I don't think so.
–Cara Chow

The abandoned blue '79 Econoline van was parked under an ironwood tree near *Pali Ke Kua* beach. Officer Moreno had drawn the short straw. Abandoned vehicles were a common problem all over the island. She tapped on her siren, to see if anyone would poke their head out of the roach coach. It was midday. "Not the best place to be, inside a hot sardine can," she reasoned. The plates were missing. She filled in the abandoned vehicle report on her laptop. High grass had grown up around the rig and the rear passenger side tire was flat. She radioed Island Towing to haul the rusty heap to the waste metal recovery site in *Kala Lui*, to be crushed and shipped off-island.

Using a yellow waterproof crayon, she wrote the citation number on the windshield. The passenger window was rolled down, and the door was unlocked. She checked the glove box for the registration. The floorboard of the passenger seat was filled with trash. She dumped out the moldy remains of a diet Coke. A ratty envelope in the glove box was stuffed with an assortment of papers. Moreno dumped the contents of the envelope out on the passenger seat, hoping to find the registration. One scrap of paper looked familiar. It was written in Japanese but had measurements in English. It was a recipe for *Goya Champuru,* bitter melon and tofu stir-fry with pork belly and eggs. She carefully unfolded a brown piece of newsprint, an old *Wai Nau Times* obituary page.

Moreno thought she recognized the handwriting as being very similar to the recipe book found in Evelyn Nalani's handbag. Without access to the evidence locker, it would be impossible to find out. She remembered Gina confessing that she had made copies of Nalani's recipe book before handing it over.

"Damn it, Gina!"

If she shared her find with Gina, there was no telling what kind of catastrophe it would lead to. She kicked herself for thoroughly searching the abandoned van. Gutierrez was right, doing a half-ass job made for fewer problems in the end.

The Sunshine Market

If you don't know where you're going
any road will get you there.
–Lewis Carroll

Moreno met Gina at Kalo's. They compared the recipe Moreno found to Gina's photocopied pages of Auntie Nalani's recipe book.

"It's Auntie's writing." Gina was sure of it. "It's a perfect match. This is our first real clue."

"I need to call this in to dispatch right now before the van is crushed. There might be physical evidence in the van, like fingerprints." Moreno paused with the phone in her hands, staring at it. "Shit! How am I going to explain this?"

"Tell Detective Alvaro that you have an eidetic memory and—"

"A what?"

"Tell him you have a photographic memory, and you suspect the recipe you found in the van matches the writing in the Nalani case. It's the truth, you did recognize the writing."

"I gotta go. If you find out something new, don't do anything without telling me. I mean it, Gina!"

"Don't worry, Carla. What else did you find in the van?"

"I found this obituary page from last February."

Gina read through the obits. Nothing stood out as unusual. "This farmworker who died?"

"Natural causes," Moreno said, anxious to get on the road.

* * *

Gina drove to the *Times* and searched the obituaries for anything unusual about the five people who had passed away during the third week of February. She remembered reading about the Philippine farmworker who suffered a heart attack after entering a field of corn that had been sprayed with pesticide. Was there a connection to Nalani? Her recipe for bitter melon didn't get into the van by itself. Maybe the blue van belonged to the killer? Gina wondered what it had to do with Sun Dairies. No doubt, there would be fingerprints in the van.

She stayed after midnight in the archive room sifting through back editions. On the twenty-third of February that year, one day after the farmworker's death, there was an article about police chief Luis commandeering a helicopter to search for an escaped prisoner named Joshua Santos who also worked for SynthCo, the biggest agrochemical company on the island.

Gina combed the ever-popular arrest logs for that year, from February to the present. In August, a local man, Denny Maka, had been arrested for a DUI. The article mentioned that Denny Maka worked as a driver for SynthCo.

* * *

The next day Gina stopped by Ray-Ray's. On Thursdays, Gina sold Ray-Ray's popular smoked pork in the popular turnout by the *Hea Hea* Falls.

Uncle was filling the left front tire of his pickup truck with a foot pump.

"Hey, Ray-Ray."

"Here comes trouble! *Howzit,* Gina?"

"How's the batch coming?" She could smell the sweet aroma of smoked pork emanating from the backyard hootch.

"Gonna be plenty of da kine ready by Thursday," he promised. "You want a beer?" Ray-Ray was more than willing to take a break from pumping up the flat.

"I heard your new girlfriend already has you wrapped around her finger," Gina teased, hoping he would spill the beans.

"You know there's nobody but you, Gina girl."

"At least tell me her name?"

"I don't know what you're talkin' about." Ray-Ray put his back into it, the tire nearly full.

"You know I'll find out," Gina taunted.

"Sylvia," he confided, out of breath. "She is amazing," He pulled off the hissing air hose and quickly screwed the little black cap on the leaking nipple. He kicked the hard tire, satisfied.

"Uncle, you know Denny Maka?"

"Denny is one loser. He lives in *Hana Kai*," Ray-Ray said, still out of breath.

"I just need to ask him a couple of questions."

"He hangs out in *Hana Kai* park most days. You want me to come with you?" Ray-Ray didn't want her talking to Denny alone.

"Thanks, Uncle. I'll be fine."

* * *

Moreno picked up Curly and Gina in front of Kalo's place. Gina pulled the seat forward, and Curly climbed into the back.

Before Curly could buckle his seat belt, Moreno gunned it down the highway. "Remind me again why we're going to the farmer's market," Curly asked.

Gina turned around and explained, "That's where Denny Maka hangs out. The guy who used to drive a van for SynthCo."

SynthCo was one of four agrochemical companies leasing land on the hot and dry Westside. Because of the year-round growing season, it was possible to grow four rotations of corn a year, making *Wai Nau* one of the best places in the world to develop and produce genetically modified seed corn.

"I get that Denny used to drive for SynthCo, but why are we looking for him?" Curly asked. "If I'm going to go to jail, I'd like to at least know why." Working a fulltime job and helping Gina was starting to wear on him in more ways than one.

"We need to ask Denny if he knows Joshua Santos, the prisoner who escaped," Gina explained.

When they reached *Hana Kai,* Moreno parked in front of the Post Office across the street from the park. The Sunshine market was winding down and the crowd was thinning.

"That's Denny's rig over there." Moreno pointed to late model black Ford F350 with a neon blue lift kit, and oversized tires.

"What's the deal with all the monster trucks?" Curly asked Moreno. Half the pick-up trucks on the island had lift kits.

"Is this guy for real?" Moreno looked over at Gina.

"I told you he was a real *haole* boy," Gina said.

"You're a guy, right? So why are you asking me?" Moreno shook her head.

"I'm asking *because* you're a woman. Does having a monster truck increase your chances of, you know . . . getting lucky?"

"Not for you," Moreno said, without inflection.

Gina stifled a giggle.

"Sorry, I just don't get it?" Curly couldn't let it go.

Moreno tilted the rearview mirror down and peered at Curly. "If a guy drives a nice rig, it tells a girl a few things. If his rig is washed and waxed, it means he takes care of what he loves. It tells a girl that he has a job, that's he's a good earner, that he has pride."

"And, the higher the lift kit, the smaller the brain," Gina added.

"Yeah, pretty much," Moreno conceded the point. "Personally, it tells me two things. One, you've foolishly put sixty grand into your toy truck. And two, you're still living at home with your parents. So, basically, you're a loser."

"Thanks, Moreno. That helps, a little." Curly thought Moreno's immaculate '69 Camaro must mean something. She did have a steady job. "I still don't get the big tires," he admitted.

"If the truck is a symbol of masculinity," Moreno continued. "Then the tires are basically genitalia."

"You mean the balls?" Curly asked.

"Exactly. The jacked suspension symbolizes an—"

"Okay!" Gina cut in. "I think that's enough about Denny's truck. Let's go find him." She swung open the long door and pulled the seat forward.

Gina asked an Auntie selling eggplant if she knew Denny Maka. The old Auntie made a face and pointed to a tattooed man sitting under a tree across the park.

Curly took the lead, strolling right up to the big man sitting on the picnic table. "*Howzit?* Are you Denny?"

Denny smoked his menthol cigarette down to the filter and flicked the butt at Curly. He stared at Moreno's breasts. "I know you," he said to her chest.

Curly held up his phone with a picture of Joshua Santos. "Do you know this guy?"

"Get the fuck out of here, *haole*! Before I crack you." Denny spit on the ground in front of Curly.

"Do you recognize this man?" Curly repeated. "It's important."

Denny stood ready to throw a punch.

It took effort for Curly not to give ground.

"*Shibai!*" Moreno stepped in front of Curly. "No worries. Denny only hits women."

"Fuck you!" Denny screamed right in Moreno's face.

Quicker than a hiccup, she shoved him, the back of his knees hitting the bench. Denny tumbled hard on top of the rickety picnic table.

"You know this guy or what?" Moreno asked, looking down on Denny.

"*Nevah* seen him."

"His name is Joshua Santos. He's a farmworker," Moreno pressed. "You worked for SynthCo driving this guy all over the place, field to field, so quit talking shit, Denny."

"Or what?"

"Tell us what you know and we'll leave your sorry-ass alone," Moreno suggested. "Or, would you rather your friends hear how you got the shit kicked out of you by one *wahini?*"

Denny looked around the park. Everyone was watching. He knew better than to hit an off-duty cop. He sat up straight and tried to make it look like everything was cool. His left hand was shaking as he lit another cigarette. "Okay. I remember this old dude. He got too friendly with one of the field nurses and got his ass sent back to the Philippines."

"When?" Moreno pressed.

"A couple months back."

"What was the nurse's name?"

"I don't know."

"Nalani?" Gina asked.

"Yeah, maybe. That's all I know. So fuck off!" Denny said defensively.

Moreno stepped closer and dropped her hands to her sides, inviting him to take a swing.

"Fuck you, bitch!" Denny yelled.

"I'm so scared!" Moreno laughed. "Let's go. This guy can't beat his own dick."

When they walked by Denny's monster truck, Moreno confided to Gina, "The sad thing is, that loser will probably get drunk later and beat up his girlfriend." Shame was a hard thing to understand.

"Truck or no truck, no way Denny has a girlfriend," Gina argued.

"Ha! You're right!" Moreno let out a relieved laugh.

Curly climbed into the backseat. "I thought you were going to kick the proverbial tires back there."

"You thought right." Moreno gave Curly a big smile in the rear-view mirror. When she first met this skinny-ass *haole*, in the park with Gina, she was worried. Curlers wasn't much to look at, but he was okay.

"You know what this means?" Gina said, excited.

"Not really," Curly admitted.

"We may have finally found a connection to Auntie Nalani," Gina explained.

"Was Auntie a nurse?" Moreno asked.

"As far as I know, Nalani retired from nursing years ago." Gina wondered if Nalani had been working for the seed company and had not told her. "We have to find this farmworker Joshua Santos. The police must think he is pretty dangerous if they commandeered a tourist helicopter to search for him. Sounds like a murderer to me."

Moreno dropped Curly at Kimo's gas station where he left his rig to get serviced. He climbed out of the backseat and gave Gina a hug and a quick kiss. "See you later."

"If you're lucky," Gina added.

Moreno pulled back onto the highway. "You want me to drop you at Kalo's?"

"Yeah, I'm starving."

Carla could tell something was on Gina's mind, but she left it alone.

When they pulled into Kalo's, Gina broke the silence, "Do you think I should tell Curly?"

"What? That you're a virgin?" Moreno smiled.

"No! About the whole Boom Boom thing."

"What? Who gives a shit about that anymore?" It made Moreno angry to remember all the assholes that piled on Gina, ruining her dream of becoming a physical therapist. "Why? Are you serious about this guy?"

"What do you think?"

"He's not my type."

Gina gave Carla a serious look. "You know what I mean."

"Girl, I never know what you mean."

"Please," Gina pleaded "What do you think?"

"Curlers is okay."

Gina let out a sigh. "Thanks, Carla."

"If you like skinny *haoles*."

Tea with Cabriole

The moon is brighter
since the barn burned.
–Matsuo Basho

Karen Klindt was a *hapa haole* in her late seventies who lived alone with her goats. The grassy meadow around Karen's plantation house was fenced with rusty pig wire.

Curly parked in front of the sagging gate. The run-down old house looked abandoned. "Seriously, someone lives here?"

"This is Karen's place, she was a close friend of Auntie's. I'm hoping she knows if Nalani worked for SynthCo or if she knew Joshua Santos. She might know why auntie went to the sinkhole dressed in her finest *kimono*."

Curly pointed to the weathered sign above the gate. *Capri Farm*.

"As you'll soon see, Karen loves her goats," Gina predicted, with a little giggle.

Back in Idaho, Curly had milked his share of goats. It was more frustrating than milking a cow, mainly because a nanny goat couldn't stand still for longer than three seconds. He carefully closed the makeshift gate behind them, remembering how goats loved to stand on top of the highest rock. A parked vehicle, to a goat, was a hollow metal peak.

Karen welcomed Gina with a big hug. They both cried a little, remembering Nalani.

Curly offered his hand to shake; Karen gave him a big hug instead. "Look, Eumaeus is coming to say hello," Karen pointed. The billy goat ambled up to Curly and half-heartedly nibbled the back of his t-shirt. "Eumaeus never goes near strangers, especially men," Karen said, surprised.

Curly did his best to act grateful to receive the stamp of approval.

"Come on in. I just finished giving the kids their bottle."

They followed Karen through the open front door. Curly noticed that Karen didn't kick off her slippers, but Gina did. Curly was unsure, so he untied his boots and pulled them off before going in.

"You better put your boots and slippers on this shelf for safe-keeping," Karen advised. She offered Curly a stuffed chair that looked like it had been exhumed from the dump. He sat down gingerly, in a futile attempt to keep his full weight off the chair cushion. A calico goat pranced on top of the beat-up sofa, abruptly pausing to do a "bit of business" before jumping and balancing on the armrest. Despite his best effort, the muscles in Curly's face registered his shock as he fidgeted in the damp recliner like a hyperactive terrier.

The goats' behavior failed to raise an eyebrow, from Karen or Gina, which made it all the more of a menagerie.

When Karen repaired to the kitchen to make tea, Curly's eyes widened. "We've gotta get out of here!"

"Relax. They're only goats." Gina had a black kid on her lap and a little white nanny was butting her kneecap.

Karen emerged from the kitchen with tea on a bamboo tray. She held it just out of reach of the frolicking goats. "Milk?" Karen asked.

"Ah, no thanks," Curly replied. He took the hot cup with both hands and smiled.

"Goat milk is good for you," Karen lobbied.

"This is fine, thanks." Curly was tempted to tell Karen that he had milked his fair share of goats, the main difference being, he had milked them *outside*. His right elbow was suddenly rammed by the spunky white kid, causing the boiling hot tea to splash on his wrist. "Faah!" Curly managed to shorten his expletive.

"That's Cabriole," Karen said, with pride. "And that's Bootsie."

Curly stared at his remaining tea and then at Gina.

Gina ignored his sour look. "Auntie, when was the last time you saw Nalani?"

The moment their hostess turned to address Gina, Curly poured the remainder of his hot tea down the side of his seat cushion. When Gina clenched her jaw, Curly knew she'd seen him out of the corner of her eye. A plume of steam rose from the cushion. *This chair's seen much worse,* he thought.

"Nalani often stopped in on Wednesday mornings on her way to pick wild ginger near Lava Rock Dam. She made flower arrangements for the lobby of the Tsuru Inn."

"I knew Auntie loved ikebana, but I didn't know it was a business," Gina replied.

"Last year, Nalani made an amazing arrangement for Mrs. Sato's eightieth birthday celebration. It caught the eye of Mr. Takahashi, the manager of the Tsuru Inn. He offered her a contract to provide flowers for the lobby. In the early morning, Nalani often took long walks and picked flowers in the wild."

"Do you know if Nalani had any other jobs, wasn't she a nurse?" Gina wondered.

"She let her nursing license expire years ago. As you know, she loved performing tea ceremony at Love Bites."

Curly looked at Gina, "Love bites?" It sounded like a massage parlor.

"Love Bites is the traditional teahouse up River Road," Gina explained to Curly, before turning back to Karen. "What did you and Nalani talk about on Wednesday morning when she came to see you?"

"The usual kinds of things. We talked about the quilt show coming up."

"Do you ever remember her mentioning a friend named Joshua Santos?" Gina asked.

"No, sorry."

"Do you remember anything else you talked about?"

"Sorry, I don't remember anything special." Karen felt dreadful for not remembering her last conversation with her dearest friend.

"Was she excited or worried about anything?" Gina could see that Karen was becoming frustrated. "Never mind, Auntie. It's not important." She knew Karen was pressing, trying too hard to remember. "Do you have any photos of you and Nalani?"

"Oh yes." Karen sprang to her feet and reached for a cake tin on the upper cupboard shelf. She opened the rusty lid carefully picking out an old black-and-white photo. "Look at those two beauties. Can you believe it? I'm twenty-three, and Nalani had just turned twenty-six." She handed the old photo to Gina.

"You're both gorgeous," Gina agreed.

"Careful, Cabriole doesn't nibble it," Karen warned.

Curly noticed that several of the photos were half-eaten. An old photo of taro terraces caught Curly's eye. "Auntie, may I take a look?" He admired how the ancient Hawaiians got the most out of every drop of rain.

"Yes, of course, dear." Karen handed him the tin, grateful the young man had gotten over his initial shyness.

Curly studied the old black and white photo, marveling at the graceful beauty of the rock terraces. "They're like rice paddies."

Karen dug around and found another old photo of the same upper valley. "When I was a girl, they used to grow rice in the old taro patches."

Cabriole was eager, convinced the brightly painted tin was filled with goodies. Karen could tell that Curly had been around goats by the way he gently kept Bootsie and Cabriole at bay while he sorted through the old pictures and postcards. "More tea?" she asked her young guests.

Gina heard Curly mumble something about having to get back to work. "No, thank you, Auntie. We have to be going. I'm helping Curly survey streams today."

Curly sprung out of his chair and handed back the tin. "Thank you so much for the tea."

Karen gave Curly a heartfelt hug and held both his hands. "You know, you're always welcome here." There was something almost prophetic about the way she said it as if she understood how cruel the world of humans could be.

"Thank you, Auntie." When he stepped into the midday sun, it took a minute for his eyes to adjust. Above the tall green grass of the meadow, a young billy and two nannies were dancing on the hood of his pickup. "No!"

"The neighbor kids cut across the pasture. Half the time they forget to close the gate behind them," Karen remarked.

Curly sprinted across the field, as the goats took turns jumping from the top of the cab onto the hood.

With Gina's help, Karen herded her flock back through the gate.

Curly started the truck and hit the wiper washer button, hoping for a miracle. Rolling down the window, he shouted at Gina, "We need to make a beeline for the carwash. If my boss sees my rig covered in hoof marks, I'm toast."

* * *

As soon as Curly walked in his front door, Hutch let out a huge laugh.

"What?" Curly wondered what was up.

"You're trending." Hutch held up his phone. Someone had posted a video of three goats dancing on top of a State of Hawaii truck.

Curly thought about the neighbor kids as he watched the video of himself chasing the goats around his truck. "I'm so screwed."

Alfred Perry's Son

All good people agree,
And all good people say,
All nice people, like Us, are We
And everyone else is They.
–Rudyard Kipling

For the sixth week in a row, Moreno had patrol with Gutierrez. After work, the prince drank beers with Detective Alvaro. She knew he must have overheard something about the Nalani investigation.

"Any breaks in the Nalani case?" she asked.

"Curiosity killed the cat. Detective sergeants investigate suspicious deaths—rookies follow orders."

"So, they're not calling it a murder investigation?"

"You should subscribe to the *Wai Nau Times*. Whatever's been released to the press is the official line. If you want to move up the food chain, you better figure out where your loyalties lie."

"What the hell's that supposed to mean?" Moreno had heard enough of the prince's wisdom for one day.

"Your friend Gina Mori might think she can stick her nose where it doesn't belong because her boyfriend is a Perry, but trust me, next time she crosses the line, she's in serious trouble," Gutierrez promised.

"What? Who's a Perry?" Moreno was confused.

"Like you don't know?" He looked at her reaction and began to wonder. "Ask Gina's boyfriend, if you don't believe me."

* * *

Moreno parked in her usual spot in back of Kalo's. She could see Gina and Curly through the window at their table. In her mind's eye, she burst in slamming Curly on the floor and cuffing him. She watched Gina lean over and give him a slow kiss. Moreno was about to drive away when Gina got up to leave. Moreno met her at the door. "Hey, Gina."

"I'm late, Carla. Gotta run."

"Okay. Don't drive like a *haole*."

When Kalo saw the look on Moreno's face, he set down his coffee mug. He didn't know what Curly had done, but if he cheated on Gina, Carla would be the least of his problems.

Moreno slid into the chair across from Curly. "Do you think Gina won't find out?"

"Find out what?" Curly asked, trying not to sound guilty.

"Did you go to *Punahou* Private School?"

"Yeah, for half my freshman year. So what? Is that a crime, officer?" He didn't tell her that he got kicked out for being in a fight. Or more accurately, for getting beat up. He'd gone out with a Filipino girl, named Ariel. He bought her a milkshake, and they made out on a park bench. The next day, Ariel's two brothers jumped him in the lunchroom. He learned too late; you don't date Filipino girls unless you're Filipino, or badass enough to beat up her brothers.

"You told Gina you grew up on the Mainland," Moreno growled.

"For the record, Your Honor, I told her that I graduated from White Bird High School. You want to see my diploma?"

"Why'd you lie?"

"When you tell people that you went to *Punahou* they make a lot of assumptions."

"Like you were born with a silver spoon up your ass?"

"Nice. I think you just illustrated my point." Curly said, defensively.

"Are you a Perry?"

"No offense, but that's none of your business."

"Gina is my friend. So, who she hangs out with *is* my business."

Curly knew he was in a corner. "You gonna tell Gina?"

"No, because you are."

The Gate

If you're going to be crazy, you have to be paid for it
or else you're going to be locked up.
–Hunter S. Thompson

Gina drove to the Westside and turned into the SynthCo field office. She needed to find out more about Joshua Santos. Was he Nalani's lover or her murderer, or both?

The guard came out of his little hut and asked, "Do you have an appointment?"

"No, but I'd like to talk to someone about—"

"Call ahead and ask for an appointment," the guard interrupted.

"Okay. Thanks," Gina reluctantly agreed.

The guard requested that she turn around and leave.

* * *

She called and set up an appointment to interview for a job the following day. She was a master at getting a job; it was keeping one that was elusive. She fell asleep in her favorite black office chair and dreamed of an owl flying over endless dunes, her left wing nearly dipping in the turquoise and white waves.

The next morning Gina put on a sensible dark blue dress and borrowed Chichi's car again. She drove to the Westside and pulled into the entrance of the SynthCo office.

"Do you have an appointment?" the guard asked.

"Yes, with Curt Simmons at 10:30. I'm interviewing for a secretarial position." Gina gave the guard her most demure smile, batting her lashes for good measure.

"Please wait in the car. I'll check to see if you're on the list." The guard went back into his little hut and used the landline. She watched him take a bite out of a malasada before washing it down with coffee. After making her wait ten minutes, the guard sauntered out with a big smile, "Sorry, ma'am, you're not on the list."

"I called the corporate office in Geneva, Switzerland. I have an appointment this morning with Curt Simmons. Thanks to you, I'm going to be late for my interview. I hope you haven't wrecked my chances of getting the position."

"Sorry, ma'am, I'm going to have to ask you to leave." The guard twirled his finger, to indicate she needed to turn around.

Gina thought she recognized a woman walking from the parking lot to the office building. Gina got out of the car and waved. The woman waved back. It was too far away to see who it was. Gina walked past the swinging car gate and yelled, "Auntie! Auntie! I have an appointment! A job interview!" Gina tried to walk through the gate, but the guard stood in her way.

"Ma'am, please get back into your vehicle. You're trespassing."

"Take it easy, big fella."

"This is your last warning!"

"This is all a misunderstanding. Call Curt Simmons and ask him yourself. I have an appointment."

"I'm calling the police."

"Fine." Gina got back in Chichi's car and redialed the SynthCo corporate office. "Hello, this is Gina Mori. I spoke with Stephanie Wyss yesterday. I'm calling from Hawaii. Stephanie confirmed that I have an appointment with a Mr. Curt Timmons at 10:30 A.M. Pacific time."

"Please hold."

Gina sat and waited, wondering what time it was in Switzerland. A *Wai Nau* county sheriff pulled in behind her. Gina watched the big man get out of his rig and unsnap the safety strap on his sidearm. "You've got to be kidding me?"

The officer approached cautiously.

She hardly looked like a hardened criminal; she had put on makeup and her finest dress. "This is all a simple misunderstanding," she explained to the deputy. "I'm here for a job interview. I can prove it, I'm on hold with the corporate office in Geneva."

"License, registration, and insurance please."

Gina looked at her phone; for some reason, the call had ended. She grabbed her purse and produced her license and proof of insurance. "It's my dad's car. I need to dig through the glove box for the registration."

"That's fine." He looked down at her license, "Miss Mori."

Gina could only find an out-of-date registration but explained that the stickers on the plates were up to date.

"Those stickers could be stolen, ma'am."

"This is my dad's car. Reverend Mori."

"Please wait in the vehicle."

Gina waited as the officer radioed in her information. He took his time ambling up to her driver's side window.

"No outstanding warrants, but your safety sticker is out of date, you'll need to get that taken care of in the next day or so to avoid a fine." the deputy sheriff handed back her paperwork and license. "I suggest calling ahead next time for an appointment."

"Thank you," she said, reading his nametag, "Officer Collins. I'll have that in triplicate next time, on that you may rely." Gina drove home frustrated. The agrochemical companies were controversial on the islands. They operated in secret, claiming that industrial espionage was a threat to their operations. Security guards patrolled the fields they leased. Getting into the SynthCo office was proving to be more of a challenge than anticipated.

She pulled over to the side of the highway and called the corporate office in Geneva. After being placed on hold for half an hour, she was told that the secretarial position had been filled.

* * *

The following Monday, a request for a restraining order, along with video footage of Gina trying to gain entry at the front gate of the SynthCo offices, as well as a copy of the police complaint, were hand-delivered to the *Wai Nau* County Courthouse. The honorable Judge Christopher Fernandez, not known for his leniency toward agitators, signed a restraining order.

Gina answered a knock at the door.

"Gina J. Mori?"

"Yes. Who are you?"

The stranger in a vintage Aloha shirt handed her an envelope. "You've been served." He smiled and walked back to his car.

Gina tore open the envelope in disbelief.

PLAINTIFF'S EMERGENCY MOTION FOR A TEMPORARY RESTRAINING ORDER AND PRELIMINARY INJUNCTION.

PLAINTIFF: SYNTHCO
DEFENDANT: GINA J. MORI
This motion is based on the following grounds.

Gina skipped to the second page.

ATTACHMENT 2c. "The trespasser, Gina J. Mori, is to maintain a distance of fifty feet from any employee, all property, and lease holdings of SynthCo and its affiliates.

"Aloo-ha!" Gina said, in disbelief. "They must be hiding something. I have to find a way to get past the guard at the gate."

The harder Gina tried to understand the events that led up to Auntie Nalani's death, the faster the shadows raced away. The harder she worked to uncover and follow the threads that led to the truth, the more frayed the fabric became. Fearing the pieces of the puzzle were too damaged to fit, a sense of despair overwhelmed her.

She fell asleep in the black office chair and awoke an hour before dawn with a crick in her neck. After her second cup of coffee, she sat on the lanai and made a mental list of the last three weeks. She had followed every lead and come up empty. Was there anything left to do? She remembered Captain Al. Why was he so agitated and aggressive at the very mention of *Hokua* Bay. It didn't make sense unless he had done something that night he didn't want anyone to know. She decided to revisit the marina.

The Wind and Leaves

Hark, now hear the sailors cry,
Smell the sea, and feel the sky
Let your soul and spirit fly,
Into the mystic
–Van Morrison

Gina called Curly. When it went to voicemail, she sent him a text: *Call me*. After waiting an hour to hear from Curly, she became impatient and drove to the harbor.

Old Pantaloon was fishing off the end of the dock.

"Hey, Gina Girl!" the old man's face lit up.

She showed him a photo of Joshua Santos. "Uncle, do you know this man?"

"No. Sorry."

"How about either of these two guys, Sammy Morita and Jay Long?" They had gone missing around the same time as Nalani was murdered. She handed him the color photos.

"The two young ones who drown."

"The paper said they were divers. Is that why you think they drowned?" she asked.

"I saw them loading their gear aboard *Sugar II*. I figured that's why you went to see Captain Al." Pantaloon reeled in his line and checked his bait.

"Do you remember what day it was when you saw Sammy and Jay?"

"Last month, I think. Sorry, I don't keep track of the days so well anymore."

"Were Sammy and Jay on the boat when Capt. Al returned to port?"

"I don't remember."

"Did you tell the police?" Gina asked.

"They never asked." Pantaloon cast his line near the old cement pylons. "Watch out for Captain Al." Pantaloon mimicked hitting the whiskey jug. "Something's off with him."

"Don't worry, Pantaloon. I'll be careful."

*   *   *

Gina hung around the docks for the rest of the afternoon and talked story with the boat crews, gently steering the conversation. "Pantaloon told me Captain Al hasn't been out fishing for more than a month," she asked the captain of *Southern Cross*.

"By noon, Big Al is too drunk to pilot a boat," Captain Ross confided. "By dinnertime, he's lucky if he can stand. The scuttlebutt is, Big Al's behind on his boat payments. There are rumors that he's about to lose his house as well."

"Divorce or a bad break up?" Gina asked.

"The *Sugar* is the only love I ever heard Big Al talk about," Captain Ross confided.

Gina spent the remainder of the afternoon watching Capt. Al from the adjacent pier. He was unshaven and looked as though he hadn't bathed in weeks. She remembered how quickly he'd turned violent the last time. If Curly hadn't been there, she didn't know what would have happened. "Not that Curly can open a bag of chips with both hands," she admitted to a golden plover running along the wooden pier. She redialed, he didn't answer.

Just after sunset, she made up her mind and drove to Kimo's store. Although it was the last thing the captain needed, she bought a case of Bud Light: coin of the realm.

Donning her pink shades, she called out, "Ahoy, Captain! I brought beer."

Captain Al's eyes lit up. "Is that cold?"

"It could use ice, but it's drinkable."

"Come aboard; don't be shy." He took her hand and grabbed the beer in the other. "Pull up a pew." He offered her a cushioned seat on the deck as he expertly ripped open the cardboard case, opened a beer, and handed it to her. "Nice and cold!" He popped open another can and took a long, satisfying swig. "What can I do ya for?"

He looked as though he'd been on a weeklong bender.

"I'm not sure why, but beer always tastes better on a boat," she declared.

"That's the goddamn truth! Cheers." He polished off the can and popped open another. "Do I know you?"

"You took me out fishing for ahi a few years back," she lied.

"I thought so. I never forget a face."

Gina took a small sip of beer and smiled. It was clear, the poor man was eaten up with guilt. She listened to his fishing stories until midnight. When they were down to the last two beers, she knew it was now or never. "Sammy and Jay were your friends."

"Damn straight."

"Pantaloon told me he thinks they drowned," she was careful to look out over the water and not at him. She immediately was sorry she had brought her old friend into the fray.

"The old Diego? That wharf rat's never been on a boat in his life. Fucking coward." Captain Al looked to the end of the pier where the old man fished.

"I went to school with Sammy," Gina recalled. "He used to bring my dad fish. I'm pretty sure Sammy was trying to get the nerve up to ask my dad if he could go out with me. He was too shy to ask me directly. Sammy was a good spearfisherman."

"Stabbing a fish with a spear isn't fishing," Captain Al explained. "There's no sport in it. The fucking fish don't even know what's happening. It's like stabbing a goddamn . . ." Captain Al's outrage quickly turned to tears. "Fucking Sammy!" He put his head in his hands and bawled. After a few minutes, he grew quiet and looked up at her. "I told those assholes it was too rough to go out. But you couldn't tell those two hotshots anything. It was gusty with lots of chop but they wanted to go. They told me their cash was good, so I took them out."

"Where?" Gina asked, not wanting to sound too curious.

"Around the point, to the south, where *Mana'olana* stream runs in and the fish are thick. I tied an extra flag on to their buoys, but I told them I was going to have a hell of a time seeing it in the chop. Those two had fished that stretch since they were kids. They wouldn't listen to me. The swell was strong that day, washing the boat back and forth twenty feet or more. I stayed out all night going back and forth searching. You have to believe me."

"I do."

"I cruised along the coast, anchored in *Hokua* Bay and rowed my dingy to *Mana'olana* beach to see if there was any sign of them coming ashore."

She took off her sunglasses and nodded her head. "I believe you."

"That's where I know you from. You and your boyfriend Peter—"

"It's okay. It wasn't your fault."

"You come here to get me to confess?"

"No. My Auntie Nalani was found dead near *Mana'olana* Beach the day after you were there. I'm convinced her death has nothing to do with you."

"It doesn't have a damn thing to do with me."

"I believe you. I promise I won't tell a soul about Sammy and Jay, but I think you need to tell your side of the story to the police; for yourself, and for Sammy's family and Jay's family. Their bodies will never be found, their families deserve to know what happened."

"I know how bad I feel; they must feel worse. I think I'd rather be dead than feel any worse." Al tossed his empty beer can overboard.

"It wasn't your fault." She hugged him and stepped on to the floating pier. "Are you going to be okay?"

"Yeah." He met her eyes. "Tell your boyfriend I'm sorry I shoved him."

"It's okay; he deserved it." She giggled.

Captain Al let out a laugh.

Gina had never heard a laugh made of pure sorrow and pain. Running down the wooden dock, tears blurring her vision, she wondered if she could bear to turn over any more rocks just to see what would crawl out. Sammy and Jay's death was an accident. Auntie may have wandered down by the sinkhole in the pitch dark and fell. It may have been an accident. Maybe no one was responsible, no one to blame.

She drove to *Mana'olana* and into the temple grounds. Chichi often fell asleep at his desk in the office in the back of the temple. She tiptoed past the office door and quietly turned her key in the side door. She lit the candle in front of the altar and held three sticks of incense over the flame. Putting her palms together, she called the Buddha's name and cried for Sammy and Jay. Not at the funeral, not since her passing, not even now could she shed a single tear for Nalani. The sick heavy feeling deep down in her chest wouldn't budge.

* * *

Chichi heard a mosquito buzzing in his ear. He shooed it away. A rooster crowed outside. The mosquito buzzed in his other ear, the rooster crowed again. "Mosquito! Go buzz in the rooster's ear!" he grumbled. Opening his eyes, he realized he'd fallen asleep at his desk again.

An hour before dawn, he found Gina asleep on the floor in front of the altar. He crept softly away to make tea. He tiptoed to the third step where he left his Crocs. The wind had filled them with dried leaves. "Haha!" Every new hiding place where he left his shoes, the wind found with ease. He slid his feet into the Crocs packed with crunchy dried leaves and let out a delightful giggle.

When he returned with tea, she was gone.

"Gina! I need the car today."

He was used to taking the bus.

What the Buddha Had In Mind

The most wrenching fear that one experiences
is the fear one feels for others. Love is like that.
When one loves, one fears for the other.
–Dharmavidya David Brazier

Gina stopped at the *Hana Kai* Post Office to check her mail. A white van, the same make and model SynthCo used to transport farmworkers, was parked in front of the mini-mart. She walked over and tapped on the window and held up the picture of Joshua Santos on her phone, the Filipino worker who had suffered a heart attack and died eight months before.

"Do you know this man?" she yelled. The two front windows were rolled up, and the engine was running. She tried the passenger side door. It was locked.

The driver came out of the mini-mart. "Hey! What are you doing?" He dropped his can of Red Bull. "Shit! It's you!" He pulled out his phone and doubled-checked.

Gina showed the photo on her phone to the driver. "Do you know this man?"

"Stay away from the van!" the driver barked. He jumped in the driver's seat and dialed 911. He rolled down the window and yelled, "I just called the police."

"And? What have I supposedly done?" she asked.

"They'll be here in a minute."

"Can't wait," she said, facetiously. The way the workers were locked up tight in the van made her crazy. People cracked a window when they left their dog in the car. When she saw the police car pull up in her rearview mirror, she got out and made a beeline.

Officer Gutierrez recognized Gina. "Stand over there, Miss Mori. I'm going to talk to the driver, and then I'll take your statement."

"My statement?" Gina asked, in disbelief. She didn't know if she was more shocked by the cop's quick response time or the fact that he was taking the nutty van driver seriously.

Gutierrez turned his attention to the man who had called in the complaint. "License and registration, please." The driver already had them in his hand. Gutierrez gave them a quick glance. "All right, Mr. Sloane. Please tell me what happened."

"I went into Kimo's to buy some smokes, when I came out, this crazy woman was trying to break-into the company van. I recognized her right away. My boss showed us a video of this *Lolo* trying to get past the guard at the SynthCo front gate. She has a restraining order against her. Call my boss; he'll tell you."

"Okay, Mr. Sloane. Take it easy. Please get back into your vehicle. This might take a while, so please be patient," Officer Gutierrez said, firmly. The men in the van sat silently.

Officer Gutierrez questioned Gina and took her driver's license. "Please wait in your vehicle." He radioed in the situation. A few minutes later the dispatcher confirmed that there was a restraining order issued against Gina Mori.

Two more officers arrived and explained to Gina that she had violated her Temporary Restraining Order. "You were served papers last Tuesday."

"There's no marking on the van," she said, defensively. "I thought I recognized a friend of mine, Uncle Fernandez. I was just saying hello."

"The driver says you tried to gain entry into the van," the older officer said.

"I only wanted to ask Uncle if he knew this man Joshua Santos." Gina held up the photo on her phone. "It's important. Call Officer Moreno, she knows."

At the mention of the rookie, both officers chuckled.

Gina hoped she hadn't thrown Moreno under the bus. The whole situation was absurd. She needed food.

"Miss Mori, I'm sorry to inform you that you're under arrest for violating the Temporary Restraining Order that requires you to maintain a distance of fifty feet from all property and employees of the SynthCo Corporation. You have the right to remain silent. Anything you say can and will be used against you. You have the right to an attorney. If you cannot afford an attorney, one will be provided to you. Do you understand the rights I have explained?"

"Can I call my dad?"

* * *

Reverend Mori walked down the long hallway of the police station counting his breaths in an effort to calm his mind. He found Gina on a wooden bench. He sat beside her. "Even as a child, you were always in the middle of things."

"You taught me the Middle Way." She tried to get Chichi to smile.

"I don't think getting arrested was what the Buddha had in mind."

* * *

Chichi drove.

Gina realized it was the first time she had sat in the passenger seat since she passed her driver's test. Wrapping her arms tightly around her, she hid her ink-stained fingers, the silence betraying the shame and indignity of being fingerprinted, treated like a criminal.

"I made you musubi, it's in the blue bag," Chichi pointed to a shopping bag on the floorboard in front of her.

"Thank you, I'm not hungry."

Chichi pulled into the temple gate and parked in the shade. Gina followed him around the grounds as he gathered up bits of trash that the wind had left. They eventually settled on the stone bench in front of the towering Kwan Yin.

"I've seen this statue since I was a kid, but I don't really know anything about her," Gina confessed.

"She is Kwan Yin, the bodhisattva of mercy," he explained.

"Where did she come from?"

"She was a gift from a wealthy temple member forty years ago. Right around the time you were born."

"Haha, very funny. You know I'm going to be twenty-nine next year."

"Feels like forty years," he teased.

"Was she carved here on *Wai Nau?*"

"Our Lady was carved in Taiwan. She took a slow boat from China."

"How did they move her, she must weigh a ton?"

"Nearly eleven tons. I remember the workers strapping cables around the thirty-foot long crate and loading her gently onto the bed of a truck. There was a long procession, more than a hundred people walked behind the smoky old rig the seven miles from the port to the temple. The workers opened the crate and carefully wrapped thick ropes around her. A construction crane slowly raised our Lady off the bed of the truck. She seemed to fly with such ease and grace. The puzzle was how to get the ropes out from underneath the base of the tall, slender statue."

"How did they do it?"

"The workers set our Lady of Compassion gently atop four blocks of ice. The ice blocks acted as temporary shims, allowing enough space to remove the crisscrossing thick braided ropes. The ice slowly melted, bringing our Lady of Compassion to rest gently on the granite lotus base, where she has endured many hurricanes." Chichi realized he needed to get the wooden ladder and clean the many blessings the ring-neck doves had left on Kwan Yin's shoulders.

"What did you say?" Gina felt a shock run up her spine.

"The ice melted and then we had a blessing service. It was very well attended." Chichi could tell something was wrong. "Daughter? What is it? Are you well?"

"I'm not sure. I remember something. It's important." It made her crazy that she couldn't finish her thought; something about the ice melting.

* * *

The Arrest Logs in the *Wai Nau Times* were nearly as popular as the Gossip Column. When Mrs. Sato saw Gina's name, she let out a small shriek.

Though she kept her own hours, every Thursday Gina sold Ray-Ray's smoked pork in the turnout by the *Hea Hea* Falls. Just before the noon rush, she backed into the shade of an autograph tree, opened Sooby's back hatch and slid out a large white cooler and black office chair. Hanging up the sign on an overhanging limb, *Smoked Da Kine,* she held up her hands to the sky and declared, "Open for business."

A brood of wild chickens delighted a gaggle of Chinese tourists tossing bread crumbs. An Indian couple stood with their backs against the falls snapping selfies. A tall German girl took a video of the plunging water with her oversized pink phone, while her pudgy boyfriend puffed on a fat cigar blowing the smoke into the face of a wild orchid.

Gina chuckled. The white orchid was effortlessly practicing Aloha, honoring the divine in another, no matter how badly they behaved. As soon as Gina spotted Mrs. Sato's car coming up the road, she knew Sato-san had read the arrest report in the morning paper. "*Ohayo gozaimasu.* Good morning, Mrs. Sato."

"Good Morning, Gina."

"Before you say anything, Mrs. Sato. It is not your fault."

"I'm so ashamed. I shouldn't have asked you to find Nalani's bag. I'm sorry, none of this would have happened if . . ."

"Don't be sorry, Mrs. Sato. I doubt the police would be investigating Auntie Nalani's death if someone hadn't forced their hand. Would you like a package of Ray-Ray's *Smoked Da Kine?*" Gina opened the cooler and picked out a choice bag. "On the house."

"No, thank you." Mrs. Sato became flustered. She had come to say something important. "You have to stop, Gina. You mustn't get into any more trouble. Promise me."

"I'm not in any trouble, Mrs. Sato. Please don't worry. The police didn't charge me with anything. The seed companies have aggressive attorneys. They filed some papers. It's all ridiculous. You mustn't worry."

"But I do. We all do."

Cheryl Taylor

Because beauty isn't enough,
there must be something more.
–Eva Herzigova

Early Saturday morning, Hutch sat on the couch perusing the morning paper he'd purloined out of the neighbor's yard.

Curly poured boiling water into the top of the red Melitta cone and waited impatiently as black coffee dripped slowly into his mug.

"This T. McKenna is a real nut case." Hutch threw the paper on the coffee table. "I doubt there's even a clubhouse for his private club. It's total B.S."

Curly laughed, wondering how it was possible to live twenty-five years and remain untouched by irony. "Of course there isn't an actual private clubhouse. I think you're missing the point."

"Then why is he always talking about his one-person private club?"

"I have no idea." Curly wasn't awake enough to attempt an explanation. "You gonna fold that paper up and get it back into Mrs. Murakami's yard before she wakes up?"

"Obviously." Hutch shook his head, he wasn't a thief. "Piko's Break is going to be awesome this morning. I'm telling you, you gotta come with me."

Curly realized it had been a few months since he had been in the ocean. "Yeah, okay." He sent Gina a short text, letting her know he was surfing until noon.

"Great! Grab your shortboard. It's gonna be slamming," Hutch promised.

Against his better judgment, Curly loaded his shortboard in the back of the truck. He knew he was going to get schooled, but he had to get back into the game some time. He realized Gina had soaked up every minute of his free time for the last two months.

Curly parked on the shoulder of the highway, and they carried their boards the half-mile through the scrub to the beach.

It was early, but already half a dozen silhouettes were bobbing up and down on the silvery breakers, waiting to catch the right wave. Curly followed Hutch, paddling to the right of the reef, ducking under the waves until they were outside the shore break.

Hutch had learned to surf in southern California where the rules of etiquette were different. On *Wai Nau*, it was rude to drop into someone else's wave. In So Cal, the tolerances were different. Not surprisingly, Hutch had already pissed off every local surfer on the South Shore.

Curly was getting the royal stink-eye just for showing up with Hutch. Content to wait his turn, Curly knew once the big waves started rolling in, all would be forgiven. He looked out at the rising sun peeking up out of the water and let go caring about the surfer social code. He smiled at Hutch to let him know he was glad he came.

Just as Hutch promised, the big sets arrived. With no wind, there was no chop. Except for the muddy water, conditions were perfect. Piko's was the most popular surf spot on the South Shore, but after a heavy rain the *Hana Kai* River spilling in a mile to the east sent a steady plume of red dirt into the blue ocean.

Curly caught a glimmer of something breaking the surface. He watched over his shoulder to be sure. "Hey, Hutch. I think I just saw a black fin."

"Probably a spinner."

Curly knew if it were a dolphin, he would have seen a dozen more fins popping out of the water by now. Dolphins hung out in a pod—they were social—sharks were not. "I think it was a shark," he looked over his shoulder.

Hutch ignored him, watching the big waves rolling in.

Curly suddenly didn't appreciate being in murky water. "I think we should go in."

"You can't paddle to shore! At least wait for a wave and ride it in." Mumbling under his breath, "Fucking Pussy." He would never live it down if Curly paddled in.

A large parrotfish jumped out of the water followed by dozens of reef fish flying into the air, desperate to escape.

Without a word Hutch bolted for shore, paddling for all he was worth.

Curly was about to protest when he decided discretion was the better part of valor and dug for shore. His feet dangling over the shortboard felt like two rubber shark lures. "I knew I should have brought my longboard," he cursed. The locals laughed as they paddled past, scurrying for dry land. Curly didn't care.

When they got to the truck, Hutch cracked open the cooler and grabbed two brews.

Though it was seven in the morning, Curly didn't argue. He was still shaking from adrenaline.

* * *

Gina came by in the afternoon. She hadn't seen Curly since she had been arrested. She knocked and tentatively opened the screen. "*Howzit?*"

"Come on in." Curly met her at the front door and gave her a hug and a kiss. She seemed a bit off. He wondered if Moreno had told her he was a Perry.

"How was surfing?" she asked.

"Curly thought he saw a shark and chickened out," Hutch explained without looking up.

Curly shrugged, not wanting to get into it. "You want some ice tea?"

"Yes, please." Gina sat as far away from Hutch as possible. She took Curly's word that his knuckle-dragging roommate would soon find his own place.

Hutch, in repose on the Chesterfield, gleefully continued to check out the babes in his new SURFER magazine. "Oh! Oh! There she is!" Hutch said, tossing the magazine on the coffee table toward Gina. "Curly's old squeeze!"

Curly came in from the kitchen with Gina's ice tea and mumbled something under his breath that Hutch recognized as, "Shut the fuck up!"

Gina picked up the magazine. "Who?"

Curly tried to change the subject. "This tea has been in the fridge for a while. It smells a little funky. Let's go get shave ice. I'm buying."

"Seriously?" Gina thumbed through the magazine. "You went out with one of these surfer girls?" Gina asked, laughing in disbelief.

"Not a surfer," Hutch corrected. "Cheryl Taylor."

Curly held up his fist and mouthed loudly to Hutch, "One more word!"

"No offense, Curly, but how did you end up dating a supermodel?" Gina got the giggles.

"I was at a club in Seattle with a friend of mine, which I hated, by the way."

"The club or the friend?" Gina asked.

"Both," he replied, bitterly. "After my first overpriced margarita, which tasted like lime Kool-Aid, I bailed. Just as I came out of the club, this guy reached under the guard rope and grabbed a woman in line."

"He groped her ass." Hutch had heard the story more than a few times.

"I didn't think." Curly's face turned red. "I clocked the guy, and he ran off. The woman thanked me and offered to buy me a drink. In my defense, I said no thanks, but she insisted. One thing led to another, and we went out a couple of times."

"Cheryl Taylor?" Gina asked, in disbelief.

"Can we talk about something else?" Curly pleaded.

"No." Gina was enjoying watching Curly squirm. "Why did you break up?"

"We went out a couple of times, that's it. End of story." Curly replayed the event over and over in his mind, wondering how his life might be different if he had made better choices.

On their third date, Cheryl came out of the club. The valet dangled her keys.

"Thanks for bringing my car. Next time, leave it running." She held out her hand for the keys.

The valet held them up, just out of her reach.

"There goes your tip, asshole. Give me my keys."

"What will you give me?" he asked.

"Give me my fucking keys before you find out!"

"How about a kiss?"

Curly had gone to the men's room. When he came out of the club, he saw Cheryl leaping for her keys in six-inch pumps.

When the valet saw Curly running toward him, he tossed the keys and disappeared into the parking lot.

"Chicken shit asshole!" Cheryl yelled after him.

Curly drove. Cheryl's five martinis were settling in.

"Why didn't you punch that guy?" Cheryl took off her shoes and rubbed her right insole.

"Should I turn around?"

"You let that lowlife get away with objectifying me," she complained.

Curly kept his mind on the road. He had sipped his mojitos, but he still had a good buzz going. He drove five under the limit, a red Lamborghini was a cop magnet.

"Well?"

"Well, what?" Curly knew she was upset, but it wasn't his fault.

"You guys are all alike. You think you can get away with treating me like a piece of meat."

Curly glanced at her long legs. Her petite black dress cost more than he made in a month.

She caught him ogling. "You fucking bastards are all alike," she slurred.

"Look, I know you're upset, Cheryl. The guy was a low life but—"

"*But* what? Because I'm pretty, it's my fault?" She snapped her head around, her tiny gold pendant swinging like a wrecking ball.

"You're not pretty—you're beautiful." He would have been smitten if Cheryl wasn't already in love with herself. She believed she was the most beautiful and desirable woman in the world. Luckily for Curly, that didn't look good, even if you were the most beautiful woman in the world. "You're a good person, but you have to admit . . ."

"Admit what?" Cheryl sat up straight. "Spit it out!"

He searched for a way not to sound like a flaming jerk. "There's a message being sent."

"A message?" She had heard it all before.

"Yeah. It's pretty loud and clear."

"Saying?" She was feeding him more rope to hang himself.

"Come on, Cheryl. Sex. The message is sex."

"Are you five?" She let out an angry laugh. "Grow up!"

"Fine," he mumbled under his breath.

"I'm not a piece of meat."

"Neither am I." His three little words were gasoline on the fire.

"Yeah, you're a fucking angel. Angel with a dick."

"I'm sorry. I get it. You're a woman, and you don't want to be objectified. Sorry for having a dick."

"You mean for *being* a dick."

He knew it took two to tango. Still, it irked him that she wouldn't own up to her part in the dance. As he drove over the Ballard Bridge, he looked out over the city. He knew he had no business driving a Lamborghini or hanging out with a famous model. The whole thing was crazy. "Your day job, those long hours under the hot lights . . ." He chuckled at the thought of anyone wanting to take pictures of him, with or without clothes on. "Those grueling photo shoots."

"What about them?"

"They result in photographs of you, which end up in magazines."

"That's brilliant, Curly. Thanks for the fucking insight."

"Magazines are objects, so in a way . . ."

"What a fucking surprise! Dick the Angel explains why it's my fault men are pigs."

"I didn't say anything about it being your fault. I only meant—"

"Yeah, you're so above all of it all." She knew he thought he was better than her. "Pull over!"

"I should drive. You've had a few—"

"Pull over, Curly, before I start screaming."

He signaled and turned into a used furniture store parking lot.

"Get out!"

"What? Seriously?"

"Out!"

He pulled out his phone; the battery was on red. "Can I borrow your phone to call a cab?"

"Just get out!"

The long walk home in the early morning gave Curly plenty of time to examine his part in the drama. The sun came up just as he reached his front steps on Beacon Hill. Feeling singed to the bone, he promised himself to never hang out with someone he didn't have real feelings for.

"You really screwed the pooch," Hutch crashed in on Curly's thoughts. "You had it made."

"It's hard to compete with a supermodel," Gina said it as a joke, but the glossy photograph of Cheryl Taylor's perfect body lingered.

He wanted to explain the shame he felt. "Cheryl's life isn't a bed of roses. She's not a very happy person. Going back into the club that first night was one of the biggest mistakes of my life."

Boom Boom

Some people think football is a matter of life and death.
I can assure you, it's much more serious than that.
–Bill Shankly

Hutch leaned his surfboard against the guardrail and looked up the highway. The swells that morning were disappointing, but he had caught a couple of decent waves, so it wasn't a total bust.

A Chevy Silverado barreled by with four old mattresses stacked in the back.

"Must be on the way to the dump," Hutch reasoned. He stuck his thumb out to the next oncoming car and gave them his best smile. It was a long five-mile walk back to town.

Two local boys came out of the brush and rinsed the salt and sand off their boards with a plastic jug of water, saving some for their feet. They looked over at Hutch and chuckled. While they were strapping their boards to the roof of their Honda, Hutch migrated closer, trying to make eye contact, hoping for a ride. He overheard them talking about Boom Boom.

"You know Boom Boom?" Hutch asked.

"One dumb fucking *haole*." They doubled over, howling with laughter. "You one clueless fuck, brah."

"What?" Hutch asked. "What do you mean?"

"Your skinny friend's *wahini*, Gina."

"Gina? Our Gina is Boom Boom Gina?" Hutch had never met a real-life celebrity.

Hutch caught a ride back to town and hot-footed it home.

Curly was washing dishes. Gina stepped out the backdoor to empty the trash, just as Hutch ran in the front.

"Dude! Gina is Boom Boom Gina! Some guys get all the luck, a supermodel, and a porn star."

"What?" Curly was used to Hutch not making sense.

"Remember that BSU game a few years back, when everyone ran out of the stadium?" Hutch ranted. "It was awesome! Right up there with Janet Jackson's wardrobe malfunction."

"English, Hutch. I don't speak Surfer Dude," Curly complained.

"The Fashion Faux Pas," Hutch clarified.

"That's French and not helping." Curly was getting irritated. "Are you talking stink about my girlfriend?"

Gina walked in through the backdoor. "Girlfriend?"

"Dude, it's about time you two came out," Hutch used his Dr. Phil voice. Even though Gina never spent the night, he was sure they were sleeping together.

"Yes, she's my friend, and she's a girl . . ." Curly knew he was only digging a deeper hole. "The point is—shut the fuck up, Hutch!"

"Yeah, shut up, Hutch," Gina blurted out.

Curly snapped his head around. He had never heard Gina talk that way. "What's he talking about? Boom boom who?"

"I just remembered, Chichi needs his car today. I'll see you later." Gina ran out of the door in tears. Curly was from Idaho; it was only a matter of time before he found out. It had been years, but it felt like yesterday.

It was an away game, the first Saturday in November. A

sold-out crowd packed into Albertsons Stadium for the conference matchup of the Boise State Broncos and the UH Rainbow Warriors. The temperature had been steadily dropping the week before the big game. The overcast afternoon had the mercury hovering at nineteen degrees.

"Third down and thirteen, Bronco quarterback, Jake Cameron under center on his own forty-two-yard line."

Gina was on the sidelines with the team, listening to the play-by-play on ESPN Radio with one earbud. "Cameron signals, changing the protection. Peterson snaps the ball with one second left on the play clock. It's a weak side blitz. Cameron spins, hands the ball to the tailback Phillips who hits the hole—no wait. It's a flea-flicker! Cameron scans the field and launches a high arcing throw to the big tight end Reynolds streaking up the middle all alone! Reynolds snares the high throw! He rumbles across the fifty! To the forty! He's going all the—"

BOOM!

A thunderous explosion echoed through the stands, sending panicked fans screaming for the exits.

Three hours later, the police released a statement to the press. Despite the panic caused by the explosion, only minor injuries were reported as the crowd surged out the exits of the stadium in terror.

ESPN confirmed that no players or coaches were injured in the explosion. The game was officially suspended, pending an investigation.

It was later determined by analyzing pre-game video, that a canister of first aid spray was left in close proximity to a propane space heater on the UH sidelines. The first aid spray was a mixture of isobutane, n-butane, and propane. Homeland Security determined that a UH trainer had set the spray canister in front of the heater after wrapping a player's ankle on the sidelines during pre-game.

The story broke nationally on the ten-o'clock news and proved to have legs.

"ESPN has just learned that a University of Hawaii assistant trainer, Gina Mori, was responsible for leaving a canister of flammable first aid spray in close proximity to a propane field heater. Miss Mori has been cleared of all criminal charges."

Homeland Security released a statement:

The space heaters were not running when Miss Mori misplaced the canister. In her testimony, Miss Mori explained, "I grew up in Hawaii. I've never been around propane space heaters."

The coaching staff of UH, under the weight of another losing season, took the brunt of the scandal. Pressured by the athletic director, the head coach informed Miss Mori that the UH sports medicine program was being reevaluated.

"I'm sorry to inform you that the funds for your internship have been canceled," Head Coach Cafferty explained.

When Gina found out that none of the other students in her program were given the ax, she thought about finding an attorney. She decided she already had enough enemies without suing the university.

The pregame video was leaked to the press. Gina's face was pixelated on the network news to maintain the presumption of innocence. A late-night host showed a clip of Gina with her face pixelated and made a crass joke about the anonymous and shapely UH trainer paying for her college tuition by starring in adult films. The story hung around into bowl season.

The cancellation of the UH vs. BSU game, combined with a one-loss season and a weak conference schedule, kept the Boise State Broncos from a much-deserved bowl game. The original unedited video clip of Gina leaving the cold spray was eventually leaked to the Boise newspaper, *The Idaho Statesman*. It didn't hurt that Gina was photogenic. There was blood in the water.

ESPN opened their college football coverage with the clip of the fans running out of the stadium in terror. An East Coast sports shock jockey, named George of the Jungle, falsely reported that the buxom Hawaiian bombshell moonlighted as an adult film actress, with the screen name "Boom Boom Gina." The nickname caught on. Gina couldn't go anywhere without being recognized and taunted with "Boom! Boom!" Irate UH fans vented their frustration of another losing season, heaping abuse on Gina. She could relate to the Chicago Cubs fan, Steve Bartman, who deflected a fly ball during game six of the playoffs. After the Cubs lost, Bartman was forced to go into witness protection because of death threats.

After a promising start as a physical therapist with a focus on sports medicine, Gina quit college without finishing her degree. She returned to sleepy *Wai Nau* Island, vowing to never go near another football field again. Without ever stepping onto the field of play, Gina had sustained a life-changing injury.

Barking Spider

Surfing is one of the few sports that
you look ahead to see what's behind.
–Laird Hamilton

Moreno opened the screen door and walked in without knocking. "Curly home?" she asked the man-child drinking a beer on the couch.

"Wow, who's the babe?" Hutch asked Curly as he came out of the kitchen.

Curly was caught off guard seeing Moreno standing in his living room.

"Check out those melons. My god!" Hutch cupped his hands in the air and squeezed.

"Dude?" Curly shook his head and whispered, "Cool it."

Moreno looked nonplussed. "So, this is your idiot friend, Eddie Haskell?" she asked Curly.

Curly busted out laughing before realizing that meant he was Beaver Cleaver.

Moreno walked over to the newly waxed surfboard leaning in the corner. "Hey, Eddie, this your new board?"

"Yeah. I haven't taken her out yet. She's a Rusty, *Barking Spider*."

"Oh?" Moreno said, impressed. She picked up the board, admiring its weight and thickness. "Nice but—"

"But what?" Hutch jumped off the couch.

"It's got a little crack," Moreno said, concerned.

"No fucking way! Where?"

"Right here." Moreno held the board up with two hands for Hutch to see.

"I don't see a—"

With one quick motion, Moreno snapped the board over her knee like a piece of driftwood. "Boom boom," she said, under her breath as she dropped the two pieces on the floor.

"What the—"

"Oh? Are you talking to me, Eddie?" Moreno cupped her hands over her ears and squeezed the air.

"Are you psycho?" Hutch yelled, jumping up and down.

Curly wasn't quite sure what had just happened, all he knew was that he had just witnessed something glorious. He bathed in a glowing white light streaming down from the heavens.

Moreno ignored Hutch and walked up to Curly, "You tell Gina yet?"

"No." The angelic music in his head abruptly ended. "I promise, I will soon."

Moreno gave Hutch one last hard look and left the way she came in.

Hutch picked the two shiny chunks off the floor. "Why did she? How could she? Why would anyone?" Hutch was in shock. He'd never witnessed the destruction of beauty on such a grand scale.

"Dude, remember how I'm always telling you not to talk about women like they're not there?" Curly asked.

"What?" Hutch looked like he was crying.

"Just now when Moreno came in, you said, "Who's the babe? Look at those melons."

"So?"

"Never mind." Curly wondered why Moreno had come by. "Moreno's a friend of Gina's. Maybe she heard about you talking smack about Gina."

"When?"

"Yesterday at Knuckleheads. You were yucking it up at my girlfriend's expense!"

"I was kidding around."

"Talking shit about someone is not cool."

"You blaming me?"

"Dude, I'm sorry about your new board, but sometimes you're an ass."

"Screw you, Curly! That bitch just snapped my board in half!"

"You asked. I'm just saying."

* * *

The next day, Hutch woke up with a dry mouth and an ice pick headache. He glanced at his signature Rusty, *Barking Spider* leaning in pieces against the wall. He checked for bars on his cell and dialed 911.

Forty-five minutes later, he answered a knock at the front door. Two police officers were standing on the front step; the female officer had her notebook out.

"Good morning, sir, I'm Officer Gutierrez, this is Officer Moreno. There was a report of an incident at this address."

"Yeah." Hutch stared at Moreno.

"Are you Kenny Hutchison?" Gutierrez asked.

"Yeah, that's me."

"May we come in, Mr. Hutchison?" Gutierrez could tell by the alcohol on his breath and his bloodshot eyes that the *haole* was nursing a serious hangover.

"I'm sorry to trouble you. I should've called to tell you it's all been sorted out." Hutch gave Moreno the evil eye.

"Are you sure? The report says breaking and entering, and destruction of property."

"It's all sorted."

"So, you don't wish to file a complaint?" Officer Gutierrez asked once more, just to be sure.

"Yeah, I'm sure."

Moreno flipped her notebook closed and silently mouthed, *Boom!* "Have a nice day, sir."

"I don't like tea."

–Kenneth Hutchinson

Over the weekend, Hutch drowned his sorrows at Knuckleheads. Halfway into his third pitcher of beer, he heard a local mention Gina. The table of locals were all staring at him and laughing. Full of Dutch courage, he strode up to them. "You know Gina?"

"Gina Mori?" the youngest girl asked.

"Yeah. Do you know where she lives?"

"No, but her dad is the Buddhist minister in Old *Mana'olana* Town."

"Thanks." Hutch rode his skateboard to the highway and thumbed a ride to *Mana'olana*. The temple gate was opened, he followed the path over the arched bridge. Halfway across, he spotted a fat golden koi in the pond below. "Whoa! Nice catfish!" He climbed the front steps of the temple.

An old man was on top of a ladder in a faded Hawaiian shirt cleaning the eaves with a wet rag. Hutch assumed the old man was the handyman.

"Is Gina here?" Hutch wondered by the little Japanese man's reaction if he understood English.

Reverend Mori looked down from the top of the ladder at the strange blond youth.

"Gina? Do you know Gina?" Hutch asked again, slowly.

"Yes, yes."

"Is she here?"

"No, she is not here."

"Tell her I came by. I need to talk to her about . . . Tell her, I'm sorry. I was drunk and didn't mean to talk trash about her."

"Would you like a cup of tea?"

Reverend Mori climbed down the ladder.

"I don't like tea."

"Oh? I have coffee."

"I gotta go." Hutch was hoping to get a look at the priest. He wanted to ask how a monk could have a daughter.

"What is that?" Reverend Mori asked, pointing at the board with wheels.

Hutch was confused. "It's a skateboard." He was unable to process how someone could not know about skateboards. "You know the priest?"

"Yes, I know him. A little." Chichi giggled.

"If you see Gina, tell her I'm sorry. Tell her . . . ask her. . . to call off her cop friend."

"I have Coca-Cola," Chichi offered, but Hutch had already dropped his board and zoomed off.

* * *

That evening Gina returned Chichi's car.

"Your boyfriend stopped by today," Chichi informed her.

"He what?" Gina was shocked. "He's not my boyfriend."

"If you say so," Chichi tried to sound unconcerned. "Interesting young man."

"What do you mean? What did he say?"

"He said he didn't like tea."

"Oh." Gina grimaced. "What else?"

"He said he was sorry he got drunk and talked about trash."

"He said that?"

"Your young man is quite a character," Chichi had to admit.

"He's not my young man."

"If you say so."

Honey Trap

My sexual preference is often.
–Anonymous

Gina worked for Estelle's Cleaning Service on Wednesdays. In her younger years, Estelle used to clean; now she did the scheduling and bookkeeping.

Gina knocked before using the key. She cracked the door and yelled, "Housekeeping!" After kicking a rubber wedge under the entry door, she pushed the cart of fresh sheets, towels, and cleaning supplies down the hall.

She had never cleaned this particular unit, but dozens with the identical floor plan. The condo was freezing cold from the air-conditioning. She opened the sliding glass door to let in the warm sea breeze. The third-story lanai had a fabulous view of Lost Beach and the lighthouse on the point.

She was amazed at how clean the place was, no sand in the carpet or shower, no spare change behind the sofa cushions or half-used tubes of sunscreen on the bathroom vanity. She checked the paperwork from Estelle. The unit was a long term lease, not a vacation rental.

She went through her routine, gathering up the dirty towels, and stripping the sheets off the bed. There was an empty bottle of *Dom Perignon* and two crystal champagne flutes on the nightstand.

She noticed the air-conditioner vent was dusty. Standing on the bed, she wiped the vent fins with a rag. A tiny camera was staring at her through the grate. Not knowing if the camera was on, she jumped off the bed and leaned against the wall taking a couple of deep breaths to get over the shock. The camera had a clear view of the bed.

"Come on Gina." Doing her best to put the camera out of her mind, she felt self-conscious as she set to work tucking in the corners of the fresh sheets. When she finished in the bedroom and the bathroom, she started on the kitchen.

She peeked in the refrigerator: a small jar of cocktail onions, a bottle of California chardonnay, and a wedge of mushroom Brie.

She replaced the flowers on the kitchen island with a fresh anthurium arrangement. Pushing her cart out the door, she locked it behind her, and let out a sigh of relief.

* * *

On her way to her next job, she decided to stop by Ray-Ray's place.

"Hey, Ray-Ray. *Howzit?*"

"Here comes trouble," Ray-Ray teased. "The batch is still in the smoker. It won't be ready till tomorrow." Ray-Ray didn't want to get into why he was running behind schedule. Sylvia was all he could think about. "I know that look. What you need, Gina girl?"

"I was hoping to borrow one of your motion sensor cameras."

"*Wat?* You got pigs?"

"You could say that."

"Okay, okay." Ray-Ray chuckled.

Gina followed Ray-Ray through his backyard hooch, a

makeshift shack packed full of old coolers, antique junk, and rusty tools. In the center of the compound was a giant pile of *kiawe* wood stacked beside the corrugated metal smokehouse. Ray-Ray's smoked pork business, *Smoked Da Kine* had almost zero operating expenses. He cut *kiawe* wood for free. If folks had problems with wild pigs tearing up their yard in the middle of the night, they called Ray-Ray, and paid him handsomely to catch the meat he used for *Smoked Da Kine.* He fed the pigs green coconuts, which were also free. Ray-Ray never talked about how much money he made. All Gina knew was he split the profits with her fifty-fifty on whatever she sold on Thursdays at *Hea Hea* Falls.

Ray-Ray stirred the small fire under the smoker, the sweet smoke billowing out along the edges of the flat roof.

"I'll have *da kine* bagged up for you tomorrow morning," Ray-Ray promised, as he unhooked the bungee cord holding the rusty refrigerator door closed. He grabbed two Longboard lagers. Gina shook her head. "No thanks. I still have a couple of units to clean."

Ray-Ray popped the top off his beer. "*Okole maluna,* bottoms up." He took a long pull. "Have a seat. You want to know something really funny?" Ray-Ray took another long satisfying tug on his cold beer. "I'm at work right now."

Gina had to admit, Ray-Ray was the master of his domain.

"I'll be right back." He disappeared into the menagerie of junk and returned shortly with two cameras. "*Wat* you think?"

"I think this smaller camouflaged one will be perfect."

"Main thing is to find out where da pigs are entering the property. It works best if you're within fifteen feet of where you think the pigs are coming. Then I set one trap. Okay, the flash is all set."

"No flash."

"So? These pigs of yours, they don't like da flash?" He chuckled.

"Something like that."

"You gonna tell me the real reason you need the camera?"

"You gonna introduce me to Sylvia, your secret girlfriend everyone is talking about?"

Ray-Ray smiled. "Don't know *wat* you talking."

"Thanks for the camera, Ray-Ray. See you tomorrow morning."

Letters to the Editor

A VIP area is nothing without not-so-important people.
–Mokokoma Mokhonoana

Editor: "Mr. McKenna, why did you decide to remove yourself from the rest of the community by becoming your own one-person private club?"

Member: "If you have to stop and ask yourself *why* then you're probably not stinking-filthy rich."

Editor: "Is that your way of saying you're afraid to answer the question?"

Member: "When I moved to the island, I had every intention of becoming a part of the community, volunteering, giving back."

Editor: "What happened?"

Member: "Although *Wai Nau* is filled with many wonderful and interesting people, I asked myself, how likely am I to meet someone as rich, intelligent, and interesting as myself? So, you can see how the genesis of becoming an exclusive club came about. Once I incorporated, it felt completely natural, as if the club had always existed."

Editor: "Aren't you just a little concerned that people will think you're arrogant and conceited?"

Member: "You'd certainly think that would be the case. But it turns out, people love celebrities, star athletes, and the filthy rich, no matter how dreadfully they behave. In fact, bad behavior increases your chances of becoming popular. Perhaps it goes back to feudal times, peasants and gentry. There's no rational explanation. Some of us are born special; that's all."

Editor: "Are you saying that you're a celebrity?"

Member: "Celebrity is Latin for cerebrum, meaning: really smart. I know, hard to believe."

Editor: "I don't want to burst your bubble, but I'm pretty sure the average American doesn't revere self-proclaimed celebrities the same way as actual celebrities."

Member: "You may be onto something. That could explain why I experienced some difficulty in Kepa'i on my way here. No one would slow down so that I could make a left turn."

Editor: "Are you saying there is a traffic problem in Kepa'i?"

Member: "Your words, not mine."

* * *

Renee, the receptionist at the *Wai Nau Times,* slipped her worn copy of *People Magazine* in the top drawer in one fluid motion just as the entry door opened.

"Keith Tanaka to see Sam Hara."

"Do you have an appointment?" Renee punched up her calendar on the screen.

"Tell Sam that Keith from the mayor's office is here."

Renee picked up the receiver just as the editor stuck his head out of his office. "Come on back, Keith."

Keith pushed out his breath in disgust when he entered the small office and sat down. "As you know, Mayor Cordeiro is committed to finding the right balance between a strong economy and protecting the environment."

"Keith, did you know that Tide was, and remains one of the worst laundry soaps ever made? It's also *Stronger than Dirt*."

"What's your point, Sam?"

"My point is, don't come in my office spewing platitudes and re-election slogans. I have a deadline to meet in three hours. If you have something to say, spit it out."

"Your paper is presenting a two-dimensional caricature of our beloved mayor, rather than representing him as the serious person that you know him to be."

"So, Keith, you're saying Mayor Cordeiro has agreed to an interview? We're all anxious to hear his views on the Avalon Club. We're dying to hear him explain how turning the North Shore into a private club benefits the community."

"A sit-down with the mayor is not very likely if you keep printing these fake T. McKenna interviews. It's irresponsible, Sam. You've really stirred things up."

"Oh? I'm sorry, Keith, for stirring things up," Sam said, in a mocking tone. "I didn't mean to make your life difficult."

"It's fake news," Keith interrupted.

"These 'fake interviews' as you call them, are in the *Letters to the Editor* section. Are you suggesting I edit the letters that citizens send in?"

"I didn't say that."

"Come on, Keith. Give our readers a little credit; they can recognize satire when they see it. Or, do you actually believe there is a one-person private club on the island? If believing made things true, I'd be a millionaire and you'd be bussing tables in McDonaldland."

"Well, you'll just have to decide which is more important: selling papers by printing malicious lies, or having access to the mayor's office."

Sam opened the latest edition of the paper and pretended to read, "The *Wai Nau Times* once again contacted city hall this week asking Mayor Cordeiro to comment on the controversial Avalon Club."

"The *Pali* golf course is rated as one of the finest in the world, but a great course can't sustain itself without amenities. If you want to attract the right clientele, you—"

"By "amenities" you mean, celebrities," Sam chimed in.

"The Avalon Club with a private airfield is modeled after the successful Yellowstone Club. It's a place where celebrities can feel safe," Keith explained.

"By "safe" you mean, "isolated and insulated from our wonderful island community." Do you know anything about the Yellowstone Club? The club founder, Tim Blixseth, borrowed close to four hundred million dollars from a Swiss bank and promptly wrote himself a check for half the money, a cool two hundred million. The private club filed for Chapter 11 bankruptcy in 2009."

"Check your facts, Sam. The club has since doubled in size and has a positive cash flow."

"Credit Suisse is one thing, this Chinese billionaire, Duane Lin, is a different kettle of fish," Sam pointed out.

"Mr. Lin is a respectable businessman. He made his money in energy drinks."

"Take it from someone who prints the news—don't believe everything you read." Sam couldn't tell if Keith was naïve, or was just toeing the company line. "You don't survive in Hong Kong by being warm and fuzzy. Lin has built his fortune on hostile takeovers. He uses a scorched earth policy on his rivals. He'll carve this island up like a hot knife through butter."

"Mr. Lin has assured the mayor and the county council that he is committed to protecting the environment."

"Have you been to China, Keith? I have. You literally need an oxygen mask to breathe. If the mayor and the council push this private club through without public participation, you're going to get your nuts handed to you in a box."

"Reactionary nonsense. The problem isn't with our mayor; the problem is your left-leaning rag publishing fake interviews from someone no one has ever met."

"Is that right?" Sam smiled and then stuck his head out the door. "Renee! Do you remember Mr. McKenna?"

Renee let out an involuntary shriek.

"You're making a big mistake, Sam."

"If you'll excuse me, Keith. Malicious parodies don't print themselves. Have a nice day."

Red Lace, Black Lace

If at first you don't succeed
Blame your parents.
–Marcelene Cox

Curly drove into the temple grounds with a giant knot in his stomach. The perfect moment to tell Gina the truth had yet to arrive. He knew it was because he was a coward. The more time passed, the bigger the lie became. Now Gina wanted him to meet her father. He had never met a Buddhist priest before. After the one and only time a girl took him home to meet her parents, he swore an oath to only date orphans.

He parked on the edge of the large grassy area. Following a winding walkway, he paused halfway across the arched footbridge and watched the fat koi swimming beneath the water lilies in the pond below.

Gina had told him to go around the back of the temple to the dining hall. He knocked and opened the door. "Hello!"

Gina called from the kitchen, "Come on back!"

The knot in Curly's stomach became a cramp. He looked at his feet. His shoelace had snapped yesterday, and he had searched high and low, but to his surprise, no stores carried shoelaces. He ended up robbing a short black lace from an old pair of shoes. It wasn't near long enough. He struggled to breathe as he walked through the empty hall to the back kitchen, wondering if he should take his boots off, before remembering his left sock had a hole in the big toe.

An older man looked up from making sushi and smiled. "Oh?" Chichi was expecting a different young man.

"Chichi, this is my friend, Curly."

"Are you sure?" Chichi asked.

"Yes, I'm sure." She gave him a stern look. "Curly, this is my father, Reverend Mori."

"Nice to meet you, sir," Curly stuck out his hand.

The older man held out his right hand covered with sticky rice, giggled and then bowed.

Curly self-consciously returned the gesture.

"Welcome, Curly-san. Would you like tea?" Chichi asked.

"Yes, please."

Gina found her favorite cup and poured.

Curly watch Reverend Mori make sushi. Within minutes, he had enough to feed a dozen people.

"So, what do you make of my daughter?" Reverend Mori asked.

"Chichi!" Gina barked, softly.

"She is, hmm . . . really smart."

"Haha! I never thought of her as smart."

Chichi's infectious laughed got the better of Curly.

"Chichi!" Gina gave her father a sour look and then turned to Curly with a look that said, "Why are you laughing?"

"My daughter is . . . hm?" Chichi took his time. "I'm inclined to say, she is . . . thoughtful."

"Nice recovery." Gina smiled.

"I meant to say, stubborn," Chichi added with a wink.

"And, she likes to eat," Curly piled on. By the look on Gina's face, he was enjoying himself a little too much. He wasn't going to like it when the lunch bill came due. Thankfully, she turned her attention back to her father.

"I thought older people became more sweet-tempered with time?" Gina asked.

"How would I know, I'm not old," Chichi shot back.

Feeling suddenly outnumbered she poured Curly more tea.

Chichi watched the young man's face as his daughter admonished him while pouring tea. The boy had a red shoelace on his right boot and a short black shoelace on his left. He wondered if there was a cultural significance to the colors. "You work for the county, Curly-san?" he asked.

"I work for the State of Hawaii, the Department of Lands and Natural Resources, surface water division. I'm a stream biologist."

"How did you two meet?" Chichi suddenly realized Gina's new friend might be an excellent source of information about his secretive grown-up daughter.

"I was gathering water samples from the *Mana'olana* stream, looked up and there she was," Curly face turned red.

"Did you know my daughter is a writer?" Reverend Mori asked Curly.

"No, but I'm not surprised. She knows how to do lots of things."

Gina was shocked when Chichi produced a wrinkled copy of a story she wrote when she was twelve. "Wait! Don't show him that!" Gina panicked.

"It's very good," Chichi said, proudly. "Everything you need to know about my favorite daughter is in this little book."

Curly admired the black cat on the cover drawn with a #2 pencil. "*Good Cat Bad Cat.* I like the title."

Chichi whispered, "Study it like a map. Later it will begin to make sense."

* * *

The next day Gina came by to borrow Chichi's car. Mrs. Sato and Mrs. Tanaka were having tea. As soon as Gina came in the dining hall kitchen, she could tell something was up.

"We heard your young man came by yesterday," Mrs. Sato said.

Mrs. Tanaka chimed in, "We understand he wears two different shoes."

"What? No. It was different shoelaces, not different shoes," Gina insisted, to the delight of the two older women who were having great fun.

Mulligan's

I idolized my mother. I didn't realize she was a lousy cook until I went into the army.
–Jackie Gayle

After responding to a fender bender, Gutierrez and Moreno finished up their patrol of the west side near Coral Sands Naval Base.

"You ever eat at the Italian place on the base?" he asked.

"Mulligan's is nice."

"You want to go out to dinner sometime?"

"What, like a date?" she asked, surprised.

"Yeah, like a date. How about this Friday?"

"Sure, why not," She could think of lots of reasons, but if he was buying, she could afford to gamble.

* * *

That Friday night, Gutierrez pulled into Moreno's driveway in his custom red Ford F-150. When she appeared in the doorway in a one-shouldered low-cut black evening dress, he was speechless.

"Well?" she asked

"Wow, you look amazing." He ran ahead and opened the pickup door for her. "You have your I.D. with you? It can be tricky getting past the security gate at the base," Gutierrez said, as he backed out of the driveway.

"I've never had a problem."

Security was tight at Coral Sands due to the top-secret radar that was being developed. Rumor had it that they could track a golf ball size object halfway around the world.

They drove west into the sun. "If we hurry, we might be able to catch the green flash," he said, referring to the green dot that appeared for a split second just after the sun sank beneath the mercury surface of the ocean.

When they pulled up to the security gate, a Marine asked for their driver's licenses. The guard looked at Moreno and stood At Attention and saluted. "Aren't Ready for Marines Yet," he said, before raising the gate and waving them through.

"What was that all about?" Gutierrez asked.

"He was making a crack about me serving in the army. A.R.M.Y. Get it? You can't blame the jarhead. They're not known for their wit."

"Oh yeah, I get it," Gutierrez lied. He remembered something about Moreno serving in Afghanistan.

A line of hungry diners extended out the open-air foyer. When they finally reached the hostess, she informed them that there was a forty-five-minute wait for a table.

"Did you call for a reservation? Moreno asked.

Gutierrez was too embarrassed to answer. "Grab a seat in the bar, I'll take care of it," he promised.

All the booths were filled, so she sat at the bar. Friday night was hopping at the base.

Gutierrez sat down next to his date with a hangdog look. "Forty-five minutes," he complained. He looked at the bartender as if it were his fault. "Bud light in the bottle."

Moreno ordered a double vodka tonic.

A short man with a trimmed salt and pepper beard swept passed them. A moment later the little man said something to the bartender. He stopped and addressed Moreno, "Good evening. Your table is ready. Please follow me. Maile, your cocktail waitress will bring your drinks shortly," he promised before setting off at a brisk pace.

Gutierrez looked at Moreno and smiled. For some reason, they were being seated right away.

The little man led them to a corner table facing the water. The sun was just sinking below the waves. "Will this be satisfactory?" he asked Moreno.

"It's wonderful, Brian," Moreno said, and waited. She stared at her chair until Gutierrez got with the program and pulled it out for her.

"So, Carla, do you come here often?" Gutierrez asked, wondering why their forty-five-minute wait had vanished. Not to mention, he had never been seated at the window before.

"I've been here a couple of times."

"They seem to know you," he gestured toward the little wiry man that had seated them.

"I thought they knew you," she countered. It gave her a deep sense of wellbeing that her two tours in Afghanistan cut some mustard, even on a Naval base.

"Yeah," he smiled proudly. *Someone must have recognized me, out of uniform,* he thought.

The cocktail waitress arrived with their drinks and a sweet smile.

Moreno raised her glass. "To your health." The ice-cold vodka numbed her lips.

When their waitress arrived, Moreno ordered a Caesar salad and the fresh catch of the day, *opakapaka*. Gutierrez ordered another beer, a cheeseburger, and fries.

"What's up with you?" he asked.

"I'm hungry."

"No. I mean, why do you hang around with Gina Mori and her loser friends?"

"Excuse me?"

"Gina Mori is bad news. If you're not careful—"

"I agreed to go out to dinner, I don't remember asking you who I should hang out with."

"I'm worried about you, Carla."

"I'm a big girl. I can take care of myself. You're the one I worry about." *Because you're dumb as a rock.*

"You're pushing your luck," he warned.

"You can push your luck when you're pulling your weight," she shot back.

Their food arrived. He made small talk, but she ignored him.

When they were through eating, the waitress came by to check on them. "Do you want to see the dessert menu? We have our famous Hula Pie and—"

"Nothing sweet tonight." Moreno declared in no uncertain terms.

Gutierrez kicked himself and asked for the check. Dinner was costing a small fortune, and not only was he not getting lucky, but the ride home was going to be a long one.

Fun Meister

I made a chocolate cake with white chocolate.
Then I took it to a potluck. I stood in line for some cake.
They said, "Do you want white cake or chocolate cake?"
I said, "Yes."
–Steven Wright

Gina sat under her front lanai in her favorite black office chair and sipped tea. The early morning light filtered through the palms. She heard the familiar squeaky springs of Ray-Ray's old truck long before it rounded the corner. A gentle pineapple rain wafted on the breeze. A green gecko leaped from the lanai railing onto a red leaf of a sprawling ti plant.

Ray-Ray waved as he went by with a full load of green coconuts to feed his pigs. The wild pigs he caught were too gamey tasting for all but the most hardcore local. Coconuts sweetened the meat. And they were free, if you didn't mind climbing a coco palm.

Estelle pulled up in her cleaning service van. "Hey, Gina. *Howzit?* Did you hear, Fun Meister's having a party tonight."

Gina grimaced. "No way, not after last time."

"Come on, Gina, the Fun Meister doesn't remember," Estelle promised.

"I'm pretty sure she does."

"Who keeps honey in a gallon jar?" Estelle placed the blame squarely where it belonged.

"Yeah, really," Gina agreed. The honey incident *was* an accident.

"You have to come. Ray-Ray is bringing his new girlfriend, Sylvia Mautembaum. She is making him convert to Judaism. Ray-Ray has sworn off pork."

"For reals?" Gina giggled. "No way!"

"It's gonna be a riot." Estelle couldn't wait to meet Sylvia. "Are you in?" The Fun Meister's parties were always the hottest ticket on the South Shore.

Gina had to meet Sylvia. She must really be something to change Ray-Ray's stubborn ways. "Okay. But I'm taking my own car. If things get weird, I'm outta there," Gina hedged.

* * *

That evening, Gina went straight around to the backyard. The party was already heating up. She proudly carried a big bowl of her signature potato and mac salad. She stopped to listen to Leroy giving Ray-Ray the third degree.

"Still warm from the smoker." Leroy held up a fatty chunk of pork to show Ray-Ray the quality.

"*Ainokea*," Ray-Ray declared in pidgin, *I no care*.

A crowd quickly gathered. Leroy held the golden chunk of pork under Ray-Ray's nose. It smelled sweet and heavenly.

"*No can*," Ray-Ray said, his resolve beginning to crumble. He looked over to where Sylvia was sitting with the girls.

Leroy got the giggles so bad he became light-headed.

Alan Mora came through the garage with a tray of laulau. "*Da kine*, from Benny!"

"Oh no! Stop!" Ray-Ray didn't know how much more he could take. Benny's laulau was his favorite and hard to come by.

Fighting through a side ache from laughing, Leroy explained to Alan with exaggerated seriousness that Ray-Ray was converting to Judaism. Alan and Leroy had to wipe away tears, they were laughing so hard.

"Wat?" Alan was beside himself. "Crack in the rainbow! A Hawaiian who doesn't eat pork? No Spam! Haha! No musubi. No shredded pork. No Portuguese sausage. Haha!"

As conflicted as he was, Ray-Ray couldn't help but laugh at the absurdity.

"Wat? She no kiss you if you have pig on your breath?" Alan asked with a straight face.

Leroy, in the middle of taking a drink, irrigated his nostrils with beer. "Oh, Braddah, you are so screwed."

"Wat? Like one rabbi, or something?" Alan asked, thoughtfully. "Rabbi Ray-Ray, or Ray-Ray Rabbi? Haha!"

Gina felt sorry for Ray-Ray, but there was nothing to be done. She kicked off her slippers in one fluid motion and stepped over the ocean of footwear stacked up at the back door. She walked through the crowded living room straight into the kitchen and opened the refrigerator jammed with food and beer. Wedging her bowl into the second shelf, she inadvertently tilted the top shelf off the brackets that held it in place. The bowl of marinating fish and Benny's laulau tumbled out unto the tile floor.

The Fun Meister heard the crash and came running. She was rendered speechless as she looked at Gina, the broken dishes of fish, and pork strewn across the kitchen floor.

"I'm so sorry I—" Gina started to apologize.

A low buzz, like a crowd booing, came out of the living room when they heard the news about what had happened. Gina heard, "Boom Boom" mixed in with some booing.

Estelle came in carrying a bowl of guacamole. Gina ran by, tears streaming down her face.

Good Cat Bad Cat

I believe cats to be spirits come to earth.
A cat, I am sure, could walk on a cloud without coming through.
—Jules Verne

Gina ran from Sooby into Kalo's and shook the rain out of her hair. It had been bucketing down all morning. She waited at the counter while Kalo poured hot water for tea.

"*Ua ola loko i ke aloha. He alii ka la'i, he ha Ku'ulani na,*" he said.

"Meaning?" she asked.

"Life is an echo."

"That's a long way of saying it." She wondered what he was really trying to tell her. "Thanks for the tea, Kalo." She stuffed a fiver in the tip jar, knowing it was the only way he would accept her money.

Moreno and Curly were at their regular table by the window. Gina sat beside Curly. Unconsciously picking up her fork, she took a swath of Curly's mac nut pie. "Way too sweet and the nuts are a tad stale."

"If it's so terrible, why not order your own piece?" Curly asked, half-kidding.

Gina set her fork down and stormed off.

"Huh?" Curly watched Gina drive away in the rain. He looked down at the half-eaten piece of pie and then to Moreno for support. "What did I do?"

Moreno shrugged.

"Is it about my pie?"

Moreno rolled her eyes.

"Why is she so upset?"

"Is Gina a *wahine*?" Moreno asked.

Curly immediately regretted asking Moreno. "Yeah, pretty sure."

"I don't know much about whinny-skinny *haoles,* but with *wahines,* it's never about what it's about," Moreno explained.

"That clears it up. Thanks."

"Gina isn't upset about the pie. Okay, dumbass."

"Why didn't you just say so?"

Moreno took a sip of cold coffee.

"Is she upset about the party last night?" Curly asked.

As a Catholic, Moreno had never believed in birth control. She found herself at a crossroads. The idea of this *haole* from Iowa producing kids terrified her. "There's just no getting anything past The Beav." She was still pissed off with Curly for not telling Gina that he was a Perry. "I gotta *hele*."

Moreno said something to Kalo on her way out. The big man stared over at Curly.

"So much for taking the day off." Curly had promised to help Gina run down a lead. He watched Moreno's Honolulu Blue Camaro sail by on the highway. The rainwater flowed across the pavement like miniature tsunamis. "At least I can get caught up on some paperwork." He reached into his satchel for the *Mana'olana* stream report. Instead, he pulled out Gina's children's story. He remembered the mischievous look in Reverend Mori's eyes when he handed him the worn pages. "Study it like a map. Later it will begin to make sense," Gina's father had advised.

"Good Cat Bad Cat." Curly read the first chapter slow and carefully. It seemed to him that Good Cat was not very good. She was moody and picky; she would only eat certain food. In the morning it had to be chicken; at night she would only eat fish.

Good Cat slept all day, she never did her business outdoors, and never caught mice. She couldn't be outside because she was declawed, but that never stopped her from darting out the door if it was left open a crack. Good Cat enjoyed watching people call her, as if she were an ignorant dog who comes when they're called.

Bad Cat, on the other hand, hunted mice. She never stuck her butt in your face when you petted her. She purred softly in your lap and never shed. Bad Cat had claws, but she never got into fights. She loved dry cat food, never scratched the furniture, and always did her business outside.

Halfway through the story, Curly was completely confused. "Why is Bad Cat the bad cat and Good Cat the good cat?"

Kalo came by the table and freshened Curly's coffee. Kalo never waited on the customers, they had to come to the counter to be served, but his curiosity got the better of him. "What you reading?"

"It's a story Gina wrote when she was a kid."

"No way. For reals?" Kalo was impressed. "Nothing that girl can't do." He wiped the tables on his way back to the kitchen.

"You can't do that! Cats don't come when people call." Good Cat was horrified. "We are cats! People come to us," Good Cat explained to Bad Cat.

It might have been possible to forgive Bad Cat if it wasn't for the Forbidden Feline Fault. Bad Cat regarded people as if they were cats.

"Think about your cat ancestors in ancient Egypt," Good Cat pleaded to Bad Cat. An image of a cat's head on a human body appeared in Good Cat's mind. Attributing cat traits and cat emotions to non-cats was blasphemy. "Are you trying to end the world?" Good Cat asked.

It was no use. Bad Cat was naturally inclined to be respectful, even toward people, an unforgivable transgression.

Good Cat jumped up on the windowsill, knocking off a potted orchid. The clay pot hit the hard tile, generating a most satisfying crash. Stretching out on the sunny windowsill, she explained to Bad Cat, through the window screen. "It's the most natural thing in the world. You simply think about the most important thing in the universe: yourself. Never let on that you notice anyone else unless they're doing something for you, which is the reason non-cats exist."

All of Bad Cat's behavior made her an outcast. In the final chapter, Bad Cat is banished for breaking the unalienable rules of being a cat.

Curly closed the book. What twelve-year-old kid knows the word *unalienable?* he wondered. Grabbing his cup, he headed over to the counter for a refill. "Hey, Kalo, you want to read Gina's story. It's written for kids, but I'm not embarrassed to say I need help understanding what's going on."

"Gina is not who she seems, so it follows that something she's written is not what it seems," Kalo suggested. He opened the book and read a couple of pages. "Ah! Gina is the Bodhisattva Cat."

"That helps," Curly said, automatically. "What's a bodhisattva?"

"Anyone with a spontaneous wish to help others."

Curly thought that matched his idea of Gina. "Have you heard about the Boom Boom thing?"

"Animals are not cruel. People, on the other hand . . ." Kalo poured Curly a fresh cup of coffee. "Some of my brothers and sisters believe it is possible to make themselves higher by bringing another human being lower. Gina is the opposite. She had her heart set on becoming a physical therapist. I heard she did real well in school. She came home a different girl. She can do anything, but she cleans hotel rooms."

"What happened to her mother?"

"You best ask Gina." Kalo wiped the spotless counter. "Don't be in such a hurry. One day at a time. And, Brother . . ."

"Yeah, Kalo?"

"You hurt her; I'm coming for you."

Curly pressed his lips together and nodded. Once Gina found out who he was, Kalo would be the least of his worries.

Eggplant Parmesan

You're never as good as everyone tells you when you win,
And you're never as bad as they say when you lose.
–Lou Holtz

Gina had agreed to meet Mrs. Sato for tea at the temple. The weak afternoon breeze did little to move the air in the temple kitchen.

"You didn't hear?" Mrs. Sato's right hand shook as she poured tea.

"Has something happened?" Gina asked.

"Carla's mother called me earlier this morning, crying."

"Please tell me, Mrs. Sato."

"Carla has been suspended from the police department." Mrs. Sato was beside herself. "It's all my fault. If I hadn't asked you to find Nalani's bag, none of this would have happened."

Gina's mind reeled. *Chief Luis couldn't get to me, so he punished Moreno.* "This is terrible news, but it has nothing to do with you, Mrs. Sato. It's not your fault." Gina could feel the top of her head getting hot. She counted her breath, trying to calm down, not wanting Mrs. Sato to see her upset.

After tea, Gina walked the elderly woman to her car. "Please drive safely, Auntie. It's hard to see this time of day driving west into the sun. Do you have sunglasses?"

"I don't need glasses." Mrs. Sato laughed at the suggestion.

"Of course, what was I thinking?"

* * *

Gina drove to Knucklehead's brewpub. Moreno was sitting alone drinking beer and shots. Moreno looked up as Gina slid into the booth. "Not a good time, Gina."

"I heard about what happened. I'm so sorry."

"If it gets back to Chief Luis that I was talking with you, I won't be suspended, I'll be fired. You need to leave."

"I'm so sorry, Carla, I—"

"You need to leave, Gina."

* * *

Reverend Mori received the call from Police chief Luis. He took the bus to the police station in Pai Kona and was shown into the chief's office by the duty sergeant.

Chief Luis didn't know why some kids turned out good while others were nothing but trouble from the start. Luis expected more from the daughter of a minister. Maybe Buddhists didn't teach the Ten Commandments, he didn't know. All he knew was that Gina Mori was bad news. Moreno was hardly the best and the brightest, but she wasn't the worst rookie he had ever seen. Now he would have to find another female officer who could do the job.

"Thank you for coming in to see me, Reverend Mori. Please have a seat."

"Is there something that I may help you with?" Reverend Mori didn't understand why he was there.

"I understand, Reverend Mori, that you recently picked up your daughter from this station after she was arrested for violating a restraining order. We had all hoped she would have taken the opportunity to reflect on her life choices. I'm sorry to inform you that Gina has been involved in illegal activities." Chief Luis paused to let it sink in. "I've managed to keep it out of the hands of the prosecutor for now, but I'd like you to have a talk with her. Your daughter's irresponsible actions may have cost the department one of our most promising young officers her career."

"I don't understand."

"Officer Moreno has been suspended, pending an investigation. Miss Moreno appears to have been aiding your daughter in an illegal investigation into the death of Nalani Ōta. Obstruction of official police business is a second-degree misdemeanor that carries a sentence of up to three years in jail."

"I see." Reverend Mori exhaled. "I will speak with my daughter. I am very sorry." Reverend Mori bowed. He was overwhelmed with shame but refrained from letting it show. "Is there anything else?"

"Let your daughter know that any further interference into police business, and I will not be able to protect her. She will go to jail."

"I understand. I will speak with her. Thank you, Chief Luis."

* * *

Chichi stopped at the Sunshine Market on the way home to buy some eggplant. The vendors called out to him, smiling. He tried his best to match their joyful energy.

Gina was waiting for Chichi when he got home. He greeted

her and went straight into the kitchen. She followed him, struggling to find something to say. She knew he had been to the police station. "I know you're disappointed with me."

"Are your actions you?" he tried to wiggle out of it. It was no use. He was upset. "I'm disappointed in my own efforts."

"You're the best Chichi in the world. It is not your fault." She started to cry.

"No matter." He clapped his hands and laughed. "What's done is done. Now you must decide what you're going to do with your life."

She knew he meant going back to college. "I know." She watched as he washed the long purple eggplant. "What are you making?"

"Eggplant parmesan, your favorite."

"You mean, *your* favorite," she corrected him.

"Look for the panko; I think it's hiding in the back of the refrigerator."

* * *

Jacob Cooperman and his grandmother pulled into the temple grounds a few minutes before Sunday service was to begin.

"Pagoda schmagota!"

"Grandma! You promised to be polite," Jacob said.

"I'm Jewish for Christ's sake."

"The website said it's a short service. If you're worried about getting baptized or something, I'll crack a window, and you can wait in the car."

"I knew I should have stayed on the boat," she lamented.

"What's the use of taking a Hawaiian Cruise if you don't come ashore and explore the islands?" he asked.

"You couldn't find any pagans boiling someone in a pot?"

"Quit kvetching. I'll have you back on board in time for mimosas, I promise."

"*Oy vey*! My only grandson is a Bujew."

They made their way together over the arched bridge and sat at the back of the empty temple. The old woman wondered where all the people were.

Jacob checked his watch. "The website said there was a ten-thirty service." He began to worry.

At ten minutes till eleven, Reverend Mori appeared from the wings rushing around lighting candles and incense.

"I'm sorry I am late beginning the service," Reverend Mori apologized and bowed. "Welcome to *Mana'olana* Buddhist Temple. I am Reverend Mori. Thank you very much for coming."

The young man stood. "I'm Jacob Cooperman, and this is my grandmother Mrs. Raz Soros."

"I am very pleased to meet you," Reverend Mori bowed. "Your last name, it is Cooperman?"

"Yes."

"Do you know the meaning?" Reverend Mori asked.

"Son of Cooper?" Jacob guessed.

"Yes, yes, very good. Cooperman is Yiddish for Yankel, and Yankel is Jacob. So you are Jacob Jacob." Reverend Mori giggled.

Raz joined in. "How is it you know this?" she asked, trying to size up the spritely fellow.

"Ah! In Japan, name is very important. Your name, Soros, do you know?"

Her cheeks turned red.

"Soros is Sarah, yes?" Reverend Mori asked. "And Sarah means princess."

"Raz *is* a princess," Jacob agreed.

"I will begin the service now." Reverend Mori bowed and walked to the front of the altar. He took a moment to collect himself. "This morning, I misplaced my glasses, and I do not see well without them. So, looking for my glasses without my glasses was a great challenge." He laughed. "I looked in all the usual places, but they were not there. I could hear my daughter's voice, "They are in the last place you left them." I know she is correct, but I never understand why she always repeats this same reminder."

Raz knowingly elbowed her grandson. "You see?"

"Finally, I found my old scratched pair, the prescription out of date. But! I became twice as efficient at searching for my good pair. While I was turning over cushions and reaching behind my desk, I thought of Buddha. He searched long and hard for the best way to help us to see what he came to see. We are looking through our old pair of glasses, maybe they are scratched and worn, but we are quite accustomed to them. We don't like change. We don't want to give up our view. Each of those scratches we made, our flaws are what make us who we are. We don't have another perspective to understand how distorted and unclear our view is until we try on a fresh brand new pair of lenses. Instantly, we see far! All the tiny unseen things are suddenly clear and in focus! In my case, I looked over and saw the big and little hands of the clock! I'm twenty minutes late for the service! And, I have not thought of my dharma talk. So, here we are." Reverend Mori paused. "Now, we are all up to date. Haha!" He clapped his hands and bowed. "Thank you very much for coming. I will chant now. Please stay after the service, I made sushi."

"Do you want to stay, Grandmother?"

"We're here now; don't be so rude."

Isle of the Blessed

The peach was once a bitter almond.
–Mark Twain

Curly called Gina and asked to meet her for lunch at Kalo's. There was no more putting it off; the time had come. He bought a piece of macadamia nut pie and a black coffee and sat at their usual table by the window. Gina came in and waited for Kalo's Hawaiian one-liner.

"A'a i ka hula, waiho i ka maka'u i ka hale," Kalo intoned like a chant.

For once, she recognized the Hawaiian, *Dare to dance, leave shame at home.* She thanked him and joined Curly. "What's up Curly-dog?"

He was relieved to see her in a good mood. "Don't be shy. Have a bite of pie," he said, sarcastically.

Gina was taken off guard by his willingness to share. "You're making me nervous. What's wrong?"

"Nothing's wrong."

She took a bite of pie and made a face. "The nuts are a little stale." She looked up and saw the look on his face. "What's going on?" A sudden panic overwhelmed her. "Are you breaking up with me?"

"Just listen." He closed his eyes. Things were already careening out of control, and he hadn't said anything yet. His palms were sweaty and he felt like throwing up. "My parents got divorced when I was thirteen."

"I didn't know that." She set her fork down.

"After my folks split up, my mom and I moved to the Mainland. She went back to using her maiden name. To support my mom, when she was going through a hard time, I agreed also to change my last name to Curry. We lived in a log cabin on a wilderness ranch on the Salmon River. The middle of nowhere. Fifty miles from a paved road, we're talking outhouses, no running water, our only appliance a relic of a wood stove. A year later, my mom remarried a guy named Parker. He was pretty cool. I liked him. I was excited to be moving downriver to a house with plumbing and electricity. Parker's family owned a peach orchard that sat on a tabletop mesa on a big bend of the Salmon River. It was the only peach orchard in two hundred miles. In late September, our little fruit stand on the highway would go crazy. People drove for hours to buy our Babcock white peaches."

"I've never had a really good peach," Gina confessed. "I think of peaches as soft and mushy." *What did he mean, "They moved to the Mainland?"* she wondered.

"Believe me, nothing in the world compares to a perfect white peach. A Westside Haden Mango comes pretty close," he conceded. "Have you ever spent a winter on the Mainland?"

"No."

"The trees lose their leaves in late fall. The world goes to sleep. When it snows, there's nothing but white and gray for months. The only color is a pine or fir tree." Not to mention, he thought, you could go months without seeing anyone other than a white person.

Gina knew he was winding up to say something important. It was just like Curly to nibble around the edges.

"When spring comes, the world wakes up. It's glorious. When the sap begins to run, the stems on the peach trees turn this amazing glowing pink. As soon as school was out, I'd hurry home and climb the trees, pruning the water sprouts, the limbs that shoot straight up. The idea is to keep the trees low, so the peaches are easier to pick. I knew every tree in our orchard."

"White Bird sounds amazing," she had been to Idaho once, it was *not* amazing. The more line he spooled out, the more nervous she became. *Is he moving back?*

"In the late fall, I helped pick. Parker said I was the best peach picker he'd ever seen. One could do worse than be a swinger of birches or a picker of peaches." Curly was disappointed that she didn't know the Frost poem. "It made school bearable, knowing when I got home, I'd be making good money doing something I love."

She sensed a turning point.

"When Parker's dad died, Parker's two uncles voted to sell the orchard to a real estate developer. Parker had no choice but to go along. After that, Parker came home late every night drunk. I understood. I snuck a bottle of cheap red wine and sat in my favorite old tree and chugged wine out of the bottle until I puked. It broke all of our hearts to watch the trees bulldozed down to make room for trophy homes. Parker had planted the trees with his father. The loss of the orchard messed Parker up big-time."

"How old were you?" Gina asked.

"Seventeen, my senior year. Later that summer, I received a scholarship for a small college in Washington State."

Gina braced herself. *Now, he's going to tell me about his girlfriend. I knew it!*

"When I came home to visit my mom over the holidays, things had gotten worse. I tried to talk my mom into leaving Parker. She said he was a good man and was just going through a tough time. When I graduated with a degree in stream biology, I came across a DLNR job opening on *Wai Nau*. I applied and got it."

"Why take a job on *Wai Nau?*"

"*Wai Nau?* Because tomorrow may never come," he repeated the tired tourist slogan. Gina didn't laugh.

I know you have a girlfriend. Just tell me.

"I was born on O'ahu," he blurted out.

"What? And, you didn't tell me this, because?"

"My dad is Alfred Perry." He watched and waited.

"*Thee* Alfred Perry?"

"Yep."

"What school did you go to on O'ahu?"

"*Punahou*."

"Where Barack Obama went? You didn't think it was important to tell me that your family owns half of *Wai Nau?*"

"That's a bit of an exaggeration," he could tell she was winding up to get really upset. "I didn't want to lie, Gina. Honest. I wanted to tell you a thousand times."

"It makes me wonder what else you haven't told me."

"When you tell people you went to *Punahou*, they make a lot of assumptions."

"Like that you're filthy rich?"

"My mom divorced my dad and refused to take a dime of his money. Sorry if I want to be thought of as me—not my father's son."

"You don't like your dad?"

"I don't know. I haven't seen him since I was thirteen."

Gina closed her eyes and didn't say a word. Just when Curly was about to die from her silence, she said, "Okay."

"Okay?" Curly let out a sigh of relief. "So? We're good?"

She looked him straight in the eyes. "If you have anything else you need to tell me, tell me now."

Curly hesitated.

"I'm serious, Curly." In the back of her mind, she knew he was holding something back.

Curly's face turned red. He kicked himself over and over again for writing those stupid letters to the editor. He wasn't sure why he had done it. The idea of turning the north shore into a private club made him crazy. Maybe it was watching the peach trees being cut down. Maybe it had to do with his father, who was a partner in the Avalon Development Group. For whatever reason, he felt responsible for the private club, even if it made no rational sense. He knew it was a dangerous game to poke the powers that be in the eye. Whatever motivated him to protect the island, it was nothing compared to his instinct to protect Gina from harm. She mustn't ever know about T. McKenna.

"I know there's something else. What's her name?"

"What? No. What? That's everything. I swear." His face turned redder.

She covered her face with her hands and shook her head.

He could see tears dripping down her chin.

She stood up.

Curly stammered.

"Goodbye, Curly."

He watched her walk away. "What? What do you mean, goodbye?" he shouted after her.

A table of locals eating lunch at the corner table turned around to see what the fracas was about.

Curly wanted to run after her and then checked his impulse. Kalo gave him a look that froze the marrow in his bones. He sat watching Gina through the window just sitting in the Subaru.

She looked in the rearview mirror, popped the clutch and killed the engine.

Pele and the Albatross

God might be in the details, but the goddess is in the questions.
–Gloria Steinem

Gina called in sick for her cleaning job.

Estelle was far from pleased. "I need people who I can count on. Your three units have to be cleaned by check-in time."

"I'm sorry, Estelle."

"You've totally screwed me, Gina." Estelle hung up before she said something she would regret.

Gina could ill afford to lose another job. "I am sick," she said, knowing Estelle had hung up. She couldn't imagine working or even driving. She spent the morning walking along the south coast and ended up at the far end of *Mana'olana* Beach. Instead of turning around, she climbed the barbed wire fence, trespassing onto the Perry Estate. The first private beach cove was empty, except for a plover running around sounding like a kid with a new whistle. Gina sat under a driftwood shelter out of the wind, wondering how it was possible to feel too shitty to cry.

"Curly! Why are you such a liar?" She knew her anger was directed at the wrong person. All of her hard places were suddenly glaring. Her own inability to deal with loss was causing more and more loss.

A honey bee with worn-out wings stumbled in circles through the coarse sand in front of her. She watched the disoriented little creature as the unidentified feeling in her stomach crawled up her throat. There wasn't the thickness of a worn-out bee's wing between wanting justice and wanting revenge. Nalani's death had made an invisible gash between her and the world. She was cut off, her life bleeding out into the thirsty sand.

At the far end of the cove, the bleached dunes were interrupted by a recent flow of black lava. She remembered the day of the eruption; Chichi picked her up from elementary school. He parked on the Ridge Road lookout so they could safely watch the river of molten lava below slowly make its way to the sea. She remembered the smell of the sulfur plume, the trees bursting into flame.

She emerged sideways from her makeshift hut like a hermit crab, dragging a piece of driftwood, plowing through an endless ribbon of tiny shells left by the high tide. Squeezing her eyelids tight, the sand and lava in the glare of the bright sunlight made everything seem black and white, the rippling smoothness of Pele's long black hair coming to life as it disappeared under the milky waves. She remembered a hula chant she learned in sixth grade. "*E Pele e Pele ka`uka`uli ana. E Pele e Pele hua`ina hua `ina,*" she intoned, with a force that surprised her. *O Pele o Pele, moving along. O Pele o Pele, bursting forth, creator of islands.* Your roiling hot lava engulfing everything in its path. O Pele the inescapable. Pele the destroyer. "Gina the destroyer," she whispered.

She clamped her eyes shut, wishing for a life where everything she touched didn't burst into flame and turn to ash. She lay down on the sand and fell asleep, dreaming her fingers were red-hot lava meeting the cool froth of salty waves. When she opened her eyes, starlight glistened off the wet sand at low tide.

* * *

Curly lay in bed replaying the conversation over and over in his mind, changing the order of the words until Gina listened and understood. He was right to be afraid of telling her the truth. "The truth is shit! I should have never told her I was a Perry." There was no one to talk to, no one to call. When you moved to paradise, you gave up the right to bellyache. "If you're unhappy in paradise, whose fault is it?" He imagined his friends on the Mainland rubbing their fingers together. "Hear those tiny violins playing?"

The days were tedious. The job he loved was now dull and monotonous, the nights never-ending. He lay staring at the ceiling, unable to fall asleep, churning, rephrasing every word again and again. "Why didn't I just tell her about Parker's peach orchard? Why did I have to mention my father? Good old Freddy. Alfred the Albatross. The sins of the father," he mumbled to the sheetrock seam on the ceiling.

Life Flight

One person's disaster
Is another person's talking point.
–Henry Rollins

Moreno headed to town to deposit her unemployment check and do some grocery shopping. After she passed through the gap heading east, the traffic slowed. It made her wonder if there was an accident up ahead. A fender bender on the busy two-lane *Hoku* Highway could add an hour or more to the seventeen miles to town.

Crossing Halfway Bridge, Moreno could see up the hill. Eastbound traffic had ground to a halt, and the oncoming westbound traffic was nonexistent. She had her police scanner on, but so far there was nothing on the radio. As she rolled up behind the car in front of her, she eased over the double yellow to get a better view. The hair on the back of her neck tingled. She was on probation; the last thing she needed was to get into any kind of trouble.

"Don't do it, girl."

She turned up the scanner: nothing.

"Fuck it." She turned into the empty oncoming lane and gunned it up the hill. If even one driver reported her, it would probably mean the end of her career as a police officer. Just as she came around a blind corner, a frustrated tourist was turning around. She managed to swerve, just clearing his front bumper.

She began to rue her decision as she continued to round the curve, knowing the guardrail had her boxed in. If she met an oncoming car doing the speed limit, it would mean disaster. She tapped her horn and crowded the yellow line. A school bus sat near the top of the rise. Thankfully there was still no oncoming traffic.

Seeing another frustrated tourist turning around in her rear-view mirror, she slammed on the brakes, hit reverse and glided into the vacated space before it closed. As soon as she opened her door, she smelled something oddly sweet and chemical. Grabbing a micro cloth out of her glove box, she headed up the hill holding the cloth over her mouth and nose. The sweet toxic smell grew worse as she neared the bus. She tapped on the hood of the cars she passed. Everyone had their windows up with their air-conditioning on. Wishing she had her badge to flash, she twirled her finger, indicated they should turn around. The bus was running, but she didn't see the driver or any children in the windows.

Moreno ran to the top of the hill and looked around the corner.

A green John Deere tractor had rolled off its trailer, sprawled across both lanes. A sweet syrupy mist was hissing from dozens of emitters on the twisted sprayer array on the rear of the tractor.

Moreno raced back down the hill to the bus and pounded on the door, still no driver. Her head was pounding and her throat burned from the chemical in the air. She kicked the middle of the accordion door and pried it open. When she climbed aboard, she heard the kids crying.

"It's gonna be all right," she said, calmly.

A woman's legs were sprawled out into the aisle near the back of the bus.

A girl hunched between the seats whispered in a scratchy voice, "Mrs. Tina was closing the windows and fell down."

"It's okay, honey." Moreno smiled. Another girl near the back of the bus was unconscious. Moreno felt for a pulse. She looked at the boy across the aisle. "What's your name?"

"Tyler."

"Hi, Tyler, What's this girl's name?"

"Christina."

"I need your help, Tyler. Come over here and sit with Christina. Make sure she doesn't fall off the seat. Can you help me, Tyler?"

"Okay." Tyler wasn't comfortable touching Christina, but he was too scared to argue.

Moreno checked on the driver, who had managed to climb up on a bench seat and sit up. "Are you all right, Mrs. Tina?" Moreno asked.

"I feel dizzy. Can you drive?" Mrs. Tina looked over the seats to the front of the bus. It seemed like a distant mountain range. She looked at the young woman. "Do I know you?"

"Yes, Mrs. Tina, I'm Carla Moreno. You used to pick me up on Piku Road when I was in elementary school."

"What happened?" Mrs. Tina asked.

"It's some kind of pesticide leaking from an accident up ahead. Are you okay? I need to get us out of here."

"Yes. Go!" Mrs. Tina shooed her away.

Moreno jumped into the driver's seat. The bus was still running but wedged in by tourists who were dead set on getting to town, come hell or high water. She leaned on the horn and dropped the bus into drive, kissing the back bumper of the Honda Fit in front of her, pushing the little car forward until it smacked into the SUV in front of it. The kids screamed. Moreno reversed and cranked the wheel, the lug nuts of the right front tire screeched along the guardrail, but the rear bumper of the bus cleared the car behind. She leaned on the horn and slowly backed the bus down the hill. She reached for the radio. "Dispatch, this is Carla Moreno. All units. Code Orange. Chemical spill, repeat, chemical spill at milepost four on *Hoku* Highway. HAZMAT and Paramedics needed."

"Copy that, Moreno," the dispatcher replied. "All available units, Code Orange. Toxic spill at milepost four *Hoku* Highway. All available units respond."

"Dispatch, I'm driving school bus number nine at milepost five. There is a ten-year-old girl unconscious and unresponsive."

"Copy that Moreno. Paramedics are eight minutes from your six."

A mile downwind, Moreno backed into a cane road and made a quick assessment of the unconscious girl. Her breathing was shallow and rapid. She looked out the window in frustration, convinced it had already been ten minutes or longer. She wanted to scream into the radio, "What's taking so long!" Instead, she smiled to the kids huddled around her. "Everything is going to be okay. Tomorrow I'm taking all of you to *Sherry's* to get a double shave ice. Promise." She couldn't remember where her car was; her thoughts were all out of order. She decided she was suffering effects from the chemical.

She blanked out, when she opened her eyes she was back in Afghanistan. An IED had ripped through their humvee killing the driver and Lieutenant Suggs in the front seat. Throbbing pain in her head replaced all sound; the explosion ruptured her eardrums. She watched holes being pierced in the metal side panels. They were taking fire. Grabbing her M4, she forced open the door and rolled out on the sand, taking cover behind a chunk of fender. Through the smoke she saw the muzzle flashes and returned fire.

She emptied her magazine, feeling the recoil of her rifle without hearing a sound.

Moreno opened her eyes when two paramedics boarded the bus. The older one immediately checked the unconscious girl. The other leaned in close to Moreno to check her breathing and pulse.

"Hey, Walters," she croaked. She had worked with him on dozens of emergency calls. "How's the girl?" she asked.

"Her lips are blue, and her breathing is shallow but steady. What's her name?" Walters asked.

"Christina."

"Christina, you're going to be fine." Walters said in a caring voice before turning to his partner, "Call for Life Flight. We need to get her on a ventilator ASAP."

"What's wrong with her?" Moreno asked.

"Too soon to tell. The dispatcher reported a chemical spill. Did you see anything, Carla?"

"A tractor tipped over on the highway was leaking a chemical. It smelled syrupy sweet."

"Christina's symptoms are consistent with exposure to a pesticide. If it's an organophosphate like chlorpyrifos, it inhibits plasma cholinesterase. How are you feeling, Moreno? You don't look so good."

"Thanks, Walters." She batted her lashes and managed a smile.

Thirty minutes later Christina was life-flighted to O'ahu, where she remained in a coma.

* * *

The *Wai Nau Times* did a series of front-page articles on the incident.

> Christina Chrisanto, the eleven-year-old daughter of Wilfred and Sarah Chrisanto, remains in a coma for the third straight day at Children's Hospital on O'ahu. Carla Moreno, a suspended Wai Nau police officer and decorated Afghanistan veteran, was first to the scene and found the driver of the bus, Tina Medeiros, unconscious. Moreno drove the bus to safety, saving the lives of twenty-three children and the driver. Tina Medeiros is recovering at the Westside Hospital.

Sam Hara interviewed the semi-truck driver, Donnie Turner. According to Turner, a tourist in a red mid-size crossed the double yellow line and struck a jeep. Turner said he braked and his trailer jackknifed, causing the farm tractor on his trailer to roll over into the oncoming lane. "It was a miracle no one was injured," Turner said.

Police Chief Luis confirmed that a Mr. Dale Blevins of Cedar City, Iowa, was cited for inattentive driving. The agrochemical giant, SynthCo, refused comment on what, if any, chemical had leaked from the plastic tank on the rear of the John Deere tractor.

Three days later, Sam Hara received an anonymous lab report from the DLNR. Traces of the neurotoxic pesticide, chlorpyrifos, were found in the ditch bank near the scene of the accident. Sam did an internet search and printed out the OSHA guidelines for chlorpyrifos. "Wow, this is some nasty stuff," Sam said, as he scanned the page.

The next day, a front-page article in the *Times* reported that chlorpyrifos, a pesticide classified as an organophosphate, was found at the scene of the toxic spill. The article gave a brief history of organophosphates. The chemicals were not originally invented for agriculture. During WWII, the Nazis developed organophosphates as nerve gas. Chlorpyrifos is in the same family of chemicals as Sarin gas. Sarin is classified as a weapon of mass destruction and was outlawed in 1994 by the United Nations. Chlorpyrifos has been in use as a pesticide since 1961. The *Times* article cited a long list of legal challenges attempting to ban the pesticide.

The Ninth Circuit Court of Appeals gave the EPA a deadline of March 31, 2017, to take final action on the 2007 petition to ban chlorpyrifos in the United States, as it is in Europe, Singapore, and South Africa. A risk assessment of the EPA found no acceptable safe level of chlorpyrifos in drinking water. In June 2017 the EPA top Administrator, Scott Pruitt, met in secret with the CEO of Dow Chemical, the largest producer of chlorpyrifos in the United States. A week after Pruitt's secret meeting with CEO Andrew Liveris, the EPA reversed its push to ban the pesticide. *The New York Times* confirmed that Dow Chemical spent 13.6 million dollars lobbying in 2016.

Geoffrey Andrews, a spokesperson for SynthCo, refused comment.

Sam Hara flew to O'ahu to interview Christina Chrisanto's parents, Wilfred and Sarah Chrisanto.

Wilfred met Sam in the hospital lobby. They knew each other from volunteering at the annual *Wai Nau* Days festival.

"How are you holding up, Wilfred?"

"Christina is still in ICU. Her doctor told me her condition is improving. She was conscious for a couple of hours this morning."

"That's great news. Did she say anything about what happened?" Sam knew it was insensitive, but he had a job to do.

"No. Christina couldn't . . . she's not able to speak yet."

"Do the doctors know what she was exposed to?"

"Sorry Sam, you know I work for SynthCo. I've signed a non-disclosure agreement. I'm sorry."

"I get it, Wilford. I'm not asking you to reveal any trade secrets about how they grow corn." Sam tried to make him feel at ease. "I understand why you don't want to be quoted. I give you my word. I can protect my sources; it's the law."

"I'm not going to debate the law with you."

"Has SynthCo offered to pay for Christina's hospital bills?" Sam asked as he got up to leave. "You have insurance through the company don't you, Wilfred?"

"Sorry, Sam. I can't talk about it. This entire conversation is off the record."

Sam knew when people were coached, how else could Wilfred know to say it was "off the record?" It was clear, SynthCo was in damage control mode. If he couldn't get the story from the horse's mouth, there were other ways. He knew the Westside watering hole where Wilfred went for a beer after work. ThWe paper had an expense account for a reason. It was a nasty bit of business. Still, if someone had to buy rounds and stay till closing, it was better the editor-in-chief take one for the team than some part-time beat reporter.

Sam flew home and hung out at the Westside Steakhouse bar for the rest of the week, buying drinks for whoever came in. Friday night, two old Portuguese regulars, Ed Souza and Armand Elias rode their ponies into town and proudly tied them up to the hitching post in front.

A Romanian couple walking by stopped and asked if they could take a photo.

"Ole Sally here is my designated driver," Ed proudly introduced his horse to the tourists before striding into the bar like the

Durango Kid.

Sam sipped his bourbon and managed to stay relatively sober until last call, when he ended up trading shots of Maker's Mark with Wilfred's best friend, Ed Souza. Ed's voice slurred as he told Sam how Wilfred and Sarah had been through the wringer. Sarah was beside herself about what had happened to Christina. She wanted Wilfred to quit his job. Wilfred was scared to lose his job with the seed company, fearing they would fall behind on their mortgage. They had almost lost their daughter, why make matters worse by losing their house? SynthCo was covering all of Christina's hospital bills. He couldn't quit his job now.

* * *

The next day, Geoffrey Andrews, the Vice President of Operations for SynthCo, came by the hospital for a private meeting with Wilfred and Sarah. He invited them into a private conference room. A thermos pitcher of coffee and brioche were on the table.

"Please have a seat, Mister and Misses Chrisanto. Can I get you anything, a cup of coffee? Thank you so much for taking the time to meet with me. The company understands that this is a very difficult time for you. The board of SynthCo in Switzerland asked me to meet with you in person."

"Thank you, Mr. Andrews," Wilfred said. "Can I ask what this is all about?"

"Certainly, Mr. Chrisanto. The company understands that you are unable to work at this time. We want to extend you paid leave for as long as you need it. I'm also pleased to inform you that the board has voted unanimously to pay your mortgage in full.

"I don't understand, Mr. Andrews?" Wilfred said, suspiciously.

"We're all anxious to put this terrible tragedy behind us. By the grace of God, your daughter is recovering well and . . ."

"And what?" Wilfred had been around long enough to know there must be a catch.

"It shows here your mortgage has a balance of three hundred ninety thousand, seven hundred dollars and sixty-three cents. If you could initial here and sign here."

Wilfred quickly perused the documents. "What is this second page?"

"Oh, this just basically states that you won't seek any further damages from the company. We already know that—"

"You're saying the company will pay our mortgage if we promise not to sue?"

"We at SynthCo feel that in your time of need—"

"But, why would we sue the company? Why do you want us to sign this paper?" Wilfred didn't understand. "Do you think . . ." He couldn't bear to say it out loud. "Do you think she? Are you saying Christina might not recover?" Wilfred stood.

"No, of course not. Please, Mr. Chrisanto, sit down. I'm sure Christina is going to be fine."

Wilfred grabbed Sarah by the hand. "Come on, sweetheart. Let's go."

Sarah tried to calm her husband down. "Wait, Honey, we should think about this."

"We can talk about it later." Wilfred stared at the vice president of operations until the man in the suit reluctantly stood up to leave.

"This is a generous one-time offer. Please think about it. We're only trying to help." Andrews reached out his hand to shake, but

Wilfred didn't want to shake, fearing the lawyer might take it to mean he was entering into an agreement.

Three days later, Sam Hara heard from Wilfred's best friend, Ed, that SynthCo had tried to limit the company's exposure by offering to pay off the Chrisanto's mortgage in exchange for agreeing to not seek any further damages. Sam ran the article, exposing the company's attempt to pay hush money, knowing full well that it put the *Times* in the crosshairs of two of the most powerful institutions on the island, the Mayor's office, and the agrochemical giant SynthCo. The multinational agrochemical corporation leased most of the public land and water rights on the island. Sam knew the clock was ticking on how long he would remain editor. "What the hell, I might as well go out with a flash and a bang," he said to himself. In the meantime, the word had gotten out that he was standing drinks for anyone who came through the door. The bar in Westside Steakhouse was standing room only.

The Washington Post ran a front-page article about the continued use of chlorpyrifos, despite the EPA warnings. The article cited the chemical spill on *Wai Nau* and Christina Chrisanto. Twenty-four hours later, a pro bono attorney working for Earthjustice showed up at Children's Hospital promising Wilfred and Sarah Chrisanto that their case would make it to the Ninth District Court, possibly higher. It would take five years, but a multi-million dollar lawsuit was in the offing. The pro bono attorney predicted that SynthCo would offer to settle the case before it went to trial.

After two weeks of fighting with his wife and sleepless nights in the hospital lounge, Wilfred called Sam Hara. "I don't know which devil to trust," he confessed to Sam. "The company's lawyers or the environmental lawyers."

"SynthCo is doing everything in its power to limit the exposure of the company." Sam immediately regretted his choice of words. "It's standard practice for any corporation."

Sam explained that the Earthjustice attorneys wanted as much publicity as possible. Christina's accident had all the makings of a high-profile court case. Sam believed that the pro bono attorney's primary interest in the case was to get chlorpyrifos banned in the US, as it was in Europe where SynthCo is based. Sam employed all the diplomacy he could muster to explain how the well-being of Wilfred's family was not necessarily at the top of the environmental lawyer's agenda. It wasn't cut and dried.

"What do you think I should do, Sam?" Wilfred asked.

Sam could tell Wilfred was exhausted from the stress. "You don't need to decide anything right now. You mustn't feel pressured by either side to sign anything. When Christina is safely home, and you've all had a chance to recover from the trauma, then you can weigh your options. Just be with your family, Wilfred."

"Thanks, Sam. I'm sorry I was so rude to you the other day."

"I should be the one apologizing. Just block out the noise. If something comes up, day or night, don't hesitate to call me."

Sam felt like he had exploited his friend's confidence by writing the articles. As editor, it was his job to shine a light on events and portray them in a balanced and professional manner. If it meant he lost his job or a good friend, so be it. It was unclear if any crime had been committed. There was no agency investigating the incident. Sam decided after closing time he would write an article asking why there was no investigation.

The federal and state regulations for transporting chlorpyrifos were strict. It was possible there was negligence involved. If the pressure on the plastic tank had been released prior to transporting the tractor, the whole catastrophe might have been avoided. Whether or not SynthCo broke the law, one thing was clear: the agrochemical companies needed to be more transparent about how they conducted their operations on the island. SynthCo was as secretive as a shadow government, wielding every bit, if not more power than the county officials. Agriculture was a trillion dollar a year business. Sam knew full well that he had thrown himself into its gears. He had as much chance of stopping the Pacific plate from moving as he did bringing the agrochemical companies to heel, nevertheless he couldn't stand by and ignore events.

Sitting in his new haunt, the Westside Steakhouse bar, Sam awaited the call from the owner of the *Times*. "Another round for the house!" he called to Joni, the bartender.

Councilwoman Yamamoto

I'd rather regret the things I've done
than regret the things I haven't done.
–Lucille Ball

On Saturday morning, three days after the bus incident, Moreno made good on her promise. The parents of the children on the bus wanted to throw Moreno a party to thank her for her heroism. She told them to meet at Sherry's Shave Ice. She was buying.

Moreno waited for the call from Chief Luis. If she had been on active duty during the rescue of the children and the bus driver, she was certain she would have received a commendation. After three days, she lost patience and called Gutierrez. "What's going on?"

"What do you mean?" he asked, in a flat monotone.

"Why hasn't Chief Luis called me about my reinstatement?"

"How should I know?"

"Come on, Gutierrez. What have you heard?"

"The department hired a female officer two weeks ago to fill your spot."

"What do you mean, fill my spot?"

Gutierrez didn't want to get into how he felt about affirmative action. "That's all I know, Carla. A call is coming in on the radio.

I've got to go." He hung up without waiting for her reply.

Just after Moreno got back from her morning run, there was a call from Councilwoman Yamamoto's office. The councilwoman's assistant, Melissa Keys, asked her to come by the county building for a face-to-face meeting at 1:30.

Moreno parked in the back lot where she didn't have to worry about anyone opening their car door into the side panels of her Camaro. She climbed the marble steps to the second floor.

Miss Keys greeted her. "Please follow me."

They walked directly into the councilwoman's office.

"Welcome, Miss Moreno. I'm Councilwoman Gayle Yamamoto. Thank you for agreeing to meet with me on such short notice." The two women shook hands. "Please, have a seat."

"Can I get you something to drink, a cup of coffee?" Melissa asked.

"No, thank you." Carla sat on the edge of the leather chair and did her best not to say what was on her mind.

"Thank you, Melissa, that will be all for now." The councilwoman waited for the door to close. "You must be wondering why I asked you here."

"The thought crossed my mind," Moreno admitted.

"I've been looking into your case."

"My case?" Moreno was confused.

"I'd like to ask you a few questions regarding your suspension from the W.N.P.D."

"Sure, why not?" Moreno figured she didn't have much to lose at this point.

"Why were you suspended?"

"I was told by Chief Luis that I was on temporary suspension pending an investigation."

"An investigation into what exactly?" the councilwoman asked.

"It has been alleged." Moreno started again, "Some have suggested, that I discussed an ongoing murder investigation with an individual outside of the department."

"And, did you?"

"Allegedly."

"And you 'allegedly' did so, knowing it might cost you your job?"

"It's complicated."

"Would I be correct in assuming that you shared information with your friend, Gina Mori, about the Nalani murder investigation?"

"Allegedly."

"Theoretically, if such information was passed along to Miss Mori, is there anything you'd care to share with me?"

"I don't understand."

"I think you do. What has Miss Mori learned about the death of Nalani Ōta?"

"I have no idea. I haven't been in contact with Gina since my suspension."

"Are you interested in continuing to work for W.N.P.D.?"

"I'm good at my job." Moreno realized it might be within the law to discuss her situation, but something about the councilwoman's demeanor kept her from letting her guard down.

"I can help you, if you help me." The council woman's voice softened.

"I've answered all of your questions honestly."

"So, you have nothing further to add?"

"That's correct."

"All right, Ms. Moreno. Thank you for your cooperation. We'll be in touch."

Later that afternoon, Councilwoman Yamamoto called Police Chief Luis and reminded him that she was chairman of the committee that approved his budget. She asked whether the police department might not benefit from having two female police officers.

"I'm required to hire one female officer," Chief Luis reminded the councilwoman. The department's affirmative action requirement was bad enough without having a woman from the county council telling him how to do his job.

"This is a courtesy call, Chief Luis. I've spoken with the mayor, and we both feel that officer Moreno has shown she has what it takes to wear the uniform."

"That's hardly the—"

"I'm glad you agree. Have a nice day." She hung up and pressed the intercom. "Melissa, I need you to set up an appointment with Gina Mori, as soon as possible. Thank you."

* * *

After getting his ear chewed off by Mayor Cordeiro for forty-five minutes, Chief Luis reluctantly called Moreno. "You're to resume your duties on Monday. It goes without saying that any contact with Gina Mori will mean the end of your career," Chief Luis reminded her. He added that during the remainder of her six-month probation, Moreno would not be allowed to ride solo, work night shifts, or log any overtime.

The following Monday morning, the duty sergeant paired Moreno with officer Gutierrez.

An hour before the end of their shift, Gutierrez broke the silence, "You can't say I didn't try to warn you about Gina Mori."

"I don't want to talk about that bitch," Moreno growled.

Gutierrez was glad Moreno had finally come to her senses. Gina Mori was bad news. She deserved to clean toilets. He was glad Moreno was back, but he missed her spicy attitude. She had lost her cockiness, which was a good thing, except for the fact that she sat beside him all day on patrol without speaking. "Cat got your tongue?" he asked.

"What?" She looked at him, her bottled-up frustration ready to explode. "You want something, Gutierrez?"

"Nah."

They finished their patrol cruising the neighborhood above the old pineapple cannery. "You wanna grab a beer after work?" he asked.

"I'm babysitting my niece."

"Your sister's kid?"

"I don't have a sister."

"Older brother?" he asked.

"I'm the oldest."

It was like pulling teeth. "What's up with you? Are you pissed off at me, Carla?"

She pushed her breath out. "I don't know. I wonder how Chief Luis knew Gina and I used to hang out?" she asked.

"What do you mean?"

"You tell me."

"I never said a word," Gutierrez said, defensively.

"You're telling me you're never down at Knucklehead's drinking and talking stink about Gina with Detective Alvaro?"

"What about it?" Gutierrez was getting worked up. "Everybody knows Gina Mori is trouble."

"What if your auntie was murdered? You telling me you'd just sit around on your hands and wait for that lazy-ass Alvaro to find the killer?"

"Reel it in, rookie," Gutierrez warned.

"You asked," she said, sarcastically. "If you can't handle it, then don't get in my face."

Gutierrez pulled over and slammed on the brakes. "For your information, *rookie*! Detective Alvaro is a professional. He sent all of the physical evidence from the Nalani case to the crime lab on O'ahu. The forensics came back. There were minute traces of methamphetamine in the silk fabric of the victim. A synthetic blonde hair was found at the scene as well. It matches a brand of cheap blonde wig available at local costume shops. Detective Alvaro is pursuing several lines of inquiry. Satisfied?"

Moreno rolled down the window. "I'm babysitting my niece, Ariel, until nine. Maybe we can grab a drink after?"

Gutierrez took a couple of breaths to calm down before pulling out into traffic. "Yeah. All right. That would be great."

* * *

The next day on patrol, Gutierrez asked Moreno, "Where do you want to eat?"

"I heard the Greek food van by Kepa Beach is good."

"Seriously? What, like goat burgers?"

"I'll buy," she offered.

"I'll try anything once."

Gutierrez pulled in the gravel parking lot and found a spot in the shade. When he saw the old beat-up van, he changed his mind. "Go for it. I'll pass."

"Suit yourself." Moreno stepped up on the wooden platform to order. "*Howzit,* Hafeed?"

"Hey, Carla! Our very own island hero!" He slid open the window screen. "It's good to see you. Congratulations on getting your job back. Looking good!" He had a soft spot for women in uniform. "You want the special?"

"Yeah, one special to go. And can you make a cheeseburger for my dumbass partner?"

"No problem. I'll make a burger that will make him wet himself."

"Thanks, Hafeed. One more thing." She handed him two folded twenties with a note. "Give this note to Gina. It's important."

"No problem. One special, one special burger. Anything to drink?"

"A diet coke and a large black coffee."

Hafeed tucked the folded note in his billfold and handed Moreno back the two folded bills. "Your money's no good here. Take a seat; I'll bring your food out when it's ready."

"Can I ask you something, Hafeed?"

"Of course."

"What is it with you and Gina?"

"I could ask you the same," he shot back while lighting four burners under four different size pans. He could tell she was sincere. "Gina is special. She was born with a talent."

"The girl who finds things."

"Do you know what a sommelier is?" he asked.

"A wine taster?"

"It's not something anyone can do. Gina has the gift. The average person has about five million olfactory receptors in their nose that send messages to our brain to discern over a trillion different tastes and smells. Gina is different, she is off the chart."

“I have no idea what you’re talking about,” Moreno meant it.

Hafeed thought of a way to break it down. “Gina appreciates good food.”

“That’s why you put up with her? She’s a picky eater?”

“Something like that.” Hafeed gave up. Either you understood food was the living breathing source of life, or you didn’t. Hafeed moved with extraordinary speed as he sliced an onion and tossed it in the pan before setting to work dicing a handful of fresh parsley. “So, what’s *your* deal with Gina?”

Carla stared at the blue flames under the pans. “I don’t know anymore.”

The Money Drop

There is a gigantic difference between earning a great deal of money and being rich.
–Marlene Dietrich

Hafeed called Gina and then drove by her place to deliver Moreno's note.

Gina was sitting in her favorite office chair under the front lanai. She hugged Hafeed.

He sat down and handed her the note. "Carla's got her job back. Everything is cool, back to the way it was," Hafeed sounded cheery as possible, neither of them believing a word of what he just said.

Gina read silently while thinking out loud, "Minute traces of methamphetamine were found in the silk of Nalani's *Obi*. That means there might be a connection to Steve Jade and Kai Shin, the owners of Speed Thrills. Maybe they know the woman who flips her cigarette in her mouth. Wait! A synthetic blonde hair? Maybe she is a brunette, or maybe *she* isn't a she?"

"Excuse me?" Hafeed wasn't following.

The murderer was a drug user, or more likely, a drug dealer, Gina reasoned. A user was interested in their next fix. A dealer had more to gain and more to lose. What connection was there between Nalani and a drug ring? "Maybe Nalani was just in the wrong place at the wrong time and saw something?"

Dealers need a way to launder their cash, Gina thought. Having a legitimate business, like an auto parts store would help, but it was hardly ideal. After meeting Kai and Steve, she didn't get the impression that they were the brains behind the operation. It would be easy enough to smuggle drugs inside of a custom muffler, but it would be suspicious to deposit large amounts of cash into the bank from an auto parts store. Before making accusations against legitimate business owners, she needed evidence.

Despite Moreno sending her the note, Gina knew her obsession to find Nalani's killer had cost her Carla's friendship. If she could find a solid lead, maybe she could mend their friendship. Curly was another matter.

If Kai palmed the money at the racetrack, it made sense that he would handle the cash drops. That evening, Gina waited outside of Speed Thrills and followed Kai up the volcano on *Pau Hana* Road to *Maka* Street. He turned down a steep driveway. She drove by, parking at the top of the hill and used binoculars to watch the house. It was a long shot, but maybe an accomplice would stop by.

* * *

The school bus drove by Sooby and woke Gina just before dawn. The knot in the back of her neck felt like a baseball. She called Estelle and found out that Kai didn't use a cleaning service. If she wanted to look around, she would have to break-in. *Too risky,* she thought. *If I get caught, I'd get six months in jail, not to mention, it would probably ruin any chance of finding Nalani's killer.*

The following Friday afternoon, Kai left Speed Thrills and headed west on the Koku highway with Gina following three cars back. He turned right at the Stone Church on to Canyon Road. Climbing the steep grade, Gina lost sight of Kai's Mitsubishi. She stood on the accelerator watching Sooby's temperature needle climb into the red. When she topped the grade, there was no sign of the Mitsubishi.

Kai pulled over on a long straightaway, just before the Perry Canyon Park entrance. Gina was going eighty when she spotted Kai's car. She instinctively hit the brakes and then blew past the parked car, knowing if she stopped it would be a tip-off. She gunned it up the hill and pulled onto the shoulder around the first corner. Grabbing her binoculars, she ran back around the bend, listening for oncoming cars. She braced her binoculars against the trunk of a tree just as Kai emerged from his crème sports car with a duct-taped bundle under his arm. He walked to the edge of the irrigation ditch and looked up and down the road before tossing the gray package into the swift-moving canal. Hurrying back to his car, he spun a quick U-turn and was gone.

Gina ran back to Sooby and made a U-turn on the blind corner. She floored it down the straightaway and skidded to a stop in the gravel turnout Kai had used. She ran along the ditch bank, painfully aware that she might be running toward her death. The distinct sound of a two-stroke dirt bike screamed and sputtered down the ridge through the Koa trees.

A hundred years earlier, engineers and immigrant workers built a system of irrigation ditches throughout the island, tunneling through mountains, diverting the precious water from dozens of streams and rivers.Sugarcane was a thirsty crop. C&H, The California and Hawaiian Sugar Company, was wildly successful, making billions in today's money. Gina stopped to study a fresh set of boot prints in the dry red dirt. A motorcycle had recently spun a donut. She was too late.

Manny's

Whoever said, "Diamonds are a girl's best friend," clearly never owned a dirt bike.
–Anonymous

On the drive down the canyon, Gina realized that whoever was behind the meth operation was highly intelligent. She remembered Kai taking the money at the racetrack and Steve passing the drugs. Even if they were caught, the drugs and the money were separate. The evidence would be circumstantial and would never hold up in court. Likewise, the money drop seemed foolproof. Whoever collected the money could simply say they found it floating in the ditch while they were riding their dirt bike. She couldn't be certain where the motorcycle would encounter the bag of money floating down the ditch, so a remote camera wasn't an option. This level of sophistication meant one thing: she was dealing with professional criminals.

Gina knew it was virtually impossible to pay for everything in cash without raising a red flag. Dirty money needed to be run through a legitimate business. It was possible for an auto parts store to wash a portion of the cash, but a better fit would be a restaurant with a liquor license. She knew from her days working as a cocktail waitress that restaurants made more money selling alcohol than serving food and customers often paid with cash. Her theory was a long shot, probably not much better than randomly picking names from the phone book. When she got home, she made a list of all the restaurants on the island with liquor licenses. "I wonder how many restaurant owners drive pickups with dirt bikes in the back?"

There were two businesses that rented Harleys to tourists, but Manny's was the only shop that sold and serviced dirt bikes on the island. Manny's also serviced small engines, like mowers.

Chichi took care of the temple grounds, which entailed mowing two acres of grass. Gina had learned to drive the riding mower when she was ten. If she helped Chichi mow, he would buy her a shave ice.

The next morning, Gina stopped and had breakfast with Chichi.

"I know that look," he said. "What's happened to the car?"

"Nothing. The car is fine. But I think the mower needs a tune-up?" she declared.

"Eh?"

"Ray-Ray is coming over with his pickup to take it to Manny's."

"It was running fine last week. Uncle Kenji just replaced the spark plug and wires."

"I know, but Ray-Ray volunteered. He wants to do something to support the temple."

"Fine, Ray-Ray can mow the grass."

"Chichi!" she gently scolded him.

He knew something was up, but he couldn't work it out. At least she wasn't getting into trouble with the police.

Ray-Ray backed his trailer up to the Lawn Mower Museum; the garden shed filled with a menagerie of dead riding mowers. The curator arranged the exhibition with the oldest dead mowers piled at the back, with the recently deceased stacked closest to the door. The only mower currently in working order barely fit in the shed. The brackets holding on the engine cover had long since rusted off. Gina used to pretend the bare engine was a tiny locomotive, a miniature version of the small diesel locomotives used to haul sugarcane from the fields.

Gina pulled the choke, started the mower and drove it onto the trailer. "If Chichi asks, tell him you're donating the tune-up."

"Huh?" Ray-Ray shook his head. He didn't want to know.

Gina couldn't be sure what was in the waterproof bundle Kai had thrown into the ditch, but her instincts told her it wasn't a box of chocolates—it had to be cash. Finally, she was getting somewhere. A drug operation might be reason enough to kill.

Ray-Ray drove to Manny's and pulled around to the back. The yellow sign on the loading dock read, "Warning. Avoid serious injury—keep your hands off my bike!" As usual, the repair shop was jumping. The front of the warehouse had all the eye candy, the latest new bikes. There was a poster on the wall with a blonde astride a Yamaha. Gina chuckled as she read the quote in Kanji and then in English, "Good girls sit. Bad Bitches ride."

Ray-Ray was disappointed when Gina stuck him with waiting at the service counter, while she disappeared into the showroom to check out the new bikes.

When the young salesman saw Gina, he blew off the two customers he was helping. "*Howzit?* I'm Brian. Welcome to Manny's. How can I help you?"

Gina was eyeing the Kawasaki and the amazingly cheap Taotao beside it. "Are these Chinese-made bikes for real?" she asked.

"They're better than they used to be. But, they're not for the serious rider," Brian informed her. "I haven't seen you in here before. I'd remember." He took a couple of steps closer to the merchandise.

"My ex-boyfriend is a serious rider. I guess when you own a fancy restaurant you can afford a nice bike. He probably paid cash." She let that sink in.

"What's he ride?" Brian liked how she let him know she was single.

"Don't remember. But I can tell you; he paid more attention to his bike than he did to me." She climbed on the Ducati and felt the clutch and the brake levers. She fed the salesman more general information, hoping he would fill in the blanks. "I should have known better than to get involved with a man who owns his own bar."

"You may not have had the best taste in men, but you're sitting on the nicest bike on the showroom floor and talking to the best ride."

"Excuse me?"

"The best rider," Brian made the small correction and then smiled. "I know how to get the most out of her, the bike I mean." He placed his left hand over her right hand on the throttle and gunned it.

Gina pulled her hand away and got off the bike. "So, Brian, are there any other salespeople working today?"

"Yeah." Brian could tell she wasn't into him. "Dale's in the back. I'll grab him for you."

Gina decided she wouldn't be quite so flirty with Dale. As soon as Dale emerged from the break room, she realized there was no need to worry. She gave the older salesman an encore performance, how she'd been wronged by her man, lacing her sad story with the few facts at her disposal: her ex bought his bike with cash from the bar he owned. Just when she was about to call it a day, a light went on behind Dale's eyes.

"Paid cash you say?" Dale scratched his chin. "I know you're too much of a lady to tell me his name, but by any chance does this scoundrel of yours happen to own the Waiola Surfrider?"

Gina smiled. "You're right, Dale. A lady never kisses and tells."

She found Ray-Ray in the back of the repair shop talking story with Manny. "Come on Ray-Ray. Let's go; I'm starving."

"Where are you taking me?" he asked.

"I don't know. Where do they serve Kosher lunch?"

Ray-Ray laughed in appreciation. "You one mean girl."

King's Tide

Never give up, for that is just the place
and time that the tide will turn.
–Harriet Beecher Stowe

The King's Tide, the highest tide of the year, happened twice a year when the moon and the sun were in alignment. Gina walked *Mana'olana* Beach in the early morning light. High surf, with help from the King's Tide, had cut a massive wall into the sand carrying away half the beach overnight. The pounding waves and wind spit chunks of white foam around her feet. The city lights of O'ahu made a faint glow on the horizon across the channel, turning to a brilliant red and orange as the sun rose from the waves.

She sensed a subtle shift. A Kona Wind from the west stirred the palms overhead.

* * *

Tremors coffee house in Waiola was packed. Gina ordered a Volcano Affogato: two scoops of vanilla gelato and two shots of espresso. She sat in Sooby and watched the choreographed procession of delivery vans backing in and out of the alley behind The Surfrider, the top restaurant on the North Shore.

She savored the last spoonfuls of her treat when a man dressed in chef's white came out the back door into the alley. With one quick motion, he flipped his cigarette in the air, catching it in his lips.

A long slow bolt shot up Gina's spine. She tried to process what she had just seen. The espresso and the sugar from the gelato didn't help. Squeezing the steering wheel, Gina's whole body spasmed. Staring at the man in white, she recalled exactly what Tom Scrum had said about the young woman he saw climbing into a beige Honda Accord. He was around five foot ten. She imagined him in a blonde wig. With a little makeup, the man in the alley could easily pass as a woman.

The Surfrider opened at five. Wearing her pink sunglasses, Gina strolled through the parking lot. Security cameras faced every direction, two on either side of the main entrance. She smiled at the hostess and walked into the dark bar.

"What can I get you?" the bartender asked.

"Vodka tonic, please. Who's cooking today?"

"Jimmy Lang, the chef."

"Tell Jimmy that Sophie is here to see him."

"You'll have to talk to Satoshi, the manager. I'm not allowed in the kitchen." Meaning he was scared to go into the kitchen. He had heard plenty of horror stories. Prep cooks never lasted more than three months for a reason. Chef was scary enough when he didn't have a knife in his hand.

"Ask Satoshi to come and see me." Gina left a twenty on the bar, thinking it was a fat tip, and then wondered if it was enough to cover the price of the drink. She found a booth and tried to figure out a way to get eyes on Jimmy. She took out her phone and found a recent *Times* article about the Surfrider and Jimmy Lang.

She watched as the photo slowly loaded. It was the same man she had just seen in the alley. She left her drink untouched and ran out into the fresh air. After three months of searching, the feeling at the bottom of her stomach told her she had finally found Nalani's killer.

She looked up Jimmy Lang's street address and drove by the palatial home overlooking Pahuna Bay. She dialed Estelle and called in a favor.

* * *

The following Tuesday morning, Gina joined the Pahuna Bay cleaning crew. She went about her work with efficiency while managing to take detailed photos of every room in Jimmy's house. She took several close-ups of the Chinese painting in the living room.

Red Pole

If you drink three cups of wine,
you will be unable to cross the mountain ridge.
–Shi Nai-an 1296-1372

Gina showed Chichi the photo on her phone. "Do you recognize the artist?" Gina asked.

"I don't remember the artist, but this is a Chinese painting called Red Pole. It depicts the popular character Wu Song killing the tiger," Chichi explained. "It's from the classic Chinese novel, *Water Margin.*"

"Why is the painting called Red Pole?"

"It refers to the weapon used by Wu Song."

"Is this Wu Song a good person or a bad person?" she asked.

"Hmm? No simple answer. Wu Song is one of the 108 bandits or spirits that escape and roam the countryside in fourteenth-century China. Wu Song's leader, Song Jiang, is a kind of Chinese Robin Hood. Their hideout is in a marsh which is why the novel is called *Water Margin.*" He gave his daughter a penetrating look. "I've been trying to interest you in art and literature for years. Why the sudden curiosity?"

"No reason. I saw this painting in a condo I was cleaning and liked it."

Chichi gave up all hope that she would tell him the real reason.

Gina researched and learned that the Triad, the Chinese Mafia, refer to their top enforcers as "Red Pole." It was a rank of lieutenant. Gina wondered why a lieutenant of the Chinese mafia would be on *Wai Nau* and why he would want to murder Auntie Nalani. Gina remembered reading an article in the Honolulu Sun detailing how a Hong Kong-based triad smuggled chemicals used for the production of methamphetamine to O'ahu.

Duane Lin, the Chinese billionaire backing the Avalon Club, was based in Hong Kong. Gina understood that a five-hundred million dollar real estate investment might be reason enough, in some people's mind, to end an old woman's life. As far as she was aware, Nalani seldom visited the North Shore. If there was a connection between Nalani, Jimmy Lang, or Duane Lin, she had no idea where to look. She could understand why T. McKenna might get under Duane Lin's skin, but McKenna was busy writing his ridiculous letters to the paper, while Auntie Nalani was in *Mana'olana* cemetery.

Although Gina couldn't prove it, she was convinced there was a link between Steve Jade Kai Shin, and Jimmy Lang. She also couldn't prove that it was cash wrapped in the duct-taped bundle that Kai had tossed into the irrigation canal, but there was no way it was innocent behavior. She'd gone to Kai and Steve's business and asked about a woman who flicked her cigarette in her mouth. The two must have known at the time that she was asking about Jimmy Lang. Odds were high that they told Jimmy Lang about a local woman asking about him. Hanging around the Surfrider would be risky. The place had cameras all around it. She was grateful she had kept her oversized pink sunglasses on when she was in the dark bar, or had she? She took them off to look at her phone. She reminded herself that she was dealing with professional criminals, and criminals were paranoid. If she wasn't extremely careful, she would be discovered. One mistake, instead of finding Nalani's killer, she would end up just like Nalani, face down on the cold ground.

Blackmail

Heck, what's a little extortion between friends?
–Bill Watterson

Gina met her old classmate, Tammy Chang, at Hafeed's for lunch. Before they could pick a table, Hafeed sprang from the back of the van with a damp towel and wiped the dust off two plastic chairs.

"Please come, sit in the shade," he beckoned with a bright smile.

"Tammy, this is the chef I've been telling you about. Hafeed, this is my friend Tammy."

"It is a pleasure to meet you, Tammy. Can I bring you something to drink?" he asked.

"Two mint teas and two specials, please," Gina took the liberty of ordering, knowing Hafeed always did his best work when he was unfettered by the menu.

Gina whispered, "Whatever he makes, you won't believe it."

"Okay?" Tammy was tempted to remind Gina that she worked at the finest restaurant on the island. Instead, she unfolded her paper napkin and got ready for whatever greasy food was coming her way.

Within minutes, Hafeed reappeared with four plates of appetizers.

Before Tammy could ask about the various dishes, the cook disappeared. She dipped a corner of pita bread into the baba ganoush and took a small bite. "Oh, this is delicious!"

When Hafeed brought the mint teas, he was delighted to see most of the first course had disappeared.

Halfway through the main course, Tammy was sweating from the spicy fish. She whispered to Gina that the food was intoxicating. When Hafeed brought the baklava for dessert, Tammy thanked him and told him it was a crime that he was cooking in a van on the side of the road.

"Thank you." He wanted to brag about all the famous kitchens where he had worked but reminded himself that his life depended on keeping a low profile. *If I can't seduce a woman with my cooking, what right do I have to call myself a chef?*

"Tammy works at the Waiola Surfrider." Gina crashed in on his thoughts.

"Oh really?" Hafeed tried to sound interested.

"Chef Lang is always on the lookout for a sous-chef," Tammy informed him.

Her saucy smile aroused him, despite hearing the words "sous" and "chef" together.

"I can put in a good word for you if you'd like?" Tammy offered.

"I'm so happy you enjoyed lunch." Hafeed smiled and stared at Gina.

Gina ignored the thousand unsaid things in Hafeed's glance. "Thank you for the wonderful food, Hafeed. You're an artist."

"You are too kind," he countered. "Come back soon." He ambled back to his van, feeling equally proud and broken. Tammy loved his food but then insulted him by suggesting, *if* he were lucky, he could work under a hack like Jimmy Lang. Suddenly the rust bulging under the faded blue paint of his van felt like a blistering rash. Only a brief moment before he was living the life: he owned his own business a stone's throw from the beach, he was his own boss, kept his own hours. Now, it all seemed shabby. His dreams washed out to sea by the sweet breath of the goddess Tammy. He flipped the closed sign on the window and set to work on the stack of dirty pots and pans.

The next day Gina stopped by the van before the lunch rush. Hafeed was raking up leaves and trash under the picnic tables.

"Hi, Gina. I don't open for another hour." He could see she wasn't there to eat. "What's up?"

"I have a lead on who killed Auntie Nalani."

"Oh?" He thought for a moment. "Please tell me it isn't Tammy."

"Stop holding your face, it's not Tammy. But . . ."

"*Al'ama*! I knew something was up when you showed up with the goddess."

Gina loved Hafeed, but he was such a drama queen. "Are you through?"

"Yes. Tell me, what you've learned."

"We know Speed Thrills is a front for selling methamphetamine, and we know that the police found traces of meth on Nalani's *kimono*."

"Yes, I remember the twins, Steve and Kai." Hafeed gestured for her to continue.

"It looks as though there's a connection between Steve and Kai and Jimmy Lang."

"What connection?"

"I saw Jimmy flip a cigarette in his mouth."

"And? That's it?"

"Not just that. It's a lot of little things that all add up. The other day I followed our friend Steve up the canyon road and watched him drop a bundle of cash in an irrigation ditch. I'm certain it was Jimmy Lang who picked up the money and sped away on a motorcycle. He's washing the drug money through his restaurant and bar."

"Hold on. You saw Jimmy picking up the money? You should tell the police," he advised.

"I didn't exactly see the money."

"But, you saw Jimmy picking up a bundle of drug money?"

"I didn't get a good look, but I'm sure it was him. When I was in Jimmy's House, there was a painting and . . ."

"Wait! You broke into Jimmy Lang's house? *Al'ama*!"

"No, I was cleaning and . . ."

Hafeed knew Gina well enough to see where all this was going. "Are you fucking kidding me? Do I look like a sous-chef?"

"Of course not! You're one of the greatest chefs in the world. Nothing and no one can refute this." She was glad he interrupted her. She almost blurted out that Jimmy Lang was a triad lieutenant. That would have scared him off for sure.

"It's all beginning to make sense now, why you brought the goddess Tammy here yesterday—to blackmail me! You want me to be a fucking sous-chef!"

"Blackmail? That's a bit harsh."

"That nut job Jimmy Lang is famous for chasing his staff around the kitchen with a skinning knife!"

"It's just for a couple of weeks. I need someone on the inside."

"*Neik!*" he cursed. "Ask your goddess friend to spy for you."

"She's a cocktail waitress; she's not allowed in the kitchen."

"Better yet—why don't *you* get a job at the Surf Rider?" Hafeed suggested.

"Remember, I went into Speed Thrills and asked Steve and Kai if they knew a woman who flips her cigarette in her mouth? I'm pretty sure they knew I was asking around for Jimmy Lang. If I go poking around the restaurant . . ."

"So, you want me to close my business and go work for a psychopath?"

Gina got up to leave. "I'm sorry, Hafeed. I shouldn't have come by."

"That's it? You're giving up?"

Gina didn't answer.

He knew she would never stop. "*Neik!*" He owed her. When he made his escape three years ago from O'ahu, Gina picked him up hitchhiking. He ended up sleeping on her couch for a year, rent-free. It was Gina who had found the used food van. She had loaned him a thousand dollars for the down payment. "If I do this, we're even." He didn't like owing anyone.

"If you do this, Hafeed, I'll owe you."

"What if I don't find out anything?"

"Then I'll owe you double," she promised.

"I don't know."

"Tammy told me your food was intoxicating."

"She said that?" Hafeed let go of his face, his eyes widened.

"She whispered it."

Hafeed made an exaggerated sigh of surrender. "I'll need Tammy's phone number to tell her that I'm interested in the job."

She jotted the number down of a scrap of paper. "Don't call her before 10:00 A.M."

Hafeed snapped up the note. "I know all about working nights."

Back in the Game

Cooking is about passion, so it may look slightly temperamental in a way to the naked eye.
–Gordon Ramsey

Hafeed had planned to lie in the weeds and slowly work his way up through the ranks. On his first day, the Sous-Chef de Cuisine, who prepared sauces, was a no-show. Hafeed volunteered. Having witnessed the abuse the sous-chef endured on a daily basis, the rest of the kitchen staff didn't want any part of it. Hafeed glanced at the recipes and set to work. He could make the twenty-three basic sauces in his sleep.

When the head chef, Jimmy Lang, came into the kitchen, Hafeed immediately felt the tension.

Brian, the number two prep cook, vanished into the walk-in freezer. Gordon, the number three prep cook, busied himself peeling potatoes.

Jimmy gave Hafeed a stern look and sampled the *béarnaise*. "Too much tarragon and it needs more lemon."

"Yes, Chef."

Jimmy was impressed by the smooth consistency and velvety feel but kept the severe look on his face to let the newbie know he wasn't in the least bit impressed.

Not without effort, Hafeed smiled and nodded through the litany of petty criticisms. Having an intimate understanding of the politics of running a kitchen, he knew Lang's words had nothing to do with the taste or texture of his sauces and everything to do with the one simple rule: *Top Dog never lets anyone forget who is Top Dog.*

The following day, Jimmy sampled the *velouté* and *béchamel* sauce. He grunted and said nothing, which was not only a compliment, it meant Hafeed had moved up the food chain.

Within a week, Hafeed was all but running the kitchen. He barked at the staff if an order went out without being perfect. Hafeed had forgotten how badly he missed being in the game. Days, and then weeks went by, and he soon forgot why he was there.

* * *

On a busy Friday night, just after the peak of dinner service, an older man came through the double swinging doors into the kitchen unchallenged.

Hafeed snapped his head around. "May I help you?" he asked.

The old man walked straight past him without a word and into Lang's office.

"Jimmy, how are you?"

Lang tossed a sample menu over the tray of cocaine and smiled. "What a surprise! How are you, Sid? Have you eaten?"

"Yes, of course. I had the pan-seared scallops with mushroom risotto. It was good."

Jimmy sensed a small reservation in his silent partner's thick Romanian accent. "I prepared the scallops myself," Jimmy informed him, defensively.

"They were good," Sid repeated, stopping short of mentioning that his scallops were undercooked. He liked his seafood firm, not soft and translucent. "Martha and I were just on O'ahu and dined at Legend's Beach House. The scallops were huge and cooked to a turn."

"A very fine restaurant," Jimmy conceded with a smile. Soon he would have the cash to buy out his partner, until then he had no choice but to put up with the doddering old fool. "Did you see the article in *Wai Nau Magazine*? We were rated number one on the island."

"Yes. Number one on *Wai Nau*." Sid bit his tongue. He wanted to mention that there were only a handful of fine dining establishments on the island. "Legend's is number one in all of Hawaii." The old man held up his index finger to indicate number one and then pointed at the cocky younger man. "We want to be number one."

Jimmy gave Sid a severe look that said two things loud and clear: *you're a "silent" partner and—my food is superior in every way to that hack Roy Chu's—no matter what anyone may have said or written.* "We're establishing a reputation for fine dining. It takes time. By this time next year . . ." *I will be through with you,* Jimmy silently finished his thought.

"The next time you are on O'ahu, you should dine at Legend's," Sid advised.

Jimmy felt the same sense of shame well up in him when his father derided him in front of strangers. "You're not a man," his father would pronounce venomously. "You cry like a girl when you skin your knee." The cocaine whipped his anger like a runaway team of horses as he imagined slicing the old man in two with a single stroke of his long Kanpeki knife. "Thank you for stopping by, Sid. I'm glad you enjoyed your meal. I really should get back in the kitchen and help with the last hour of the dinner service," Jimmy said, in a calm, steady voice.

"Yes, of course. I'll see you next week. You are coming along fine, young man," Sid said, with pride.

* * *

Gina called Hafeed and arranged for them to meet at Rey's Taco van for lunch.

Hafeed gave Gina a big hug. "Are you sure you can risk being seen with me?" he asked, sarcastically.

"Why? Because you look like a terrorist or because you're an infamous food snob?"

"I have a discerning palate." Hafeed peered into the taco van with suspicion. "Is the food any good?"

"Rey makes an amazing fish taco. So, don't go all Michelin stars on me." To be on the safe side, Gina made him sit at the far picnic table while she ordered for both of them.

When she brought the food, Hafeed peered inside the double-layer of corn tortillas. "More cabbage than fish." He plucked out a handful of shredded greens before taking a bite.

"What have you found out?" Gina cut to the chase.

"Hmm?" he mused with his mouth full. "The fish is fresh, not frozen. Opah, possibly ono. The sauce is sour cream based, not yogurt. There is dill, cumin, smoked paprika—"

"What have you found out about the chef at the Surfrider?" she interrupted.

"Lang is an okay blade man, but his food is too salty. The most egregious thing—he uses mediocre oils. Even in his salad dressings!"

"That's not what I meant."

"He lacks the depth of human feeling to ever be a chef. The man has no soul."

"Hafeed?"

"I'm serious, Gina. Lang is in love with the *idea* of food, but he has no heart. He understands nothing! Food is life!" Hafeed exclaimed.

Gina reached up with both hands and pulled her hair in frustration. "Have you noticed anything suspicious?"

"More suspicious than not having a soul?" Hafeed realized it was pointless trying to make her understand.

"Have you noticed anything illegal?"

"After hours I have a few drinks with the staff, you know, to unwind."

"To flirt with Tammy, you mean."

Hafeed tried to act hurt, but his smile gave him away. "Lang's office is adjacent to the kitchen. He disappears in there, sometimes during dinner service. No doubt tooting fat lines of coke." Hafeed lived the lifestyle for many years. "There's a small window into his office, but the blinds are always closed. A couple of nights ago, an old guy sitting at table six wandered into the kitchen and walked straight into Lang's office. I held my breath, expecting Jimmy to lose it. The two of them were in there for a while chatting. I found out later from Mckinnon, the bartender, that the old guy was Sid Margolis, Lang's silent partner."

"That's interesting. What do you know about this guy Margolis?"

"He immigrated to America from Romania in the early seventies and started a piano school in southern California. Evidently, he created his own teaching method. According to Mckinnon,

Old Sid has produced several generations of concert-level pianists. The guy must be ninety."

"Margolis doesn't sound like a drug kingpin. I wonder why he put up the money for the Surfrider?" Gina asked.

"According to Mckinnon, three years after his wife died, Margolis married his housekeeper, a much younger woman. They have a teenage son who is a child prodigy. Margolis sold his piano school business and lives in *Wai Nau* full time. Mckinnon claims Margolis doesn't know anything about the restaurant business and probably invested for tax reasons?"

Gina hugged Hafeed. "Aside from being an artist with food, you're a damn good covert operative."

"I know." Hafeed smiled.

"We're one step closer to cracking this," Gina said, wanting to believe it was true. "How are things going with you and Tammy?"

"We're friends." The goddess Tammy was out of his league. "Maybe if she knew I was a super spy, as well as a world-class chef?"

"She knows," Gina reminded him.

"What's not to love?"

"I love you." Gina squeezed his shoulder.

"A lot of good it will do me." Hafeed turned serious. "You keep saying you and Curly are on the outs, but it's pretty obvious you two are . . ."

"Are what?"

"Remember, my dear; I lived in Egypt for many years. I know when someone's floating down that river in North Africa: Da Nile."

Eumaeus

Through pride we are ever deceiving ourselves. But deep down below the surface of the average conscience, a still small voice says to us, something is out of tune.
–Carl Jung

Before a Use Permit for the private club could be approved by the county, the Avalon Development Group was required to complete an archaeological survey and an Environmental Impact Statement. A Mainland firm, GEO Consultants, was hired to do the E.I.S.

Curly was given the gate code that accessed the upper valley in order to verify the E.I.S. He took *Wai ʻapo* Valley Road that skirted Uncle Kahawai's place before snaking up the south side of the basalt canyon. A wall of rain met him as he topped the hill soaking the report sitting on the passenger seat. He rolled up the window catching glimpses of the seventh fairway through the border of palms and fuchsia bougainvillea. The sprinklers were running despite the heavy rain. *The Pali* was a thirsty two-hundred and thirty-acre course.

The Chinese developer, Duane Lin, had made a commitment to make improvements, promising that once again *The Pali* would be in the running to host the PGA Grand Slam. A recent *Times* article quoted Lin as stating, "A great course cannot sustain itself without the proper amenities."

Curly stopped at *The Pali* clubhouse restaurant for lunch. When the clouds opened, his table by the window had an amazing view of *Wai ʻapo* Beach below and the *Pali* cliffs above. "The rest of the world makes this place look like a country club," he quipped to the waitress, who gave him a smile and a blank stare. It made Curly crazy that Uncle Kahawai's old farm below would soon be polo grounds. Did Pebble Beach have polo grounds? He didn't want to know.

After paying his bill, he visited the spacious men's room, tiled head-to-toe with slabs of Brazilian marble. The private showers and koa wood lockers shocked Curly. The gold fixtures seemed over-the-top if that was possible. A signed life-sized photo of Tiger Woods stared down at him. "Nice watch," Curly complimented the legend as he strolled by. He wondered how they planned to make the place more upscale, other than to hire security guards to keep riff-raff, like himself, from sneaking in and ordering a twenty-five dollar tuna melt.

He drove to the end of the road, entered the gate code, and took the muddy dirt track up to the upper reservoir. He took photos of the earthen dam and inspected the cracked concrete around the spillway.

Dark clouds to the east threatened. He decided to use the rest of the afternoon to survey the stream. Hau trees choked the bank making it nearly impossible to access the water. With help from the E.I.S. map, he located a trench that had been dug near the bank as part of the cultural survey. According to the report, no artifacts had been found. Either due to the heavy rains or a highwater table from being so close to the stream, the trench was full of water. He noted that a fabric barrier was required around the trench and a tarp over the mound of dirt to prevent the silt from washing into *Wai ʻapo* stream. Surveying the area, he found stacked lava rock walls that were probably part of a terrace system used to grow taro. He made a note. The E.I.S. had no mention of the old terraces. Either GEO Consultants were lazy and incompetent, or had been instructed *not* to find anything of cultural significance in the upper valley.

On his way home he took the winding back road, the long shortcut Gina had shown him. He was free to go where ever he liked, but he felt banished. *The one person I want to see doesn't want to see me.* Nearing Karen Klindt's farm, he surprised himself by turning into her rutted driveway.

Eumaeus the billy goat was waiting by the gate. Curly looked over his shoulder as he securely fastened the gate, remembering how the neighbor kids had played a trick on him last time. It was close to dusk. He hoped the little rascals were home having supper.

Eumaeus followed a step behind all the way across the wide meadow. "Hello, Auntie!" he called out.

Karen emerged, gathering her gray hair out of her face. "Who have you brought, Eumaeus? The king of Ithaca returns."

"It's Curly. I'm a friend of Gina's." He paused, wondering if he should have said, I *was* a friend of Gina's. "I met you a couple of months ago."

"Yes, I remember. Come in; I was just making some minestrone. Nothing like hot soup on a chilly evening."

Upon hearing Karen's kind invitation, Curly was surprised by the wave of emotion that welled up in him. He wanted to tell Karen the whole woeful tale of his exile. "I'm sorry to come crashing in on you unannounced."

"Don't be silly," Karen said, from the kitchen. When they met, she had a feeling he might be back.

After they finished their steaming bowls of minestrone, Karen got down her cake tin, and once again introduced Curly to all of her people, dead and alive. She handed him one of her most cherished photos. "This is Isaac Brown. He was a Scottish sailor."

Curly noticed a bit of color light up Karen's cheeks. He wondered if they were lovers. For some reason, he assumed Karen had always preferred the company of goats to people, before realizing she was not sharing old photos of goats. All the photos were of people, except one. He picked it out of the pile, a black-and-white picture of a small valley with a maze of beautiful taro terraces. "Do you know where this photo was taken?" he asked.

"Is there anything written on the back?"

"No. Nothing." He thought he recognized the drainage. "May I take a photo of this?"

"Of course."

Curly took out his phone and snapped a couple of shots of the old black-and-white. He suddenly realized that maybe it was rude to only show interest in the one photo without any of Karen's friends in it. "I'm a stream biologist," he said, by way of apology. "I'm curious if this photo was taken on *Wai Nau*."

"I'm quite sure it was. Hawaiians grew taro everywhere before Europeans arrived. When the Chinese and Japanese arrived to work the sugar cane, they had grown rice in the taro terraces. After the war, everything changed."

Curly grew up near Pearl Harbor. December 7th, 1941 was a song in the background that never stopped playing. He never stopped to think about how deeply the music was still affecting people's lives.

"How's Gina?" Karen could see the sadness in the youth's face.

"She's well," he said, automatically. "It's been a couple of weeks since I've seen her, but I've heard that she's doing great."

In her youth, Karen had met the love of her life—he sailed away—that was that. Isaac Brown was not the kind of man you could forget, even if you wanted to. "Gina is one of a kind." She gently tapped his arm to let him know she understood.

"I better hit the road." Everything he was feeling was being telegraphed across his face. He had to leave before he broke down.

"You're welcome here anytime. You know that?" Karen gave him a hug.

"Thank you for the delicious soup." He stood at the doorway. "Can I ask you something, Auntie?"

"Please."

"When I arrived, you mentioned something about the king of Ithaca?"

"Oh yes." She paused, wondering how to explain. "Eumaeus was the loyal swineherd of Odysseus. When King Odysseus returned home from the Trojan War, after twenty years, to his surprise and dismay, no one recognized him. The once-mighty king ended up sleeping on the swineherd's floor," she explained.

"I don't remember that part of the story."

Tiger Pit

Now gathering
Now scattering
Fireflies over the river
–Natsume

Gina's plan uncoiled in her mind like an open chord on a Hawaiian steel guitar. Uncontrollable factors warbled in and out of pitch like a far-off ragged chorus singing, "Don't do it!"

She didn't have the complete picture and realized she probably never would. There was only one way to learn the truth—she had to ask Jimmy Lang.

The porous threshold of sleep spilled over into morning. Gina awoke with her legs kicking, feeling like she'd been spit out by something bigger than the earth. Glancing over at the well-thumbed copy of Sun Tzu's classic on the nightstand she intoned, "All war is deception."

* * *

The next morning on his way to work, Curly drove by Uncle Kahawai's driveway just as the low clouds thinned, revealing the high *Pali* above. Curly pulled over and took out his phone to check his messages. He felt like he was standing right next to something, waiting to remember why he was standing there. He flipped through his photos. "That's it!" He found the photo of the taro terraces. The *pali* in the background was the same. "This photo was taken near here!" He drove to Kahawai's house and ran across the meadow. "Uncle! Uncle!" He found the big man near *Wai 'apo* stream pushing a wheelbarrow. "Uncle, I have to show you something!"

Curly showed the old man the black and white photo on his phone. "Do you recognize where this photo may have been taken?"

"I know the very spot."

Curly followed Uncle Kahawai up a small rise. The old man stopped and pointed up at the high basalt cliff.

Curly held up the phone so they could both see. "A perfect match, it could have been taken yesterday."

Uncle Kahawai nodded and smiled proudly.

"Do you know what this means?" Curly was beside himself. "This photo proves that taro was grown on your farm."

Not wanting to spoil the youth's joy in the obvious, Kahawai didn't tell the boy that he had known this his whole life. The meadow was taro before it was graded to plant pineapple.

"This photo is physical proof, the kind of proof that will hold up in court. This means your land carries the original water rights from the time of the Great Mahele. The old water rights supersede all other claims and rights. It's the law."

"I don't understand."

"You don't have to sell your land, Uncle. You can divert water from *Wai 'apo* stream and grow whatever you want. Not only that—" Curly began jumping around in excitement. "You have the last word on how the water is used upstream. The golf course now needs to ask you for permission to use the water in *Wai 'apo* reservoir." Curly's mind reeled. "I have to call Gina." He looked at his phone: no reception. "Uncle, I have to go. I'll come back as soon as I can with more information." He shook Uncle's hand and ran back to his truck.

* * *

Hafeed dialed Gina, but it went straight to voicemail. He sent a text: *CALL ME!* He called Curly and it also went to his voicemail. "Doesn't anyone answer their phone anymore?" Hafeed realized the beep had already happened. "Curly, this is Hafeed. I know you and Gina are on the outs, but I'm worried about her. Gina's convinced she found Nalani's murderer. His name is Jimmy Lang. He's a real nut job! You know how Gina is. I think she's planning to confront Jimmy. We need to find Gina ASAP! I'm calling Carla right now. Call me back!"

* * *

Wrapped in a turquoise scarf, wearing a wide-brimmed sun hat and sunglasses, Gina parked outside the city limits of Waiola and walked the rest of the way into town. Jimmy Lang's red Porsche Cayman was in the Surfrider parking lot. She slipped a note under the wiper blade and hurried away. By the time she made it out of the parking lot, she convulsed, throwing up acid into her mouth. There was no turning back now. When she reached Chichi's Subaru, she sat in the driver's seat until the wave of panic subsided.

* * *

Curly listened to Hafeed's message and then dialed Gina's cell, it went directly to voicemail. He sent her a text, *Call me, Gina. It's important!*

When Hafeed didn't pick up, Curly left a message and a text. He called Moreno, who thankfully answered.

"Hey, Curlers. How did you get my number?"

"Gina's in trouble. She thinks she found the murderer. We need to find her."

"Take a deep breath. I'll call Kalo's Café and make a sweep through *Mana'olana*. Don't worry; Gina can take care of herself." Moreno hung up wishing she could believe her own bullshit.

Curly took the bypass and headed north on Pahua Road, Gina's preferred route. He drove to the end of the road and asked the lifeguard at *Waiwai* Beach.

"I haven't seen Gina in months. How's she doing?"

Curly handed him his business card. "Please call me if you see Gina, it's important. Thanks." He ran back to his truck.

It was *pau hana* Friday and the traffic was bumper to bumper. He remembered it was the Bon Dance at *Mana'olana*. He called Moreno.

"Did you find Gina?" asked Moreno.

"No sign of her. By the looks of the traffic, I'm an hour or more away from *Mana'olana*. If you find her or hear anything, please call me. Hafeed's got me in a panic."

"Take it easy, big guy. I told you, Gina can handle herself," Moreno used her cop voice to mask her concern. "Don't drive like a *haole*."

* * *

Gina parked at the end of the road and hurried up the river path, her *kimono* preventing her from taking longer strides. She kicked herself for not arriving earlier. The last rays of the sun illuminated soft red clouds to the east. Paper lanterns were already lit along the footpath that circled an ancient Hawaiian heiau. Kalo told her that when he was a boy, his mother would take him to this heiau when he was sick. It was a place of power and healing.

A chorus of screechy whispers emanated from the tall bamboo that obscured the old teahouse. Kammie Sato was waiting beside the small entrance; her golden *kimono* shone in the fading light. Every detail of Kammie's appearance was in contrast to the wild surroundings. Her hair was perfect, tied up in the traditional style, with an ornate abalone comb with three miniature showers of plumeria blossoms on her left side.

"What are you doing here, Kammie? Didn't you get my message?" Gina panicked, already her plan was not going according to plan.

"I got your message, Gina, but it didn't make any sense. I can't just—not show up—this isn't just a job."

"I know how important the way of tea is to you, but your life is in danger. Your guest isn't coming. Auntie Nalani's killer is on his way here right now!"

Kammie could see it in Gina's face, she was serious. "Okay, I believe you."

"There isn't much time. You have to leave."

"How? There's only one path back to the road. If the killer is coming, I don't want to meet him in the dark."

"The river!" Gina grabbed Kammie's hand, and they made their way down to the riverbank. A yellow plastic kayak was propped up against a tree. "Can you paddle?" Gina asked.

"Are you serious, in my *kimono?*"

"There isn't time to change. I'll pay to have everything professionally cleaned. I promise." Together they carried the plastic boat to the water. "Get in. I'll push you."

Kammie settled into the kayak, and Gina handed her the paddle.

"You ready?" Gina asked, before gently shoving the boat out into the current. "Be careful. Don't *huli*."

Kammie called out, "What about you? Should I call the police when I get to town?"

"Don't worry; I'll be fine." Gina's *tabi* slippers and the hem of her *kimono* were soaked. She hurried back to the teahouse.

* * *

Jimmy Lang followed the string of paper lanterns along the path. He struggled to put his first visit to the little teahouse out of his mind. The chance encounter in the rainforest with the old woman was most unfortunate. It had to be done. His plan was flawless. It was impossible to believe that he had been discovered. There was no way anyone could have figured out his involvement.

The note on his windshield read: *Nalani Ōta's death was no accident. Meet me at the old Murakami Teahouse at 8:00 P.M.*

Jimmy approached the teahouse cautiously, the rice paper moon-window glowed with candlelight. After a perimeter check, he crawled through the small door and was shocked by the disheveled look of the hostess. She gestured for him to sit in the place of honor where he could view the scroll and the flower arrangement.

Their eyes met in a muted exchange.

She had expected a monster, not a fine-boned handsome young man. His eyes were dark, but not sinister. She placed her palms together and made a formal bow, *gassho rei*. Chichi's voice stalked her thoughts, "Breathe in the entire universe, exhale all delusion, anger, and fear."

Jimmy watched the clumsy girl bow. He wondered how long he would have to wait for whoever left the note. He read the scroll, "*Ichi go, Ichi e.*" One time, one meeting. *We will never meet again.*

Gina ladled hot water and rinsed the tea bowl. She unfolded her tea towel and ritually cleansed the tea bowl, careful not to touch the rim.

Jimmy studied the small room. The hut was a thrown together affair. The flickering light of the lanterns danced around the exposed rafters which had been cut incorrectly and should have been discarded.

Gina followed his eyes to the rafters. He noticed the birds-mouth cuts in the rafters and didn't bother to hide the contempt he felt.

In Japan they valued art and craftsmanship, he thought.

Nalani had called the notches, "love bites." When Gina was a girl studying *wabi-sabi,* Auntie told her the story of the lovesick young carpenter who built the teahouse. He was thinking of his lover and not the rafters when he measured. The tea aunties affectionately called it Love Bites Teahouse.

Jimmy studied the hostess's every movement. The clumsy girl nervously arranged the tea utensils. The *natsume* tea caddy did not match the set. The girl's lack of grace gnawed at him. He wouldn't hire this peasant to bus tables. Nothing could compare to the grace of the host on his first visit. It was most unfortunate that the old woman was picking wildflowers that day. He had no choice. It had to be done. He put the old woman out of his mind.

Gina offered the wagashi sweet on washi paper.

Jimmy bowed and accepted the sweet. *Just because this peasant has no grace, doesn't mean I'm without manners.* He ate the sweet bean treat and listened for any movement outside.

Gina noticed his nicotine-stained fingers, his confident smile, the cold emptiness behind his eyes. She realized she owed Hafeed an apology. *I should have listened.* As ridiculous as Hafeed seemed at times, he was an artist. Artists see beyond mere appearance. Hafeed was right; Jimmy had no spirit, no soul. Now, it was too late.

In the soft light of the paper lantern, Jimmy saw it in her eye. "No one else is coming?" His question a statement.

The wind settled, quieting the bamboo. The birds ceased their evening's song. A hush fell like silent snow, gathering all around her. She carefully scooped out the green tea powder, her hands shaking. After ladling hot water into the tea bowl, she whisked the bitter green tea with a steady motion until it became light froth. With her left hand under the bowl and the right surrounding, she bowed and gently placed the bowl in front of the guest.

Jimmy bowed and picked up the tea bowl with both hands, turned it once to the right, and drank. He took a second swallow, draining the bowl.

The bitter silence rang in Gina's ears.

"Life and death are not complicated," Jimmy informed his disheveled host. "We are born. We live. The time arrives for all of us when the cost of our lives is paid in full by our death." Jimmy flipped a cigarette in his mouth and lit it in one smooth action.

She had never felt so naked or exposed. In the inescapable silence, it became clear, Jimmy was going to kill her. "You've been to our teahouse before; an older woman served you tea."

"Yes." Jimmy cleared his throat. It was an evening he would never forget.

"One month later you lured her out to the sinkhole and murdered her." Gina poured the hot water into the tea bowl and rinsed it.

Jimmy took a long draw from his cigarette and peered at his prey.

"I know everything." Gina met his eyes as she carefully folded the tea towel.

Jimmy laughed. "It's obviously the first time you've served tea." He leaned back and smiled.

"You have a painting of Wu Song in your living room."

"You dared to enter my home!" Jimmy struggled to regain his calm. It would not do to kill her in anger.

"I was working. I'm a maid."

"Ha! You make tea like a maid," Jimmy sneered and relaxed. "You should have stuck with scrubbing toilets."

"You're a Red Pole, an enforcer for the Triad."

Jimmy's laugh sent a wave of panic up Gina's spine.

"The scroll you chose begins to make sense," he observed. "*Ichi go Ichi e*. One time, one meeting. This will be your last."

* * *

Curly ran through the crowd of dancers searching for Gina. He noticed the long line in front of Gina's booth. Reverend Mori was manning the shave ice machine. "Have you seen Gina?"

"She called to say she would be late. Can you help? Please." Reverend Mori asked, looking at the ever-growing line. "I'm supposed to be offering the prayer in a few minutes."

"Did Gina say where she was going?"

"Mirabelle Sasaki thought she saw Gina driving up River Road. She needs to come soon and run her shave ice booth."

"What's up River Road?" Curly asked, doing his best not to sound too concerned.

"There's an old tea house up the path at the end of the road."

"If you see Gina, please ask her to call me," Curly said, calmly. He walked a few paces into the crowd and then ran back to the parking lot.

Curly's roommate, Hutch, was leaning on the hood of his pickup.

"Have you seen Gina?" Curly asked.

"Why? What's wrong?" Hutch could tell something was up.

"I think Gina's in trouble. She's not answering her phone. Hafeed thinks she found the person who killed her aunt and she's using herself as bait."

"Let's go!" Hutch jumped in the passenger seat. "Where are we going?"

"Upriver." Curly stood on the gas pedal and careened out of the parking lot toward River Road.

* * *

Steve Jade and Kai Shin were waiting at the end of the road when a Tokyo businessman pulled up in his rented BMW dressed in a formal black *kimono*. Kai confronted him as he stepped out of the vehicle, "Hey! What are you doing here?"

"I have an appointment for a private tea ceremony."

"It's canceled," Kai informed him.

"There's been some mistake; I made a reservation six weeks ago. I was assured that—"

"Leave now!" Kai said, firmly. He stood with his feet apart in a kickboxer stance.

The businessman looked into the two men's eyes and saw his life pass before him. He scrambled back into his car and sped away.

Curly swerved as the headlights appeared from around a sharp corner. He couldn't see who was driving the luxury sedan. "Did you catch the plates?" he asked Hutch.

"Not a chance. That guy was flying." Hutch turned around watching the taillights vanish. "How many bad guys are we talking about?"

"I don't know. My gut tells me we better be ready for a fight." Curly had never been to the end of the road. He braked when they came to the turnaround. A grey Camry, Chichi's Subaru, a red Porsche, and a crème Mitsubishi Lancer were parked near the trailhead.

Steve and Kai heard the rig coming up the road. Jimmy Lang had broken protocol and called them directly at the store, instructing them to wait at the end of the River Road and not to let anyone pass. When they heard the rig approaching, they hid in the trees and watched as two *haoles* jumped out of a 4x4. It was clear they weren't late for tea. Kai's adrenaline kicked in. "We need to head up the trail and scout for the right place to jump them."

* * *

The limousine stopped in the middle of the street. Mr. Lin's bodyguard got out first, wanting to accompany him into the crowd.

"I will be fine. Stay with the car." Lin ordered.

Paper lanterns strung like spokes of a wheel hung above the smiling dancers. The sights and smells of the Bon Dance reminded Lin of his own rural village in Gansu. His first love, Yu Yan, was from a wealthy family. He looked across the circle of dancers dressed in their brightly colored happi-coats, remembering how Yu Yan's eyes lit up when they met, all those years ago. He wanted to ask her to dance but was ashamed of holding her hand with his rough stained fingers. A flood of memories overwhelming him. He looked at his manicured hands, seeing the invisible stains from climbing the dung heap of Hong Kong. He strolled through the crowd beyond the light of the lanterns, called by the sound of the river. The young boy who left the village for the city had watched both his parents work themselves to death. He long believed that village boy had died as well. He followed the riverbank, pausing on a boulder that jutted out into the current. The full moon peeked out from a cloud. Lin took a deep breath of the soft ocean air, the gentle breeze stirring the silvery palms making a sound like gentle rain. He closed his eyes and was once again the awkward boy awaiting his Yu Yan beside the river.

Kammie could just make out the dark shapes of the overhanging branches on the far riverbank. She let out a sigh of relief when she saw the lantern light reflecting off the water. She paddled toward the familiar sound of the music. The bow of the kayak hit a set of rapids. Afraid of tipping, she overcompensated and rolled over backward, screaming as she went under.

Lin heard a scream from across the wide river. A pair of lily-white hands flashed on the surface of the water before disappearing. Kicking off his shoes and pulling off his suit coat, he picked an angle and dove in, swimming across the current to the far side of the river.

* * *

"You were sloppy," Gina goaded.

"Careful, maid," Jimmy warned. "Tell me who told you these lies you are spewing and I will let you live."

"There's a witness that places you at the scene, wearing a blonde wig."

"Not likely." Jimmy smiled, knowing he had an ironclad alibi. He was in his kitchen when the old woman died.

"She was my Auntie." Gina's voice was so low she didn't recognize the sound. "Her name was Nalani."

"Are you talking about the old woman who wandered around in the middle of the night and fell in a hole? I read about that in the paper, a tragedy."

Gina knew from Moreno that time of death was determined to be just before midnight. "You took great pains to plan Nalani's murder. Prior to your meeting, you cut a tree limb near the edge of the sinkhole, leaving six inches on the trunk to use later as a hook. You took the green limb, bent it into a loop and placed it in your walk-in freezer with some kind of mold,so that a block of ice locked the two ends of the limb together. How am I doing so far?"

Jimmy took a long pull from his cigarette before flicking the butt out the small door.

Anger flashed across Jimmy's face, convincing Gina that she was on the right track.

"Bringing your murder weapon with you in a cooler, you lured Nalani to the sinkhole. After rendering her unconscious with chloroform, you untied her *obi,* looping it around the green limb locked in ice. Leaning Auntie's limp body over the edge, you hung the green loop over the stub you left on the tree trunk. With the pressure on her lungs from hanging from her *obi,* Auntie couldn't cry out for help. She hung there in terror while you drove to the Surfrider." Gina took a breath to control her anger. "The ice holding the loop slowly melted, and the green limb let go, slipping from under Nalani's *obi*. She fell to her death around midnight while you were in your restaurant unwinding from a long hard day."

"I never knew maids had such wild imaginations." Jimmy slowly drew another cigarette out of the pack and lit it. "How did you ever dream up such a tale?"

"The ground was dry, except on the top of the ledge near where Auntie fell. I felt the damp ground. Nalani's *kimono* was also damp. I found a green limb stripped of its leaves lying under the tree where it had been cut days before. It was more curved than it should have been."

"A tree branch and a patch of wet ground. Quite the smoking gun?" The smug look on Jimmy Lang's face turned into a cold stare. "People will wonder why you fell into the river." Jimmy's smile returned. "What a pity. Didn't you know, maid, it's impossible to swim in a *kimono*?"

"I know how you killed Nalani. Tell me why and I won't struggle. Tell me the reason why you killed her and I promise I'll walk down to the river on my own."

He looked at the tea bowl and the charcoal brazier. "The old woman who served me tea," Jimmy paused to find the words. "She was a true artist. It's impossible to believe you're related." Gina's coarse manners repulsed Jimmy. "I've been entertained by the most famous geishas in Japan. Witnessing her grace . . ." Lang's voice broke. "It remains one of the most profound experiences of my life."

"I don't understand." Gina was confused.

Jimmy paused to regain his composure. "I found myself . . . overwhelmed." The beauty of the moment had left him completely exposed. The old woman had seen him as if he were a naked child. A month later, in the middle of counting the cash with Kai Shin, this same woman walked into the clearing near Lava Rock Dam. She had looked at him in the same piercing way, holding a bucket full of wild ginger.

Gina's heart pounded, she forgot to breathe. "What are you saying? You killed Nalani because she saw you crying?"

Jimmy struggled to arrange his thoughts. He didn't owe this peasant an explanation. "The old woman was in the wrong place at the wrong time."

"What do you mean?"

"She saw something she shouldn't have."

"The money drop in the canal?" Gina asked.

When the old woman came out of the rainforest, Jimmy couldn't believe it. Kai Shin almost killed her on the spot. Afterward, Jimmy devised the canal drop so no one could happen upon the money exchange by accident. Now, somehow, the skinny niece of this same old woman has found out everything. "What do you know about a canal?"

"What's wrong with you?" Gina had never seen a monster. She was prepared for Jimmy to be insane. Instead, he was simply pathetic. "How could you murder Nalani, the sweetest person in the world?"

"How did you find out? Were you hiding at the cave? Tell me! How do you know about the canal drop? Did the old woman tell you about me?"

"Wu Song killed a tiger. You killed an old woman! How can you live with yourself?"

"Who else knows?" he asked.

"No one."

"Why should I believe you?"

"You're the liar." Gina wept, not bothering to cover her face. The sadness she had been holding back burst through the levee. "It doesn't matter now. Nothing matters now."

"If you wish for a quick and painless death, it matters," Jimmy explained. "Tell me who else knows." Just as he was about to pay off Sid Margolis, his greatest fear of losing the restaurant was becoming a reality.

Gina rose from her knees with surprising ease. "I'll walk down to the river. I keep my promises." She couldn't bear the thought of him touching her.

Jimmy gestured. "*Dozo,* after you."

She bowed under the low doorway. The weight of the earth lifted. She could breathe again.

Jimmy followed close behind.

The moonlight through the clouds illuminated the gravel path. Gina felt the spirit of Auntie Nalani walking beside her.

Jimmy scrutinized the cadaverous shadows following close behind and wondered if they longed to witness the moment of death?

* * *

Curly raced up the trail following the lanterns, his imagination taking oblique paths to unspeakable places. What if the murderer was driving the black sedan they passed on the road? *What if he is getting away?* He had to find Gina. That was all that mattered. He turned just as something heavy battered the back of his head, sending him somersaulting down the bank toward the river.

*　　*　　*

Kammie struggled to hold her head above water, her wet *kimono* dragging her under the current. She ripped at her *Obi,* but it was tied at the back.

Lin called out, "Are you there?"

Swallowing more water, Kammie coughed and let out a weak cry and gulped more water.

"Roll on your back. Relax. Breathe. I'm almost there." Exhausted and out of breath, Lin put his head down and fought his way through the water, refusing to give up.

Convinced she was going to be washed out to sea, the stranger's voice gave Kammie courage. She tilted her head back and tried to float.

*　　*　　*

The bamboo squeaked and whispered, each leaf a shining black blade. The moon hid behind a cloud. Jimmy felt a sense of unease. He didn't know how the girl had found out but she had to die. *I'll catch a flight to O'ahu in the morning and be back in Hong Kong in twenty-four hours.* Shadows began to take on form. His breath caught in terror. *Father was right.*

Gina had found Nalani's killer. Now, she searched desperately for a way to forgive him. What would Chichi say? What would the Buddha say? She didn't know. Jimmy was a coke head, not that it excused what he had done. It was no use, her heart was not big enough to forgive.

Jimmy felt a curious tingling in his fingers. "Time is up, maid. Tell me, how did you find out? Tell me, and I promise you'll die quickly."

The moonlight glimmered off the water. Gina turned around to face the end.

Jimmy took a step toward her, his feet and legs were suddenly unresponsive. He lunged toward her and fell. "What? What have you done?" he asked, his right cheek pressing against the sharp gravel.

Gina kept her distance. "Be subtle, even to the point of formlessness."

"Sun Tzu?" Jimmy's eyes grew wide. "The tea?"

"Defeated by a leaf." She took a moment to let it sink in. "The bitterness of the tea masked the taste of the benzodiazepine."

The previous night she broke into the *Mana'olana* Pharmacy and stole Valium, Rohypnol, and Ambien. She put a handful of the pills in the blender with the bitter green tea powder.

"No matter," he whispered, unable to move his limbs. "I *will* kill you."

She reached into the generous sleeve of her kimono for her cellphone. Her hands shaking, she dropped it. She picked it up off the gravel and played back the recording of his confession. "I hate the thought, but you'll probably enjoy prison."

"Gina! Gina!"

Gina heard Curly's voice near the teahouse. "I'm here! By the river!"

Curly ran down the path and nearly tripped over the body lying face down. He wrapped his arms around Gina and held her close. "I was worried you were going to do something crazy." He looked at the man on the ground "Who's he? Is he all right?"

"Meet Jimmy Lang. He murdered Nalani."

Hutch lumbered down the path out of breath. "Hey, Curly, did you tell Gina how I just saved your ass?"

"I thought I'd let you tell it." Curly knew he'd be hearing the story for the rest of his life, but he didn't care.

"What's wrong with him?" Hutch kicked the man lying motionless, to see if he was alive.

"He's had a bit too much tea," Gina explained, as she dialed 911.

Poolside

Most of us enter journalism and join news organizations because we care about the greater good. We strive to comfort the afflicted and afflict the comfortable.

–David Shuster

Sam Hara sat in the teak lounge chair next to Curly. They were just out of range of the kids splashing in the pool. "Toxoplasma gondii," Sam said, to no one in particular.

"Excuse me?" Curly asked the stranger.

"You're Julius Curry." Sam put out his hand. "Or is it Julius Perry?"

"Do I know you?" Curly shook the man's hand.

"We've met."

"Sorry; I don't remember."

"You work for the DLNR," Sam stated.

"That's right, Surface Water Division."

"That's how you know that cat feces carry Toxoplasma gondii," Sam explained.

Curly stood. "I'm sorry, this conversation is a little too bizarre for me. If you'll excuse me."

"Say hello to Mr. McKenna when you see him."

Curly froze. "Who did you say you were?"

"Sam Hara. Before I moved to *Wai Nau* to take the job at the *Times*, I was a beat reporter in Honolulu for thirty-five years. Many of my friends and sources on O'ahu were homeless living on the streets. In other words, I can spot a real bum from a fake one a mile away."

Curly laughed. "I've been told *haoles* all look alike."

"They do, especially the dumb ones."

"What is it you want, Mr. Hara?" Curly knew his secret was bound to get out.

"I was curious if our mutual acquaintance, Mr. McKenna, was going to be writing any more letters about his exclusive club?"

"I couldn't say." Curly gestured at the local kids swimming in the Avalon Club pool. "It appears these days that private clubs are not all they're cracked up to be." Duane Lin had changed his mind about the Avalon Club being separate from the community and had opened the resort to locals. They could swim in the pool and use the gym for free.

"I think it's fair to say that Mr. McKenna had a hand in changing some minds about what it means to be a part of a community," Sam offered.

"It's more likely that the lovely Miss Kammie Sato had more to do with Mr. Lin's sudden conversion," Curly set the record straight.

"Perhaps? Opening the gated communities is a promising sign," Sam agreed. "But there are plenty of other challenges facing our island."

"Now that you mention it, Mr. McKenna did say something about an industrial dairy. . . thousands of dairy cows living too close to endangered habitat." Curly knew the dairy would be a disaster.

"Did you know, Mr. Curry, that the circulation of the *Wai Nau Times* has tripled in the last six months? Instead of cold calling to beg for subscriptions, I've had to hire a full-time assistant to answer all the calls coming in. Even Renee Algar, our receptionist, is busy. She blames your friend Mr. McKenna."

"Hmm? So, what's the job pay?" Curly asked.

"Half of what the DLNR pays, and no benefits."

"Tempting." Curly laughed. "If I see Mr. McKenna, I'll ask him if he's interested."

"A word of advice." Sam glanced over to the other side of the pool. Gina was making a beeline. "Remind Mr. McKenna not to forget to ask his special friend before he makes any big decisions. Come and see me at the paper, I'm serious."

"Thanks, Mr. Hara." Curly shook his hand.

"Call me Sam." He tipped his hat as he passed Gina.

"What did Sam Hara want?" She gave Curly a quick kiss on the lips.

"I'll tell you later. Care for a swim?" He was curious to see what she had on under her towel.

A big kid bounced off the end of the diving board and made a perfect cannonball. The splash reached Gina. She shivered and sat down. "I think I'll sit in the sun for a minute and warm up. Was there something you wanted to ask me?"

"Either you have really good ears, or you know something."

"I'll tell you a secret, Curly. Your cheeks turn red when you're hiding something."

"Sam offered me a job." It was the truth.

"Does the paper need a stream biologist?"

"He thinks I'm a good writer," he lowered his voice.

"Quit niggling and spit it out, Curly."

"I'm Terence McKenna." He watched her smile fade. "I wanted to tell you a thousand times."

Gina bit her lower lip. "Why? Why would you write those stupid letters? And, why would you not tell me?"

"It was stupid. I'm sorry. The idea of a private club taking over the north shore made me crazy. Maybe it reminded me of the peach orchard being bulldozed. I don't know," he said, throwing up his hands in surrender. Her expression changed. He couldn't decide if she was thinking or if she was so pissed off she couldn't speak. "Can you forgive me?"

"Depends."

"On what?"

"Do you have a girlfriend on the Mainland?"

"What? Seriously? Is that what you've been worried about?" He could see her eyes tearing up. "You should know by now; you're the one and only."

Her cheeks flamed.

He leaned over and kissed her.

Another big splash reached them. Gina shivered and laughed. She looked at all the local kids playing in the pool, having fun. Only a week before it was impossible to get past the guard at the gate unless you were a member or staying at the Avalon. "You did this, Curly. Or should I say, you and Terence McKenna? You changed Duane Lin's mind about building his private club."

"Your charming friend Kammie Sato may have had a little something to do with it," Curly added.

"So, are you going to take the job at the paper?"

"Hell no!"

Proclamation

The human brain is a wonderful thing.
It starts working the moment you are born,
And never stops until you stand up to speak in public.
–George Jessel

The Kahuna Ballroom at the *Wai Nau* Bay Resort was packed for the award dinner. The lavishly catered event was co-sponsored by Duane Lin and the Chamber of Commerce. Several individuals were being honored for their service to the community. Officer Carla Moreno was presented an award by Councilwoman Evelyn Yamamoto for bravery and outstanding service. "Bully" Dan Mecham, a retiring firefighter, was also recognized for his lifetime of service to the community.

The woman of the hour, and the reason for the all the O'ahu TV news station cameras was *Wai Nau's* own Gina Mori.

Gina waited on stage, sweating under the hot lights.

With orchid leis piled up to his ears, Mayor Cordeira went on a great deal longer than fit the occasion. The TV cameras were like optical pheromones that excited the politician's brain stem. His speech started out promising, mentioning Gina, before quickly descending into one of the mayor's canned self-promotions. The local audience knew the drill. It wouldn't be over until the fat man sang. After exhausting every self-aggrandizing metaphor at his disposal, with his signature warbling falsetto, the mayor sang *Aloha Wai Nau*. The local Hawaiian version of Wagner.

During the anthem, Gina mouthed the words and imagined Mayor Cordeiro wearing a Brunhilda cow horn helmet, which oddly enough, helped her to keep a straight face. She wondered if the awkward tradition of government proclamations had its roots in the Kingdom of Hawaii.

Karl Kawakura, Chair of the County Council, handed the scroll to Mayor Cordeiro. He turned to Gina and read the proclamation.

"WHEREAS, kindness, harmony, gentleness, humility, and patience are characteristic of the words, actions, and life of Gina J. Mori,

WHEREAS, the State of Hawai'i recognizes that it has a vital role in identifying, protecting its citizens from, and responding to threats that may have significant impact on our individual and collective security and

WHEREAS, Gina J. Mori exemplifies hard work and passion, and the spirit of collaboration with the *Wai Nau* Police Department to apprehend the leader of an international drug ring and bring a murderer to justice;

THEREFORE, I, Bento Cordeiro, Mayor of *Wai Nau*, do hereby proclaim today to be GINA J. MORI DAY.

After an eternity of adjectives and non-sequiturs, praising Miss Mori for her bravery and determination, the Mayor finally presented Gina with her award and proclamation. The big man leaning over and gave Gina an awkward hug, nearly crushing her.

Curly thought the mayor must have stepped on Gina's toes, by the pained look on her face. Her pasted-on smile shifted slightly as she stepped in front of the microphone. She made a small bow and looked first at Chichi and then to Curly. Two large screens to either side of the stage projected a close up of her face.

The large banquet room became still. Everyone set their forks down and waited in silence for Gina to speak.

Gina adjusted the microphone on the podium. A high-pitched squeal came through the speakers. She jumped back, knocking the binder off the podium that contained the mayor's speech. It hit the hollow stage with a loud thunk.

The audience laughed. Those who knew Gina thought it was perfect. A table in the back of the hall began chanting, "Speech, speech, speech!"

Curly noticed a man in a dark suit come in through the side door. There was something oddly familiar about him. He sat down at the VIP table just behind Curly.

Gina cautiously approached the microphone. She could see Curly looking over his shoulder at the VIP table.

Moreno noticed Curly not paying attention. She tapped him on the shoulder and gave him a look.

Curly looked up and met Gina's eyes. He felt a knot in his stomach. Curly realized that the man sitting right behind him, between Duane Lin and the president of the Chamber of Commerce, was his father, Alfred Perry.

As soon as Gina's eyes met Curly's, a sense of calm filled her. She took her time and looked around the large banquet hall at all the familiar faces. "Thank you all so much for coming. I would like to ask for a moment of silence to remember Auntie Nalani."

A warm hum filled the room.

Gina bowed her head.

Curly bowed, but stole a glance around the room at the solemn faces, many with their eyes closed in prayer. He realized most of them had known Auntie Nalani.

After a few minutes, Gina looked up at the sea of familiar faces. She searched the room for Mrs. Sato and Mrs. Tanaka. She found them sitting beside Ray-Ray. She held up the acrylic plaque. "It is an honor to receive this award, but it's not what I'm moved by. I'm overwhelmed by your presence. Thank you all for taking the time out of your busy lives to be here. Together we are this island. We are *Wai Nau*."

The audience roared in delight.

"It should be Uncle Kalo up here. I can hear Uncle's few simple words in Hawaiian. Most of the time I have no idea what he's saying," she admitted.

The banquet hall burst into spontaneous laughter.

"Though I don't understand the words, I feel in my heart I know what Uncle is saying. We know aloha means to share breath, to recognize and share our spirit with another person. When I was a little girl, I would stay up late and watch the old movie channel with my father. He loves the old comedians. I remember watching Jack Benny being honored. He stepped up to the podium and said, 'I don't deserve this award, but I have arthritis and I don't deserve that either.'"

The hall burst into laughter.

"We love you, Gina!" Ray-Ray called from a back table. The crowd began shouting, "Gina! Gina! Gina!"

It was just as Chichi had told her so often, *what we create in our minds is an illusion*. She had always felt, *believed*, that she didn't belong. She stepped back from the microphone and made a formal bow to her father and slipped off the stage. She spotted Commander Abrams, sitting in the wings at a small table just to the right of the sound technician. Abrams had recently been appointed to the top job at the Coral Sands Naval Base. Gina approached his table. "May I join you?"

Abrams stood. "Yes, please have a seat, Miss Mori."

The mayor, sensing the lull in the festivities, grabbed the mike. "How about another warm round of applause for our very own Gina Mori?" The mayor led the polite applause. The audience once again returned to their desserts as the mayor read down a long list thanking all those who helped to put on the event.

"Congratulations, Miss Mori, on your well-deserved award, though I'm curious as to why you invited me?" Commander Abrams asked. "You mentioned on the phone that it was important. I don't mean to imply that your award isn't reason enough." He didn't want to sound disrespectful, but he had important matters that required his attention.

"Thank you for coming, Commander Abrams." Gina reached into her handbag for a manila envelope. "I'm confident you'll want to see these." She poured the contents of the envelope on the table and spread out photographs of different men, all with the same woman. "Do you recognize any of these men?"

"Yes, I recognize all of them. They work on the base." The commander gave Gina a concerned look. "These scientists are working on a top-secret radar system. May I ask you, Miss Mori, how you came to be in possession of these photos?"

Gina didn't want to get into how Hafeed had helped her to hide a motion-sensor camera in the potted palm tree across the hall from unit #8 of the Lau Kana condominiums. "These men were photographed coming and going from a condominium in Lau Kana. Do you recognize the woman in each of the photographs?"

"Now that you mention it, yes. She works at Mulligan's, the Italian restaurant on the base." Commander Abrams wondered where all this was going.

Gina paused as the waitress refilled her water glass.

The commander followed Gina's eyes.

Gina watched as recognition washed over the commander's face.

"Excuse me, young lady," Abrams asked. "Don't you work at Mulligan's?"

The waitress pulled a strand of blonde hair away from her face and flashed a bright smile. "Yes, Tuesday through Saturday."

"What's your name?" asked Abrams.

"Marcia." She smiled with her mouth closed, showing off her dimples.

"Your real name is Emily Simpson," Gina interrupted.

"Excuse me?" The waitress laughed nervously.

"You have a security breach, Commander. Miss Simpson has been running a honey trap on these five married scientists who work at the base. You'll find a hidden camera in the bedroom of unit #8 of the Lau Kana condominiums."

"A honey what?" The waitress stood frozen with the water pitcher in her hand.

Commander Abrams was fully aware that the MSS, Chinese Military Intelligence, was operating on the island. He stood and signaled to a man standing in the wings. "Miss Simpson, this is my chief of staff, Lieutenant Reynolds. He will accompany you to the base, where we would like to ask you a few questions."

"I'm sorry," she said. "I don't know what this is about, but I can't leave until after the tables are cleared."

"I must insist." Commander Abrams whispered to Reynolds. "Presume she is armed and dangerous. I'll be along directly."

"Yes, sir." Lt. Reynolds took Miss Simpson gently by the arm and escorted her out the side entrance.

Abrams turned to Gina and lowered his voice, "How did you arrange for Miss Simpson to be serving at my table?" Abrams asked.

"I didn't. She's very good at her job. I'm sure she always manages to be your server at Mulligan's," Gina offered.

"Now that you mention it." Abrams mind reeled. An investigation into base security would impact his career. "Forgive me, Miss Mori. I didn't quite follow the reason for your award today. But, I can assure you, the US Navy is most grateful for your help. We'll be in touch." Abrams shook Gina's hand and slipped out the side entrance.

Gina found her seat beside Councilwoman Yamamoto, directly across from Mayor Cordeiro and Police Chief Luis. She eyed the desserts and wished her stomach was more settled. The chocolate cheesecake with Oreo crust was calling her name. She reminded herself, more often than not, desserts at resorts look fantastic, but taste like convenience store cake.

A man with A man with a trimmed gray beard, wearing a burgundy blazer, wove his way through the maze of diners to the Table of Honor.

When Mayor Cordeiro spotted the man coming his way, he sat up in his chair.

Gina watched with interest as a man in the loud suit bent down and whispered something in the mayor's ear.

"What are you doing here?" The mayor asked, doing his best to sound unconcerned.

"I received an urgent call from your office. They said you needed to see me on an urgent matter," the man explained.

"Are you Dr. Sturgis by any chance?" Gina asked.

"Yes, I'm Dr. Sturgis. What's this all about?"

Sam Hara nonchalantly tapped the record button on his phone and went back to eating his cheesecake.

Councilwoman Yamamoto exchanged glances with Gina and reached into her handbag for an envelope. "Dr. Sturgis, I'm Councilwoman Evelyn Yamamoto." She unfolded a document. "Could you please tell me if this is your signature?"

Dr. Sturgis froze. "Excuse me? What's this regarding?"

"It is a simple enough question." The councilwoman handed the Certificate of Death to the doctor. "Is this your signature?"

Dr. Sturgis read the deceased man's name on the certificate and looked over at the mayor.

"Why are you looking at our mayor?" Councilwoman Yamamoto put a little steel into her voice. "Did you want to ask the mayor if it's your signature?"

"Yes, it's my signature. I demand an explanation. I just traveled from O'ahu, and now I'm being—"

"If I may?" Gina interrupted. "I might be able to shed a little light on the situation. Dr. Sturgis, do you recognize Jacob Clemente's death certificate?"

"Medical records are private," Dr. Sturgis snapped.

Gina continued, "In the Cause of Death section you indicated: *Cardiac Arrest*. Then in section #37 Manner of Death, you checked the box: *Natural*."

"You've no business asking me about this!" Sturgis raised his voice.

A few guests at the tables nearby turned to see what the commotion was about.

Sturgis lowered his voice and looked at the mayor. "This is hardly the time or place to—"

"But it is the perfect time and place," Gina interrupted.

Dr. Sturgis became agitated at being interrupted yet again. "If you will excuse me, Mr. Mayor. I can see this is all some sort of misunderstanding."

Councilwoman Yamamoto stood. "You must be tired from your flight, Dr. Sturgis. Please have a seat, I must insist." She gestured to an empty chair.

Sturgis sat down. His face, which had been red with emotion only moments before, and lifeless as stone.

"I recently received an autopsy report from a Dr. Bautista, a medical examiner in Manila." The councilwoman handed Dr. Sturgis the medical report. "Dr. Bautista's examination revealed that Jacob Clemente's cause of death was consistent with being in contact with an organophosphate nerve toxin, possibly the pesticide chlorpyrifos. Dr. Bautista's medical report is interesting because records from Mr. Clemente's employer, SynthCo, show that chlorpyrifos had been sprayed in the field where Mr. Clemente was working less than three hours prior to his death."

Dr. Sturgis didn't respond.

"Do you practice medicine on *Wai Nau,* Dr. Sturgis?" the councilwoman asked.

"I'm a licensed M.E. in the state of Hawaii."

"That's not what I asked." The councilwoman's tone was increasingly sharp.

Police Chief Luis leapt to his feet and pounded on the table. "Once again, Councilwoman, you have overstepped the mark. I must insist that this ridiculous attack on Dr. Sturgis come to an end. You have no authority to—"

"Sit down," the councilwoman demanded. "I'm not through speaking."

"You can't order me to sit down!" the police chief barked.

Guests at neighboring tables all turned and listened to the fracas.

The mayor held up his hands and said in a low voice, "Please calm down everyone. I suggest we continue this discussion tomorrow in my office."

Gina looked at the mayor and smiled. "Did you know, Mayor Cordeiro, that Jacob Clemente was not alone when he entered that field of corn on the morning of the twenty-second of February? His friend Joshua Santos was with him."

"I must confess, Miss Mori; I don't understand what any of this has to do with you."

"I confess, Mr. Mayor, that's not quite the confession I was hoping for." Gina smiled, but she was not happy. "Perhaps you simply don't recall. No matter, I'm sure Chief Luis remembers Joshua Santos."

"Who?" Chief Luis was doing all he could not to leap across the table and arrest the young woman.

Gina shuffled through the contents of her thick file looking for a photo.

Councilwoman Yamamoto addressed the mayor, "I should mention that last month I hired Miss Mori as my executive assistant. She's been helping me to look into irregular activities surrounding the death of the farmworker, Jacob Clemente. Judge Christopher Fernandez signed a number of warrants that have benefited our investigation.

"Found it!" Gina held up a photo obtained from airport security of Chief Luis standing beside Joshua Santos. She handed the photo to the mayor. "It's possible that you don't recall picking up Mr. Santos at the SynthCo field office, or driving him to the airport, or escorting Mr. Santos to his gate at the airport, but I would have thought, Chief Luis, that you would remember commandeering a helicopter from Paradise Helicopter Tours on the twenty-third of February at 8:21 A.M. to search for an escaped prisoner. This is your signature; is it not?" Gina passed the document to the mayor. "Mr. Mayor, your secretary booked a one-way ticket to Manila for a Joshua Santos." Gina handed the mayor a copy of the receipt. "Everything was going according to plan until Mr. Santos went to the restroom and gave Chief Luis the slip."

"I don't know what you are driving at, Miss Mori, but if you think I'm going to sit here and listen to your unsubstantiated accusations for another minute you're mistaken. One more slanderous word out of your mouth and you'll spend the night in jail," Chief Luis assured her.

"Oh?" Gina looked over to the table where the SynthCo execs were eating and then waved to Moreno.

Carla escorted an older man to the Table of Honor.

Gina stood. "For those of you who have not had the pleasure, may I introduce Joshua Santos,"

"Thank you for coming, Mr. Santos." The councilwoman stood and shook the older man's hand. "I'm Councilwoman Gayle Yamamoto. On my word of honor, Mr. Santos, you've nothing to fear. Please tell us, do you see the man who picked you up the morning after your friend Jacob's death and drove you to the airport?"

Joshua pointed to police chief Luis. "This man came to the bunkhouse. He showed me his badge and said he was the chief of police. He said I was being sent back to Manila. He said if I ever spoke of Jacob's death to anyone, I would go to prison. He put me in the back of a police car and drove me to the airport."

"Lies!" Chief Luis couldn't think of anything else to say.

"I'm curious, Mr. Santos. How is it you missed your flight to Manila?" Gina asked.

"I told the chief I needed to go to the toilet. When I got in the restroom, I used all the cash I had to buy a young man's red sweatshirt. I pulled the hood over my head and hurried for the exit. When I got out of the airport, I ran into the cornfield across the highway."

Gina continued digging through the papers stuffed in her folder until she found the Hawaiian Telecom records and tried to pass them to the councilwoman.

The councilwoman shook her head. Gina had done all the groundwork, she deserved to see it through.

Gina looked around the table and took a deep breath. "I'm sure most of us remember reading in the paper how Chief Luis commandeered a civilian helicopter to search for an escaped prisoner named Joshua Santos who fled into a cornfield. Judge Fernandez signed a warrant allowing us access to the cell phone records of several key people in the investigation. It appears, Mr. Mayor, that you spoke with police Chief Luis on the phone just moments before the Paradise helicopter left the helipad that morning on February twenty-third."

Gina looked closer at the Hawaiian Telcom phone bill. "Mr. Mayor, according to the record, you also called Dr. Sturgis several times on the previous day, the twenty-second, the day that Jacob Clementé died. Is Dr. Sturgis your doctor?" Gina paused to give the mayor a chance to confess.

The mayor had his hands over his bald head. "Please, Miss Mori, try to understand the situation from my position. Yes, it's a terrible tragedy that the poor man died, but there is nothing nefarious here. No crime was committed."

"I imagine that's a matter for the courts to decide," Gina suggested. "What is it they say? It's not the original act; it's the attempted cover-up. And by the way, Mr. Mayor, 'the poor man' has a name, Jacob Clementé."

"There wasn't time to do a thorough autopsy," the mayor explained, with righteous indignation. "We couldn't be certain what had caused Mr. Clementé's death. For all we knew, he died of natural causes. What was certain is, the poor man's death would be used by the environmental groups to force the seed companies to move their operations off-island. Over a thousand jobs lost! A disaster for the hard-working families that I was elected to represent. And that's why this needs to remain between us."

Gina laughed. "You can't be serious?"

"The truth is, there wasn't time to do a thorough autopsy," the mayor insisted.

"You and your buddies at SynthCo saw to that," Gina said, unsympathetically.

"Congratulations on your award, Miss Mori. Now if you'll excuse me." Mayor Cordeiro got up to leave.

Sam Hara picked up his phone to see if it was still recording. "Mr. Mayor, any comment for tomorrow's paper? I'm thinking Special Edition."

Cordeiro made a low growl like a caged animal.

"I'm sorry, Mayor Cordeiro, I didn't catch that. Did you have a comment about the alleged cover-up of Jacob Clementé's death?" Sam asked. "No? How about you, Chief Luis? You seem to have had a bird's-eye view, so to speak. Nothing? Okay. How about you, Councilwoman Yamamoto? Do you have a comment?"

"That depends, Sam. Have you been recording this entire conversation?"

"Councilwoman, this is hardly my first rodeo," Sam beamed.

"I imagine the state attorney general would be very interested in your recording, don't you?" Councilwoman Yamamoto asked.

Gina stood. "I hope to see all of you in court. Now, if you'll excuse me, I'd like to celebrate with my friends."

Gina got up, strolled across the crowded ballroom, and sat between Chichi and Curly across from Moreno and Joshua Santos.

"Slumming it with the little people?" Moreno teased.

"I couldn't have done any of it without your help," Gina said, earnestly.

"Hey, where's Eddie Haskell?" Moreno looked around the room, disappointed.

"Hutch heard you were going to be here," Curly explained.

Hafeed was sitting two tables over with Sid Margolis, the silent partner of the Surfrider. When he saw Gina, he came over with a big smile. "Guess who is the new chef of the Surfrider?"

"Congratulations, Hafeed!" Gina gave him a big hug. "What are you going to do with your van?"

"I've decided to give it to a friend. She's starting up her own shave ice business. What do you think?"

Gina kissed him. "Thanks, Hafeed. Maybe for the summer. I've always wanted a shave ice shack."

"This is better than a shack," Hafeed reminded her.

"You're right." she knew how dear the van was to Hafeed.

Curly reached over and hugged her. "Congratulations on another new venture." He was amazed by all her different jobs. "What are you going to call it?"

"Gina's," Moreno suggested.

"I think I'll call it—Shave Ice Paradise."

"What did you mean, for the summer?" Chichi asked.

"I've decided to go back to school in the fall," she announced while hugging her father.

Kalo looked around the table at the smiling faces. "*Mohala i ka wai ka maka o ka pua.* Unfolded by the water are the faces of the flowers."

Eyeballing Curly's chocolate cheesecake, Gina grabbed a fork and took a big bite.

Kalo let out a big belly laugh.

Curly acted hurt, though he had saved it for her.

"Hey!" she said, with her mouth full. "Pretty good."

About the Author

Mark Daniel Seiler is an award-winning author and musician who lives on the island of Kaua`i. His debut novel, *Sighing Woman Tea* was a winner at the Pacific Rim Book Festival 2015, nominated for the Kirkus Prize, and *Foreword Reviews* Indies finalist. Mark's second novel, *River's Child,* was awarded the Landmark Prize for fiction, Silver Nautilus Award, da Vinci Eye finalist, Eric Hoffer Award Short List, Next Generation Indie Book Award Finalist, Literary Titan Book Award, National Indie Excellence Award Finalist, Independent Press Award Distinguished Favorite, CYGNUS Book Awards for Science Fiction Finalist, Reader Views Reviewer Choice Award. Mark describes himself as a life-long learner, who got a very late start.

Visit Mark at www.markdanielseiler.com